MORE THAN JUST A HAIRDRESSER

by

Nia Pritchard

D0994796

HONNO MODERN FICTION

Published by Honno
'Ailsa Craig', Heol y Cawl, Dinas Powys
South Glamorgan, Wales, CF6 4AH

The author would like to stress that
this is a work of fiction and no resemblance
to any actual individual or institution
is intended or implied.

A catalogue record for this book is available from The British
Library.

Published with the financial support of the Welsh Books Council.

ISBN 1 870206 851
9781870206853

Cover illustration: Kim Smith
Cover design: Graham Preston
Printed in Wales by Gomer

ACKNOWLEDGEMENTS

I would like to thank Caroline Oakley for all her
guidance and advice; Helena Earnshaw at Honno
for her enthusiastic support; and all the wonderful
characters I've met along the way who have inspired
me to write this story.

ONE

New Year's day, a day when many wake up claiming 'never again'... Shirley was no exception. Her pink fluffy bed covers hid her almost completely except for the red painted toenails that peeked from beneath the duvet. Clues to last night's celebrations were scattered around the room, from her silver glittery party dress to the half empty wine glass on the bedside table. Shirley rolled over, looked at the clock and groaned. Her blonde shoulder length hair looked halfway decent but the make-up smudged around her eyes gave the game away – last night had been party time. She rolled over the other way, waited a few minutes, but it was no use putting it off any longer, she had to get up: her bladder could wait no longer. Dragging herself out of bed Shirley pushed her feet into the hot-pink fluffy slippers and struggled into the bathroom in her matching short pyjamas. Holding her head she stepped over a pile of clothes on the landing and gingerly made her way down the stairs, ducking to avoid the Christmas decorations that had realised Christmas was over and fallen down all by themselves.

Bodies lay in various states in the living room, empty bottles and cans strewn around the place. The table still set up with the remains of last night's spread had obviously been a welcome sight for one guest who was tucking into stale crisps and congealed dips.

Shirley gave half a smile as she attempted the obstacle course of bodies, clothes and empties and made her way to the kitchen. Even the kettle boiling was too loud for her today. She put together her sure-fire hangover cure and renegotiated the obstacle course. Once back in the comfort of her bedroom, hangover cure in hand, Shirley kicked off her fluffy slippers, snuggled back into her cosy bed and reached over for her new pink diary from the bedside drawer. She opened it at the nice clean first page and smiling in anticipation set about recalling last night's celebrations.

Tuesday, January 1
<u>10 am</u>

Dear Diary
Oh my God, I feel totally wrecked. I've still got the whirlies. It was worth it though, well I think it was. What a party. It was mint! Fireworks in more ways than one! I'm really suffering, just got up cos I need the loo.

Feel a bit more like meself, though, after a mug of tea with three sugars and a bacon buttie – always does the trick.

Back to last night. I had a New Year's Eve party. Loads of peeps came. Oli – he works for me in Cuts 'n' Curls. Bent as a nine bob note but me best friend and I love him to bits. Me mum and Auntie Dilys, Mum's sister, came. Me kids: Jason, he's sixteen and Fiona, she's fourteen. They had a few friends over. I think it's Jason's friends who are still lying on me living room floor actually. They were great but I think they'd drunk more than they let on. The sick on the landing and the fact they were both in their beds fully clothed gave the game away a bit.

A few clients/friends turned up: the factory girls, we do their hair every Friday...that's another story. They'd pass for the Russian shot put team no problem. Not the most glam, but absolutely fantastic girls, a real laugh. Susan had gone all out an' all with her new black dead tight top she'd bought especially for the party. It had 'Gorgeous' written in silver glitter across her forty-four double G knockers. The mere fact that she's five foot two, size twenty-four and one front tooth missing has absolutely nothing to do with it! That's the type of fun loving girls they are; don't give a shit!

A few neighbours – Ted and Pam from next door. Pam uses more peroxide in a month than we do in work in a year, and he likes to wear her knickers – say no more, but they like a drink and they were a laugh. Frank and Fay from over the road – the quiet ones, well so I thought until Frank decided to do the Full Monty, much to Auntie Dilys' delight and Fay's disgust. He was in full swing in more ways than one. Fay had a right go at him, but he didn't give a shit. He loved all the attention. She chucked a drink over him in the end but that just made it worse cos at least, before, he was trying to cover his bits up with his hands, with drink in his gob he had no choice but to wipe it off did he? Using both his hands and the new dress he'd got Fay as a Chrizzy pressie!

We were having a great time. Oli turned up at eleven. He'd been around town first, but I knew he'd turn up before midnight. We were in the middle of a boogie when he came. I'd got one of them free Christmas hits CDs in the Sunday paper. It was great. All the usual Christmas songs that you can all sing along to, which we all did, mint!

Oli was on his own, wearing a red net top and black leather pants, teamed up with a diamond belt. He'd put in some Chrizzy earrings, a reindeer headband on his head, and a mound of tinsel round his neck. He looked like a member of a Right Said Fred tribute band who'd had a scrap in The Christmas Shop.

"Wow, I never said it was fancy dress. You look like a friggin' Christmas tree!" I giggled.

"Well, got to get into the spirit hon'. Fetch us a drink, me gob feels like an Arab's flip-flop. Hey, you've scrubbed up well for an old bird," he said looking me up and down.

"Cheeky bastard. I'm only thirty-six remember. Hey, I thought Gus was coming with you," I said, handing him a large G+T, complete with straw and little umbrella.

"He's coming later, hopefully in more ways than one, babe!!!!! I left him in Frankie's."

I should've known then that it would all go pear-shaped. Gus is the biggest flirt this side of the Mersey. If he were mine no way would I leave him in a bar in town, full of well-nice fellas, especially on New Year's

Eve. Ten minutes to midnight and me mum and Auntie Dilys were busy fussing with getting drinks for every one. Jason and Fiona were pissed with their mates. No sign of Gus and Oli was busy texting him.

"Everyone outside, the Woods over the back fence have got some fireworks, everyone out to have a Dixie," I shouted over the music. Well there was no point me buying some as well was there? We may as well watch theirs! More money to buy the drinks with, eh?

Bang on midnight they let off the fireworks and we all cheered. Well except Oli. He was well pissed off... no sign of Gus.

"He's switched his friggin' phone off, the bitch. Our first New Year together. I'll kill him."

"Maybe he couldn't get a taxi or he's too pissed or something," I said.

"Yeah, you're right. Happy friggin' New Year, Boss."

"Happy New Year, Oli."

So the night went on. Oli was still upset, I could tell, but we had a laugh and a few dances, listened to Frank and Fay's row and went to bed at four! No wonder I feel like shit today.

Smiling to herself, Shirley put her diary in the drawer and lay back in bed, pulling the covers over her head in the hope of sleeping off the effects of the night before. Engulfed in happy memories of the celebrations she drifted off to the land of fun.

Several hours later she woke to a quiet, clean house. Her mother had called round and, horrified at the mess, had taken it upon herself to do the decent thing. She'd made Fiona, Jason and the friends that were still around clean the house from top to bottom. The place was cleaner than before the party started.

"Hey, what's been going on here then?" Shirley enquired still wearing her pyjamas and make-up smudged all over her face.

"Well we thought you deserved it, Mum, giving us all that party an' all." Fiona replied.

No mention was made of the fact that it was their gran's idea but since they'd been responsible for getting rid of any unwanted lingerers they'd thought no more of it.

The house was back to normal and so, remarkably, was Shirley's head. All was well, a lazy afternoon watching TV and eating the rest of the seemingly endless chocolate planned. Shirley's mind did, however, wander to her best pal Oli and his troubled love life, but he was bound to phone by the end of the night so she settled down to the New Year's day film, which, surprisingly, hadn't been on before. The afternoon and evening muddled into one as mum and kids ate, dozed and ate some more.

<u>10pm</u>
Oli phoned earlier. Still no news from Gus. Oli was convinced that he's shagging someone else. Thankfully, I had a message on me answer machine later. (I was soaking in a bath full of bubbles at the time, one of me Christmas pressies from Fiona). Gus had arrived home. Oli said for me not to ring back as they had a lot of catching up to do! He'd ring me tomorrow. If the giggles and oohs and aahs in the background were anything to go by I'm in for a treat.

Straight to bed after the bath. Left the kids arguing over the tele. Can't wait to speak to Oli tomorrow, but God do I need me bed now. Night, night little pink diary.

A new day and any remains of a hazy head gone for the time being, Shirley was woken by loud banging music that to her mind could only be enjoyed by anyone under twenty-two. She felt sure it would restart the throbbing in her head. It was her last day off and she was hoping to spend it in the madness of the January sales with the kids. Looking, hunting, and fighting for things they didn't really want or need, but because there was 75 per cent off they, just like the rest of the country, would have to have it even if it didn't fit that well. But meeting up with Oli was on the agenda so she'd got that to look forward to.

<u>Wednesday, January 2</u>
<u>9am</u>
I've been woken up by the sound of Jason's blaring music. The new CD he'd got for Christmas. Well I think that's what it was, was so loud you couldn't understand a word of it. Why do teenagers do that? Are they all slightly deaf so they have to have it louder to hear it, or is it just to piss everyone else off?!!!

Thought we'd hit the sales today. Me last day off. Back to work tomorrow. A nice day with the kids, and jangle with Oli later. Perfect.

With a day at the shops planned Shirley set about

preparing the breakfast. The sooner she could get off into town the better.

"Fancy a little look in town, later on today?" Shirley asked, buttering the toast.

"Oh, soz Mum, I'm going with Shaz in a bit. Thought you could give us a lift in though," said Fiona tucking into a bowl of cereal.

"Charming!" Shirley exclaimed.

"I've got a bit of money from Chrizzy to spend, so I thought I'd get something to wear in the sales. You couldn't give us a bit for a Top-up, though, could you? Then I could ring you to let you know what time we need to be picked up."

"Double friggin' charming!" she muttered throwing the toast down on the plate.

Shirley, resplendent in her new marabou-frilled dressing gown and ready to tuck into a burnt piece of sliced white toast, studied her two delightful kids: "So not only am I a mobile hairdresser, I'm a mobile bank and a taxi service," she said sarcastically.

Fiona carried on eating her cereal blankly and Jason buried his head in the *Sun*.

"Same here Ma, no can do. I'm off to play footie today with the lads. If you're givin Fi a few notes I could do with a Top-up," Jason answered not even looking up.

"Don't worry about me I'll spend me last day off alone," Shirley said pointedly.

"Nice one, Mum. You will give us a lift though yeah?" Fiona ventured through her Coco Pops.

5pm
Two lifts later and forty quid down, I was in town about

to have a coffee when me mobie rings. It was Oli.

"Hiya babes, where are you?" he asked.

"Just dropped the kids off and I'm in town, where are you?"

"Meet me in J's Coffee House at two; love ya, got loads to say," he went on.

So I cancelled Starbucks, and went to do a bit more shopping till two.

(I'm back in at last, thank God, cos me feet are killing me. What a great day though. I'm completely spent up.)

Anyway going back to this afternoon, I met Oli at two in J's and we had a great chat. Apparently Gus had got so pissed that he'd fallen asleep in Frankie's and the landlord Matt had very kindly let him stay in his accommodation above the bar. The lads had to carry him up, he was so well gone! He was so hung over that he slept until six the following day. He told Oli he had tried to ring him but there was no signal and then the battery went flat!!! Well, Oli seems happy with the explanation... He did go a bit quiet when I asked why Gus hadn't used the bar's payphone though.

Anyway he's all excited because, to make up for them missing their first New Year's Eve together, Gus has booked a weekend to Paris for them both over the internet. So now Oli wants a week on Friday off and he said he will work the following Monday on his own to give me a day off. They fly out on Thursday evening and are due back Sunday evening. Lucky bastards.

I then had to listen to all the gory details of the make up. Very nice, I don't think, especially if you haven't had a shag yourself for years! Well it feels like that anyway! I'm not actually sure how long it is, to be honest, and let's face it sex isn't everything is it? I'm so busy with everything else I've no time for a relationship and who wants just the sex? Not me, well not really, not without feeling a bit crap the next day. For me one can't go without the other, well not anymore anyway. Maybe when I was a bit younger, but now I suppose I do want a bit more; not like them factory girls, it's a different fella nearly every night of the week with them lot. I do miss the intimacy though if I'm honest, to feel wanted and fanciable, isn't that what every woman wants?

After shopping, gossip with Oli and a quick confide in her little pink friend, Shirley spent the evening listening to the kids' days, looking at the goodies Fiona had bought and getting everything ready for the following day's work. Fiona was due to tag along with Shirley and Oli in the hope of making some extra pocket money. The van had been loaded with all their equipment and was full of petrol. Back to the grind of Cuts 'n' Curls mobile hair salon!

<u>11pm. In bed.</u>
I wonder what is going on with that Gus. I think he's up to no good but Oli thinks it's all ok. I hope Oli doesn't get hurt. Meself I think Gus is a sly little shit but I may be wrong. We'll have to wait and see.

I can't believe we're back to work tomorrow. These Christmas hols have flown by. If I'm being honest, I'll be glad to get back to normal.

Shirley closed her little pink diary. Poor Oli. The two had

been close friends for years and with no man of her own, she felt an extra special bond with Oli. The kids loved him too, just like he was part of the family. Given she spent most of her time with Oli, all day in work, and he was her drinking partner she supposed it was only natural to be concerned.

She'd be glad to get back to work; she'd wanted to be a hairdresser since she was a girl, spending her pocket money on hair magazines, knowing one day she would create amazing styles for her clients. The amazing-hairstyle-type-client list was yet to happen, sadly, as the closest Shirley got to radical styling was when someone asked for a blow wave instead of rollers. Somehow that didn't matter anymore, Shirley was doing what she loved with people she loved in an environment she loved. A born gossip, she was in her element with her fun-loving clientele and she flattered herself she wasn't a bad hairdresser either.

She'd planned to take Fiona out with them the following day, so the girl could earn a bit of extra post-Christmas cash. Fiona loved going out with them – she was following in her mother's footsteps on the gossip front. Fiona thought Oli was hysterical and listened agog to all his stories. The only thing Shirley had doubts about was Fiona's ability to get up in time, so she packed her off to bed early with an alarm clock and promised her a great pay day as an incentive.

Thursday, January 3

Up and out by eight thirty. Fiona wasn't very impressed, especially as Jason was still flat out when we left. Oli for once was ready when we arrived. He's trying to keep me happy cos he wants the time off next week.

First client of the day for Oli was Marsha the Man-eater. She's got a face like a farmer's arse on a frosty morning, poor cow! She's been after Oli for ages. She wants to show him how great a woman can be, and has been trying her best to convert him for months. She insists on having him to do her hair, every week. She'll be waiting for him in her leopard skin nightie and black slippers. A right old tart, but still she's a customer.

I dropped him off outside her house. She was down for a cut and blow so I knew he'd only be about half an hour, well, if he was lucky and escaped, homosexuality intact. He could walk then with his bag of tricks to Jane's, round the corner, to do a tint there. I arranged to pick him up at 11.30 outside Jane's.

"Off you go then, soft lad," I said to him, I could see he was starting to get a bit nervous.

"I'm only doing this cos I love ya," he said pulling a face.

"I know Oli, I love you too, and so does Marsha."

"But in a different way..." our Fi laughed. "I'll protect ya."

"It'll soon be over, love, you do a great job on her, much better than me and we have to keep the customers happy don't we, eh?" I said encouraging him to get on with it.

I had a perm and shampoo and set to do for the two misses, as we call them. Two old spinster sisters who live together. We've been doing their hair for years. They're not all innocent, though. Gladys used to be a right one in her time, if you know what I mean. She used to entertain us and still does with stories from her younger days. Even Oli used to blush. They'd both been evacuated to Wales during the war and often tell the stories. I love chattin' to them cos me granddad was Welsh. He came to Liverpool to work down the docks.

We went to Wales one year on holiday, when I was a kid, and met all the rellies. All the kids took the piss out of me accent all week. Cheek! I could never understand a word they said and that was when they spoke in English!

Fi went with Oli. She loves to go with him for a laugh. And she could save him from Marsha.

I picked the pair of them up before dinner.

"Scuse the language, Fi, but that frigging Marsha. What an old tart. She's a right bomhead. Shittin' hell."

Fiona stood laughing.

"Did she give you a hard time?"

"That was the only hard thing she gave me, kid. When she sucks on a lemon it's the lemon that pulls a face. She's got a face like a robber's dog that one."

"Oh behave, you love it," I said to him.

"No way, look at me hands, they're still shaking. She'd scare a monkey out of a banana tree! She's in for the kill next time I tell ya. It was only cos Fi was there. Touching me arse to feel the material of me kecks! It's sexual harassment, that's what it is."

"It's a right laugh," said Fiona still in stitches.

"Easy day first day. Lets go for a coffee; we've got nothing now till two and that's only three more clients each. Nothing too hard," I said to them with fading enthusiasm.

Roll on five o' clock I thought, so we could get home.

We dropped Oli off and made arrangements for the next day. We'll be working together all day cos we were doing one of the old people's homes. That'll be a laugh.

Oli's house was in darkness when we got there, but Gus was due to make a romantic meal for them. Didn't look like that was happening. Oh shittin' hell not another excuse. I'll be waiting for the phone call...

They decided on fish and chips for tea. Cooking was not one of Shirley's strong points. "You can't be good at everything,' she often told Fiona. It was good looks not good cooking skills that ran in their family.

Later that evening, while Shirley and Fiona sat watching the TV, there was a phone call from Oli. Gus was still missing, his mobile phone was switched off and Oli was raging. Shirley tried to console him on the phone but Oli wasn't convinced. He thought Gus really was up to no good. Even Fiona got in on the conversation with all of her fourteen years of wisdom, which incidentally was as good advice as Shirley's. They ended up telling Oli to sit and watch TV to take his mind off it and they would do the same in sympathy with him.

"Make sure you let me know what's happening before you go to bed, love."

"Go to bed! I don't think I'll sleep ever again," Oli said dramatically.

11pm, in bed
I had a text message from Oli - Gus had returned complete with takeaway, flowers, wine and chocolates.

He was held up in work and all is forgiven.

Well as usual another eventful day. I feel knackered, and today was an easy day. It must be all the late nights catching up on me. I feel tired and a bit... lonely I suppose. This time of year can do that to you sometimes, especially if there's no one special. I wish I had someone to snuggle up to of a night. A loyal kind fella, not a tossa like Gus. I've been on me own now for six years, well apart from when I was with Ronny, and that only lasted three months. What a shit he turned out to be. Nearly as much of a shit as Mike. Mike and I have been divorced for five years now. Five years! God it doesn't seem that long.

My childhood sweetheart, then he went and broke me bloody heart when he went off with that slag Cheryl, who worked on reception in the garage where he was a mechanic. They buggered off to Scotland and we only ever hear from them on the kids' birthdays and Christmas. Bastards.

As for Ronny, what a dickhead. I met him one night when I was out with Oli. A real ladies' man he turned out to be. He was a looker, and boy did he friggin' look! He had that many jumps he could have been a trampoline in his spare time! So he was kicked into touch, and apart from a few casual flings there has been no one, no one special.

Oli's me bessie mate, we work together, have fun together. We're always there for each other. That's why I'm so worried about him now with this dickhead Gus. They've only been together six months and Gus has moved in. Oli's got a lovely place an all. His dad died about four years ago, and cos his mum and dad were divorced and Oli's an only child he was left everything.

He's not short, quite comfortable I suppose. That's why this job suits. I can't pay him loads but he's quite happy with that. The flexibility suits him. He's a right gossip and he loves to jangle with all the clients.

Oli talks about Gus non-stop. It's a pain in the arse really but I put up with it cos I love Oli. If he does the shit on Oli, Gus'll have me to answer to.

Shirley had never really had much luck with men despite being an attractive woman. She always seemed to fall for the wrong type. Mike, her children's father, had been the love of her life and he hurt her badly; after that she hadn't been keen on a serious relationship with anyone. Boyfriends are so overrated, she thought (not even convincing herself).

Shirley was a family girl who idolised Fiona and Jason. If they were happy then she was happy; she had her best friend Oli and a large group of girlfriends – what else did a girl need? Except that deep down Shirley knew that one day, as much as they loved her and how close they were, her lovely children would finally fly the nest and she would be left alone. The mere thought terrified her.

Friday, January 4
9pm
A really fantastic day. What a laugh. Fiona and I picked Oli up at nine and we spent the day in West Haven residential home. We normally do the factory girls on a Friday afternoon but they're still off this week so we arranged to go to the home. It's a lovely cozy place, more like a hotel I think. They've got all

sorts of characters there, though.

Shampoo and sets today for all the old biddies and a few trims for the old fellas. We did have one perm though, Mavis. What with all the jollies going on we forgot about her, and left it on a bit too long. It does look a bit like ginger pubes, but luckily she's got cataracts and can't see that well. I did feel guilty, though, so I took a couple of quid off; she thinks it's because it's the festive season and was well made-up!

They all love Oli, and were dead chuffed when Fi got on the piano and Oli sang Chrizzy carols with them in between the hairdos. We had a sherry with them and a mince pie, both left over from their party! Fi used to have piano lessons when she was little; it's not so cool now. I wish she'd have carried on though, she was doing so well. Anyway she can still hold a tune so the old folks were made up with her doing her bit.

They must have entertained them for about an hour or more, it was great. All the oldies and their rellies were sat around in little groups in the pink floral day room, the dominoes and cards were given the push and so was the woman who comes in to do creative stuff with them. Fair dos to her though, not to be left out she started off the clapping and the jiggin' about. Typical hippy, arty farty type, you know long hair and sandals, even in the winter, looks like she hasn't looked in the mirror for years. I think she was relieved really, even she must get a bit pissed off trying to get everyone to make them raffia baskets. Mind you, looking at her she probably has a house full of them, does them in her sleep. Anyway, the oldies couldn't be arsed, especially when there was panto-style entertainment on.

Oli got a bit flustered at one point, when a relative's

dog tried to shag his leg, much to the amusement of the old folks. I threw the dog the display raffia basket to get it to stop. It was happy to lie there then chewing the woven plastic leaving Oli free to carry on Red Coat style.

We left them all a bit pissed on sherry, singing the rude versions of the Chrizzy carols Oli had taught them.

Met up with Jason in town later and we all went for a pizza. Oli phoned Gus and surprise, surprise he came as well. We did have a laugh and Gus was dead charming tonight. What's he hiding? Anyway, I should give him the benefit of the doubt, he was ok tonight. He even paid for us all!

A great Friday, the weekend is here. Rest, relaxation here I come.

The weekend did not turn out to be the restful time that Shirley had hoped for. It did, however, turn out to be intriguing, leaving Shirley with yet more unanswered questions on the Gus front.

<u>Saturday, January 5</u>
What happened to rest and relaxation? Spent the day taxiing the kids round. Me mum phoned. Auntie Dilys was feeling a bit under the weather so would I drop them both off at the bingo at seven, save them getting the bus. If she was feeling under the weather why the frig was she going the bingo? I did ask me mum but she just ignored me. So off I went to do me duty.

"You couldn't fetch us and all at half ten could you love? It's a pig of a night, and what with Auntie Dilys not feeling herself," me mum asked.

What could I say!

"I'll treat us all to a fish supper on the way home," she went on dead excited.

Well no contest...a fish supper on a Saturday night, it was too good to refuse! Let's face it I had no other offers.

Took Fiona with me to fetch the bingo queens. Jason's sleeping over at his bessie mate, Digo's house. We were sitting outside the Odeon at 10.25. They were due out at half ten! Well, I didn't want to be accused of keeping poor old ill Auntie Dilys waiting out in the cold, it being such a pig of a night, did I?

"Isn't that Gus, mum?" Fi asked.

"Where?" Me eyes were scouring the area.

"Going into that pub over there, with those lads."

"It looks like him, but I can't be sure, I need a closer look."

Oli is like me little brother. We all love him and feel he's like part of the family. He's no family of his own, so I feel responsible for him. I'd hate him to get hurt. I know what it feels like. I had to find out if he was at risk of getting hurt.

I got out the car, I'd forgotten I was wearing me house slippers (not me hot pink mules – they're bedroom only), me Christmas box from Oli. I noticed when I was halfway across the road – two great big Rudolf heads were smiling up at me, it looked worse cos I'd got a short skirt on. I thought bollocks, if I was helping nail that cheating bastard then it was worth the humiliation.

Fiona sat in the car looking on horrified. I got to the pub and looked in through the window, it was heaving, and I couldn't see him. I stood on a plastic chair that was outside and stretched up, nearly fell off it to a load of car horns and cheers. I knew I couldn't go in but I was positive it was Gus.

I had to call it a day, so walked back to the car just as me mum and Auntie Dilys were on their way out.

"Ah, hello, Mrs Cartwright," I heard a voice from behind me say.

I looked round and much to me horror, and our Fiona's, saw the well-fit David Wilmore, Fiona's form teacher, with a group of teachers from the school, obviously out on a night out.

"Nice slippers," he said walking off.

"Friggin' hell, Mum, the shame!"

"Hey, language," I said, trying to keep myself together, pretending I didn't care when really I was in a hell of a state.

"Who's for a fish supper?" Me mum said, ignoring what had just happened.

With a bit of luck she hadn't seen, I thought.

"Ah yes, I'm starving now," said Auntie Dilys.

"Aw, feeling better, Auntie Dilys?" I said trying to hide me annoyance.

"Oh yes, love, much better now."

Typical.

We arrived outside the Golden Cod. I always have to go in and get them. Usually nobody else can be arsed, starving or not.

"You'd better stay here, Shirley. You've caused enough of a scene for one night," me mum said, getting out of the car almost before the engine had stopped.

Fiona just sat there giving me dirty digs in agreement.

I dropped them off with their fish bloody suppers and when we got in Fi sat in her room eating her food. How bloody childish, I was only out in me slippers. It could've been worse I could have been out in me friggin' nightie!

Fiona was mortified that teachers had seen her mother out in her slippers. She reckoned that some of them thought her family weren't good enough, from the wrong side of town and a bit common. She didn't really care about that, but her mum was an attractive woman who usually looked great – trendy clothes, nice hair and make-up – but to be seen like that, moseying around the place in a pair of comedy slippers was enough to make any fourteen year old ashamed. Fiona wouldn't stay cross with her mother for long, tomorrow she would come round but tonight she would make Shirley suffer. Just as long as noone mentioned it when she got back to school next week.

<u>Sunday, January 6</u>
<u>10am</u>
Still getting the cold shoulder from Fiona over the slippers incident. I've tried to see it from her point and granted I would have died if her gran had done that when I was fourteen, but I did tell her it was for a good cause. For Oli. She came round and even laughed about it, well a bit all at my expense of course. I didn't remind her that she's back in school tomorrow

though!

Tried to phone Oli. No answer so I left a message on his answer machine. Just a hi-how-you-doing kind of message.

<u>6pm</u>

Still no news from Oli. The kids and me sat down to Sunday dinner and Fiona told Jason about the slippers escapade – he thought it was hilarious, but worth it to find out if Gus was doing the dirty on Oli.

"So d'ya really think he's doing the dirty on Oli, Mum?" Jason asked tucking into his spuds.

"Not sure, but to me it does look very dodgy, don't you think?" I said to them both and they both looked as if they agreed despite the gobfuls of roasties.

Sunday is a special day; well the three of us try anyway. Whenever we can, we all sit down together for our Sunday dinner. We sit round the table, too, don't sit with plates on our knees like every other day of the week. I even go mad and buy a pudding. Everyone mucks in, well with the clearing up anyway. I do the food. Sometimes we have it at dinner time, sometimes at tea time. It all depends who's got what on. Usually it's to fit in with Jason who often has football.

He's getting to look more and more like a man everyday. I was looking at him today while we were having our dinner. He gets his height and his dark looks from his dad, that's for sure, and with all this football he's getting to look very muscular and fit. Fi as well, she's developing into a very attractive young woman too. She's grown her hair quite long now and I've put a few layers in it. She wants to have some blonde put in but I've been battling for ages with her to avoid that. Her dark hair is so lovely and glossy it would be a shame. Every now and then she threatens to go somewhere else to have it done, but she'd never go through with it cos she knows how upset I'd be. She has had a go a few times at Oli, but he's with me on this and hasn't even tried to persuade me.

It doesn't seem like that long ago I was changing both their nappies and look at them now.

Everyone thinks they both look like me and I think they do too, but they both have lovely olive skin like their dad. Mike's grandmother was Italian and the kids have been lucky enough to inherit her fantastic skin. I'm so lucky to have such great kids.

Oli's another one I'm lucky to have. I wonder what's going on with him. I wish he would ring. It's driving me mad. Should I say something or keep shtum?

9pm

Oli phoned. He and Gus have been out shopping all day getting stuff ready for their little trip on Thursday. Shit, I'd forgotten about that!

"How was your weekend?" I asked trying not to sound too obvious.

"Fab babes, I stayed in on Saturday just sorting out me clothes for the weekend, you know."

"Oh right, not out on the ale Saturday night then?" I pushed for a bit more info.

"Na, Gus just popped out for a takeaway for us."

"Oh, I thought I saw him when I was waiting for me mum and Auntie Dilys at the bingo. Obviously it wasn't him."

"Oh right. The Indian was packed on Saturday. He

was gone for well over an hour ya know."

So it could have been him. The Indian is across the road from the Odeon and next door to the pub. I didn't say anything cos I wasn't sure but I definitely have me suspicions about that Gus one and I'm gonna keep me eye on him.

TWO

No rest for the wicked.

The evidence seemed to be building up in Shirley's eyes but with nothing concrete there was no way Shirley would risk losing Oli's friendship by suggesting anything untoward was going on. She knew she had to find out more.

Shirley's mother was testing at times and always had a knack of making her feel guilty even when there was nothing to feel guilty about. It had happened her whole life. As much as she loved Shirley, her mother had always wanted her to do better. She could have worked harder in school, got a better job and chosen a better husband. This trait was one Shirley was determined not to inherit and inflict on her own children. Her mother thought she was too soft with them, but Shirley was happy and did things her way, which worked for her and the kids.

Dutiful daughter that she was, Shirley never seemed

to be able to refuse her mother's requests, no matter how unreasonable, and being an only child she had no one to share the load with. She felt responsible for her mother's sister Dilys too; since Dilys had never had children, Shirley was often called upon for support. Although Shirley's mother did a good job of looking after her, Auntie Dilys milked them for everything it was worth.

Shirley's thoughts returned to the week ahead. The school Christmas holidays were over and it was time for the kids to head back to school. Back to normal was good, except it wasn't totally normal as it was still in the back of her mind that Oli maybe in for a rough time.

She had a busy day ahead and the first port of call was one of their regulars, Barbara, and her family. Shirley had been doing Barbara's hair since the day she'd left the salon she'd trained in and gone mobile. Barbara was a regular in the salon, but so loved Shirley doing her hair she became her first mobile client.

Barbara was in her early fifties, had been married to her businessman husband for twenty plus years. They had a lovely home on the outskirts of town, a nice middle-class neighbourhood. Her collection of Royal Doulton dolls took pride of place on her mantelpiece and trinkets and keepsakes from her many foreign holidays filled the rooms.

Barbara liked to keep herself young and attractive-looking and ensured her hair was done every week, including a root touch-up to keep any signs of advancing years at bay.

Although not short of a bob or two, Barbara was very down to earth and hadn't forgotten where she came from. Brought up in the council house where her mother still lived, Barbara was proud of her roots but equally proud that she had married a local businessman and got out. Although at first he'd seemed a bit of a rogue, he also seemed an attractive choice given the change of lifestyle he brought with him. Young and deeply in love Barbara married her businessman and was living happily ever after on the smarter side of town.

Monday, January 7

Jason and Fiona back in school today after the holidays. I think they were glad to be going back; they do get a bit bored. And they're a pain in the arse asking for money all the bloody time. I've arranged to pick Oli up at ten today. No doubt I'll be hearing about Thursday's trip non-bloody stop. Spent the morning at Barbara's. We do Barbara, her sister Ann, her mum Betty, and her mum's sister Joan every Monday. That's what I love about this job. We've got our regulars and we fit them in to suit Oli and me, so we can work together and keep the clients happy. Plus the fact Oli can't bloody drive so we've no friggin' choice – I have to ferry him around. He said his New Year's resolution is to learn to drive. No chance! He likes to be chauffeured around. He's like Lord friggin' Muck.

This morning we had the four of them over at Barbara's.

"How's your love life, Oli?" asked Barbara, smiling.

"Don't ask," I said.

"Eh, what d'yer mean? It's bloody fab girl. We're off to Paris for a romantic weekend on Thursday," Oli said smugly.

"Ooooooh, a dirty weekend more like, with you," Ann said.

"Hey, cheek, I'm madly in love me. It's gonna be fan-bloody-tastic. Moonlight walks by the river Seine, candlelight dinners, wining and dining, and loads of shaggin'. Eh what d'yer think, Joan?" said Oli.

Joan giggled from beneath the drier. I didn't think she heard him properly. Good job, she thinks Oli is such a nice boy!

"I can't wait till next week to hear all about it," said Barbara all excited.

"He'll be on his own next week. I've got the day off. You'll be in for a treat I'm sure," I said.

"Hey, fair dos, don't you be overworking me next week, remember I'll be recovering from my weekend of luuuurve."

"Ah, he's all loved-up," said Betty.

More like blind as a friggin' bat, I thought, but what do I know? I'm just the silly cow who thinks that something fishy is going on. I've got no real proof.

"How about you, Shirley love, any signs of romance?" asked Betty.

"No time for romance me, Betty, I'm too busy looking after Oli."

"Behave. Listen if she doesn't find a fella soon she'll be joining a bleeding convent."

What a thought.

"You could always borrow my vibrator, Shirley love. I find it very handy," Joan said. The drier had finished and she was sitting bolt upright, ears waggin'.

We all turned to look at her, gobsmacked.

It had come to something when a seventy-year-old woman felt so sorry for me and me crap love life she was offering to borrow me her friggin' dildo.

"I mean it, queen, it's fantastic stress relief. I call

it me little pal. I got it in one of them parties. Doreen over the road had one. D'yer remember Betty, love?

"I got one for me sister-in-law as well cos she's always complaining she's stressed. I asked her next time I saw her how she was getting on with it. The silly cow had only been rubbing it on her shoulders hadn't she? When I said to her it was for stress relief, she thought it was one of those massage thingies. You should of seen her face when I told her where she should have been rubbing it!" Joan said laughing.

Every one was in hysterics although Betty looked a bit sheepish.

"Oh aye, Mum, you never said you'd been, what did you buy?" Barbara asked Betty.

Betty sat there laughing nervously, as red as a beetroot eating a great big bag of grapes. I was still in shock and Oli looked over at me waiting for an answer.

"Leave her alone, Barb. You go for it girl. I hope I'm still at it when I'm your age. It's nothing to be ashamed of, queen, though God knows how you've got the energy. It must be all them grapes you eat," Oli said laughing.

"It's not for energy she eats the grapes, it's to keep her bowels moving isn't it, Betty love?" Joan said dead serious.

We all looked at each other in complete silence, dead uncomfortable like, and poor old Betty went even redder!

"You're all right, Joan," I said trying to change the subject from one embarrassing thing back to another.

The thought of having to borrow Joan's little pal

was enough to make me want to jump on the next fella passing the front gate.

"The offer's there if you want it, queen, you know, if you want a little trial run... You could always have a party of your own, you know. You should have seen the stuff Doreen got for being hostess. Them front curtains were closed for weeks in the afternoons after her do," she went on.

"That was a turn up. Old Joan, eh? They say the quiet ones are the worst, Shirl'," Oli said when we got back in the van.

"Well she brought it home to me, Oli. I've got no fella have I? And no sign of one in the offing."

"You'll find someone babe. A real good un, like I have with Gus."

I friggin' hope not, I thought...

The revelations at Barbara's had got Shirley thinking about her love life, or more properly the lack of it, as she lay on her bed writing up the days events in her little pink diary. She wondered if it was really a good idea writing down everything that was happening in her life at the moment and decided it was. At best, it would serve as a good record of events to nail Gus and at worst she would be the talk of the street if anyone ever got their hands on it.

It was worth the risk, she needed something to confide in if she was going to keep her sanity and no one ever went into her bedroom, except for the kids, and certainly no one went looking through her drawers – she wasn't that lucky! – so she vowed to write on and record every daily event, especially the best bits of the conversations... So, back to it little pink diary!

<u>6pm</u>
Arrived home to find Fiona in a nark because Mr Wilmore had reminded her about the slippers incident, and now every one keeps singing Rudolph the red-nosed reindeer when they pass her.

<u>11pm</u>
God, maybe I should have one of those parties after all...

Shirley closed her diary, put it on her bed and stood in front of the mirrored wardrobe. Brushing her blonde tresses she removed the hair band from around her wrist and loosely piled her hair on the top of her head. Closely inspecting the fine lines around her eyes she picked out a facial wipe from the packet on her bedside table and carefully began to remove her make-up. She completed her beauty routine with a small blob of white moisturising cream with which she smothered her face and neck.

Removing her jeans and top she stood in her bra and pants and surveyed her body. Sucking in her stomach and pushing back her shoulders she posed and pouted.

"Not bad for an old bird," she laughed.

Clutching her thighs and then wobbling her now released stomach she sighed, "Could be better, though, but could be worse an' all. I have had two kids."

She reached under the pillow and brought out her pyjamas, pulling them on, then switching on her little portable television, she snuggled between the bedclothes and settled down to some reality television, a guaranteed way of drifting off to the land of nod.

*

After a night of horrifying dreams about being left on the shelf and having her diary printed in the local newspaper for all and sundry to see, Shirley woke suddenly. Her thoughts quickly turned as she remembered the coming weekend, Oli's trip to Paris. She wanted to arrange getting him to the airport and made a mental note to remind herself to ask him about it that day.

The kids had settled back into the school routine and even her mother and Auntie Dilys had been quiet and undemanding. Other than on the romance front, all seemed good with the world.

<u>Tuesday, January 8</u>
<u>5pm</u>
Had a busy day at work but managed to remember to ask Oli about his trip. "I'd been thinking, d'yer need a lift to the airport on Thursday?"

"Oh, yeah, great babes. That'll be well handy. The flight's at eight from Liverpool," Oli replied.

"Well, if you want, take a half-day Thursday to get your stuff ready, and I'll come and pick you both up at about six?"

"Oh, you're a little star. Oooh, yeah, I can get meself sorted. Six is fine babe. One other thing I forgot to mention. Any chance you could pop in and feed Mixie and give him a bit of love?"

Oh shit. Mixie is Oli's Persian cat. He thinks the world of it and God help anyone who doesn't.

"Course I will, Oli," I said feeling sick at the thought of it.

The afternoon was spent in the wholesale stocking up

on our essentials.

"How's it going, Shirl' love?" Charlie asked.

Charlie is the manager of the wholesaler's. Oli keeps saying he fancies me. I don't think he does, but wouldn't mind. He's well fit.

"Oh, hiya, great yeah. Any special offers today, Charlie?" I asked him.

"Well, yeah, how about a date with me?" he said laughing.

"Oh, aye, yeah," I said walking off to the perming solutions.

"What d'yer do that for, you silly cow?" Oli said.

"He was only kidding. He's a bit of a joker. I bet he's like that with all the girls that come in."

Oli walked off shaking his head in despair with me.

I looked over at Charlie, who by this time was on the phone. What am I thinking, Charlie was only asking for a date hardly a full on relationship and I couldn't or more importantly wouldn't go with him as a one-off. I couldn't look him in the eye next time I had to go in and buy perming solution if I did.

Dropped a very excited Oli off after the wholesalers. He thought he might start a little packing tonight.

11pm (in bed)

I wonder if Charlie was only joking. You can never tell with him. I'd die of shame if I said yes and he was only kidding. He's defo got the look, just my type. Quite stocky an' all he is. I love the head shaven look, a bit ironic really isn't it with me being a hairdresser and all. Fi always says I'm mad to like that look, she likes skinny lads with long floppy hair. If I was younger, well, yes, I can see what she sees in them, but when a fella gets older and starts to lose his hair there's nothing worse than trying to disguise it, look at old Comb-Over. Whip it off, lads, it's the only way. When Beckham whipped off all his hair I nearly peed me pants he looked so gorgeous.

Balls, I've just remembered about friggin' Mixie. I've got him to sort out while Oli's away. He's a bit of a nutter as cats go. Last time I saw him he snarled and clawed me. Well he can sod off; none of these loving shenanigans Oli gives him. Food, toilet stuff and that's me gone.

Shirley's mind wandered again to Charlie from the wholesale. Charlie was about six foot two tall, but built, towering over Shirley's five five frame. He had shaved his head, obviously to hide a receding hairline but Shirley had always thought he looked good and the bald look was sexy on good lookers. He wore fake designer labels, usually knock-off, and dripped gold chains. He could be loud and brash at times, but Oli always said it was to cover up his loneliness. Shirley wondered if that was true. He didn't seem lonely to her, he was always checking his phone for texts or chatting to someone.

She wondered what her diary entry would look like if ever she did go out on a date with Charlie as she drifted off in the mass of pink fluffiness that was her bed.

<u>Wednesday, January 9</u>
Picked Oli up early today. I've fitted a few more in for him. Well I may as well get me money's worth what with him skiving tomorrow and Friday. (Only joking, I

love him really). Some clients ask for him anyway, so I don't want to disappoint, do I?

Dropped him off at his first of the day.

"Had any more thoughts about these driving lessons?" I asked.

"Yeah I have. I don't know if me nerves could stand it, Shirl'."

"Behave soft lad, you'd be fine, no problem. Once you're driving we can do more stuff. I thought maybe have a mobile nail bar or something?"

"Oh, aye, yeah, that sounds good. I'll have to have a good think and maybe book a few lessons, see how I get on. We're still ok like this for now, though, aren't we babes?" he said, though, looking worried.

"Course we are, Oli love, it was just an idea," I said reassuringly, daft cow that I am.

"Great, I love you and how we work together. See you later."

No chance of Oli driving then!

Met up with Oli again for a late lunch. We'd both had quite a busy morning.

"I'll have to phone Gail from the factory later. Let her know I'm on me own this week, just so as she doesn't have a pile of girls wanting their hair doing," I said.

Friday lunchtime every week we go to Henshaw's factory to do the girls hair. Bob Henshaw (Comb-Over as he is known, for obvious reasons), the boss, takes a half-day every Friday, so Oli and me go in and do the girls hair all afternoon. Gail is the secretary so we sort it all out through her.

"Oh, aye, yeah, well it's only this week, they should

be ok. Soz about it though, hon'. Tell them I'll make it up to them next week."

"They love ya, ya bastard, course they'll be fine. Especially when you tell them all the gory details."

Treatments for the factory girls were always the perfect way to begin the weekend. It was guaranteed entertainment. Everyone looked forward to Friday afternoon, especially the factory girls who made the most of their boss's early departure. It was their one and only chance in a week full of toil to get themselves pampered and glammed up for the weekend – all in the boss's time of course.

The factory was relatively small, no more than thirty people working there, usually turning out plastic parts for household appliances, but on a Friday afternoon it turned into a beauty salon with hairdryers, straighteners and even colour treatments in full flow. It was the busiest the girls were all week: re-arranging the furniture, ensuring water was available and making space for everything to get underway.

This week's antics and stories, though, would have to wait until the girls got back from the factory's Christmas shut down.

All Shirley wanted was a restful quiet evening watching the TV. Sadly this wasn't to be the case – open house for teens again...

<u>6pm</u>
Back home. Didn't feel like cooking so got fish and chips for me and the kids.

"Mum, Shaz just phoned me on me mobie. She's coming round in a bit," Fiona said.

Shaz is Fiona's mate from school. A bit on the rough side but you can't choose their mates can ya? She's what some people might call a stereotypical Scouse girl. But not the 'great sense of humour and heart of gold type', no, Shaz is more the 'over-tanned under-dressed' type. She turned up looking every bit the Shaz we all know and love!

"New boots, them, Sharon love?" I asked looking down at the white plastic, stiletto-heeled, knee-high boots.

Fiona glared at me.

"Oh yeah, ten quid off in the market, they're boss aren't they?" She replied brightly.

"What does your mum say about them then?" I asked trying to be serious so as not to upset Fi.

"She's got a pair in red. I thought white, cos it goes with everything, and they show off me tan. There's a black pair there as well. They'd be well smart for you Fi," she went on.

"Great tan that, girl, for January..." I said smiling.

"Ooh, yeah, I know," she giggled admiring herself.

Fiona and Shaz went up to Fi's room to watch a DVD. Great outfit that, mini skirt, knee-high white plastic boots and a strappy belly top, to go round your mate's to watch Grease on DVD in January!

The evening didn't turn out as noisy as Shirley had first imagined when she heard that Shaz was due to make an appearance. The girls were happy watching a DVD, and apart from the odd scream and belly laugh Shirley heard very little from them.

10am
Well the big day has finally arrived. Oli and Gus are off to Gay Paree. (Scuse the pun!)

Oli's been like a loon, he's well excited. I hope it's all he wants it to be, and that Gus doesn't go wandering in Paris!

Shirley was feeling generous and decided to let the over-excited Oli have a half day to which he was delighted. He could spend the afternoon getting ready leaving Shirley on her own to finish off.

Shirley only had one client left, the unforgettable Marsha the Maneater. She didn't think that Marsha would be too keen when she found out that she wasn't getting Oli to herself for the second week in a row, but there was nothing she could do about it, only go and face the music.

Marsha was a good-time girl, a woman well the wrong side of forty; she lived alone in a tiny terraced house within walking distance of town. The whole place was decorated in animal print, from the wallpaper to the sofa, lamps to rugs; it was mostly either zebra or leopard skin material. Marsha worked in the pub over the road and often brought one of the locals back for some after hours drinking and entertainment. She thought Oli was the most beautiful thing she had ever seen, and though deep down she knew she would never have him in her bed it didn't stop her trying. It had become a bit of a game for her. Shirley rarely went to Marsha's, but today she would have to fight her way through the animal print and get on with it. Sunglasses might be called for, January or not.

5pm

Oli finished at lunchtime and I carried on. He said he wanted to get himself all ready for his weekend of love. Oh my God!

I went to see Marsha the Maneater this afternoon. I thought I couldn't give her to Oli today just before his hollies. I didn't want him stressed out completely. She had a face like thunder when I arrived.

"Where's Oli today?"

"Sorry, Marsha, I know how much you like Oli doing you're hair but he's off on his hols today."

"He never said last week," she said looking very hurt and a bit miffed.

"He must have been miles away, you know Oli," I answered.

"Gone with that boyfriend of his has he?"

"Yeah. Gus."

"I know that Gus one; he used to go out with a lad I worked with once in the pub. He broke Jules's heart. He had a load of flings, little shit. Anyway it's got nothing to do with me, except I am fond of Oli and wouldn't like to see him get hurt."

So the wonderful Gus was a serial shagger. I can't really prove he still is though can I? But with Marsha's info' now, an' all, I'm sure something is going on.

After Marsha, the next job of the day was to take Oli and

Gus to the airport. Fiona and Jason decided to tag along and took ages getting ready – French-style – for the big send off.

Shirley picked the boys up from Oli's house and Jason threw the huge suitcase that Oli had into the boot, just managing to squeeze it in. Gus only had a holdall. Oli had everything but the kitchen sink.

11pm
Dropped the lovebirds off at the airport. They had a big send off from me and the kids. Fiona was wearing a beret and waving a French flag. Jason had drawn a French moussie on his gob with my eyeliner. All for a laugh. Oli loved it. I'm not so sure about Gus. Tossa.

"Friggin' 'ell, you'd swear we were emigrating to Australia not going to Paris for the weekend," Oli said.

"We love ya. Hope you have a great time," I said, blowing kisses, as they walked off through the crowd.

Next I've got to psych meself up for tomorrow's feeding of Mixie the loony cat.

Friday, January 11
8am
I'll have to get a drive-through for lunch cos I've got to go to Oli's. Deep breaths...it's only a cat.

After the drive-through lunch Shirley made her way to Oli's house. She pulled up outside the neat semi. On the outside it looked like any other nineteen-fifties semi. Nice driveway, garage to the side, small little square patch of grass in the front with a neat flower border all around. It even had a cast iron bird bath in the middle of the garden. Inside, however, it was a different story. It was decorated in nineteen-sixties retro style, bright colours, and big designs.

Oli had wanted to keep the outside as it was when his parents had the house in memory of them. They both loved the garden. Inside he wanted to put his stamp on the place and decided to go all out on the sixties theme. Oli loved fashion and interior design. All the furniture was expensive, no cheap and nasty for Oli. The house was spotlessly clean, Oli made sure of that. Nothing was out of place. Dotted around the living room were photographs of Oli with his friends; Shirley was in every one of them. There were a couple of Oli with his parents, and one of his parents on their wedding day.

Shirley gingerly unlocked the glossy red front door and made her way into the hallway. A fresh floral smell hit her from the plug in air-freshener Oli had bought to ward off any unpleasant smells while he and Gus were away. She walked into the turquoise and white living room, no sign of Mixie. On into the kitchen, where she changed his water bowl to fresh water and mixed up the special food Oli had instructed her to give him.

Shirley walked up the stairs and into Oli's bedroom and there lying on the red silk sheets was the cat, himself, Mixie. The sheets were covered in cat hairs but Shirley had no time to sort that out, work called, so knowing Mixie was still around and hadn't been catnapped, Shirley quickly left the house locking the door behind her.

Sorted that flamin' cat out at dinner. In and out I was, thank God. Shame I had to go back there later though!

Great afternoon with the factory girls. Spent the time jangling about the Chrizzy hols and what they had been up to. They all asked about Oli and wanted the low-down of what happened after the New Year's Eve party, cos most of them were there. I played it down and never said too much. I'm not going to gossip about me best mate. It's up to Oli if he wants to tell them or not.

Gail had told the girls I was on me own so only five of them wanted their hair doing today. Usually it's the whole flamin' lot. Me and Oli are usually rushed off our feet. Well at least the girls get their hair done in work time. No use wasting a day off getting your hair done if you can get it done and be paid at the same time, eh? Well that's what Oli usually tells them anyway!

Kelly wanted a trim, Susan, Claire and Rita wanted a cut and blow, and Angie just wanted her fringe trimming and her hair straightened. Gail was keeping Dixie this week. They take it in turns just incase old Comb-Over comes back for something. He never does like, but just in case. I made the arrangements for the following week.

"Back to normal next week, girls."

"I can't wait to hear all about Oli's trip," said Angie dead excited.

"Oh, aye, yeah and we can start to plan your hen night," Susan said.

"Ooooh great, when is it?" I asked.

"Well the wedding's on the fourteenth of Feb' so

maybe a fortnight before. Give us plenty of time to recover, eh girls?" Angie said.

A hen night – that would be great. A real girl's night out. Oli would come too, of course.

I was looking forward to coming straight home but I had to look in on that flamin' cat again. I went in the bedroom to look for him only to find a great big smelly cat shit in the middle of the red silk sheets. Charming!

I was nearly sick. I had to strip the bed completely. I threw the sheets in the washer. I hope to God they'll be ok.

Fiona thinks Mixie is fretting for Oli. I think he did it cos he knows I'm looking after him! That cat's a proper sadist.

9pm
Just had a text from Oli on me mobie.

"Bonjour babes, havin a gr8 time, c u l8er Oli xxx."

Saturday turned out to be pretty quiet with the highlight of the day being the feeding of Mixie the monster cat. With no boyfriend on the scene, best mate away, and kids busy with friends there was little else for Shirley to do but sit and daydream.

Saturday, January 12
1pm
Went round to sort out the shittin' cat. Phew, no shit today. I thought I'd better give it a bit of a stroke. Big mistake, it nearly took me bloody hand off! So it's

no more Mrs. Nice Guy from me.

I know I shouldn't have but I couldn't help meself – I had to have a little nosey at Gus's stuff.

I looked through his wardrobe; he's got some beautiful clothes. Oli's bought most of them for him, I bet. I had a look in a few pockets and in one found a box of matches. I shook it, sounded just like matches but when I opened it there was a tiny piece of paper folded neatly at the bottom of the box. I unfolded it and found a mobile number on it. I put the number in my mobie and put the piece of paper back in the matchbox and the box back exactly where I had found it.

2pm

I wonder what Charlie from the wholesaler is doing now? If he asks me out again, I think I'm gonna go for it. I can always pretend that I'm kiddin' if he says he is. I still haven't had chance to phone that number yet either. I want to do it at home so I can put 1471 in front of the number so they can't trace back the call. Listen to me, eh? I sound like a real private dick, tracing back bloody calls.

7pm

I've just dialled that mobile number I found in Gus's pocket. It went straight to answer machine. Thank God, really, cos I hadn't planned what I was gonna say!

Some fella's voice came on and said he was unable to get to the phone, but if the call was about the job to please leave your name and number and he would get back in touch.

I don't really know what to make of it now. It all seems innocent enough. Maybe Gus is looking for another job, although Oli hasn't mentioned it and why would Gus hide the phone number like that if it was just a job?

<u>Sunday, January 13</u>
<u>1pm</u>
Took Fi and Shaz with me to feed Mixie. Shaz was still wearing the white plastic boots only today she was wearing an even shorter skirt with them and a plastic white jacket to match.

"You not cold, Shaz love?" I asked her.

"I don't feel the cold, me," she said.

It must be all that fake tan she puts on herself. Today she looked almost orange.

I could've screamed; Mixie purred no end for Fi and Shaz. They thought he was amazing. Well I've still got the scratches to prove what a vicious little shit Mixie really is.

I sorted out the bed, so hopefully Oli an' Gus will never know about the shit incident. Oli prides himself in the fact that Shitzie, oh sorry, Mixie has never shit outside his litter tray!!!

"D' yer think the cat is gay as well?" Asked Shaz on the way home.

"What makes you ask that, Shaz?"

"Just wondering, you know, the way it prances round in that diamond collar, it looks like a gay cat that's all," she went on.

Sometimes I wonder about that girl.

The last day of feeding Mixie – hurrah – Shirley was looking forward to the return of her best mate and the end of her cat-sitting duties. There would be many stories of the Parisian interlude she was sure, but she would have to wait until after the pick-up to hear all about it.

<u>11pm</u>
Picked the Froggy queens up from the airport. It was just me and Fi that went. Jason had been offered a few quid to move some stuff for Alf, an old fella who lives near me mum and Auntie Dilys.

Oli and Gus were made up with the trip. Oli talked non-stop with the odd almost French word thrown in. I went in to their's for a quick coffee. Mixie glared at me, and I gave him a right dirty look. Childish – again – but after the shenanigans with the shit I couldn't help meself. Oli was like a little lap dog, with Gus running around after him, carrying in all the luggage and it was him that made the coffee. Gus said he was knackered and went to bed leaving Oli and me and Fi to it. I thought he was dead rude.

"He's knackered, poor thing, we've had a packed weekend and he's back to work early tomorrow," Oli said keeping Gus's part. "He's been a real love all weekend."

"Ok." I said to him. I wasn't convinced at all.

Fi looked over at me, but Oli didn't notice. He was too busy digging through his suitcase looking for the pressies he had bought for us. Perfume for me and Fi and aftershave for Jason. Bless him.

We arranged the work for tomorrow. Barbara and co. changed to Tuesday this week cos sex mad

Joan has got an appointment at the hossie. Maybe it's something to do with over-usage of her little pal! So now Gus is going to drop Oli off at nine in The Bay Tree residential home, and pick him up at five. What with Oli not driving it's the only thing to do... Maybe this will encourage him to start lessons.

"Oh nice one, babes. I love The Bay Tree. The owner always spoils me. I bet she'll make a cracking dinner, girl."

No chance of that then!

Shirley woke up to a dark drizzling day little realising that Monday 14th January would change her life. Nothing much had been planned, it was a day that started out like any other. Breakfast, kids off to school and a coffee whilst reading the paper before the day proper kicked off.

She was due to have the day off in lieu for working alone while Oli was away in Paris. She had planned a look in town; she wanted to exchange a couple of the Christmas presents from her mother. She'd have to do it alone just in case anyone let slip and told her mother she wasn't happy with the gifts – otherwise she'd hear no end of it.

Shirley lived close enough to town to walk in when she was feeling energetic. The drizzle had eased, but Shirley carried her umbrella in her bag just in case. She didn't want damp frizzy hair just in case she saw someone she knew. Shirley always made sure her hair was immaculate. She couldn't understand any hairdresser having messy hair. Hardly a good advertisement...

Town was quiet; everyone had spent all their money over Christmas or in the sales. Shirley walked past an

Easter display in one of the larger stores, rows of small chocolate eggs lined up ready for purchase. No sooner had one holiday finished the shops were keen to promote the next even if it was a while off. Shirley wasn't bothered, she picked up one of the eggs: she always had been a sucker for the consumer society. Alongside the eggs, she noticed Valentine's cards; she picked up one of the funny ones, read the message inside and smiled. Back it went on the shelf; she had no one to give it to, the little chocolate egg would have to suffice for now. Valentine's Day was a little while off; maybe there was still a chance to send a card she thought, even if it was only to Oli, still a few weeks to go.

Shirley managed to change her unwanted Christmas gifts. One was a gift set in a scent that Shirley had liked in the early eighties. Fortunately her taste had moved on – or so Shirley thought. She managed to swap it for something more suitable and up to date. She would swear blind when she saw her mother next that the perfume she was wearing was the original one. Perfume smells differently on different people would be her story and she'd be sticking to it.

The other gift was a jumper. There was nothing wrong with the jumper, provided you were sixty-five... Shirley decided to get a younger, trendier one in the same colour and if her mother ever asked would swear blind it was the same one. Her mum wouldn't be told, so Shirley accepted all presents offered and then did her swaps in secret.

And then, as Shirley wandered around aimlessly watching Liverpool go by, she unwittingly fell upon the truth about the dastardly Gus.

<u>Monday, January 14</u>
<u>5pm</u>
OH...MY...GOD.

What a day today has been. I was in town when I saw Gus. He was buying flowers from the market. I followed him a bit to try and catch up with him, just to make sure Oli got off ok this morning.

I thought it was a lovely gesture, flowers an' all, to carry on the romance after the Paris trip. Maybe he was in love after all! I couldn't believe me eyes when I saw him walk over to this fella, give him a hug and hand over the flowers. I was friggin' gobsmacked.

They were sat on the wall in the square and to me definitely looked pleased to see each other. I thought maybe I could get away with following them, but I realised I would need real proof not just circumstantial stuff (as they say on the telly!). I thought it was worth the risk of losing them: if I was to be believed I would need photographs. I ran back to the market like a loon on extra-loony-juice. I grabbed a throw-away camera from a market stall, threw a couple of quid at the fella and dashed back to where all the action was. I prayed that the dickheads would still be sat on the wall. The fella was there, Gus was nowhere to be seen, though. I was gutted. He'd gone, or maybe I had imagined the whole thing.

Next thing I saw Gus walking over to the fella carrying two takeaway coffees. He'd been to the coffee shop across the way. He never makes Oli a coffee; in fact he never does anything at all for Oli, well not what I have seen of the pair of them – apart from the luggage last night, and it's poor Oli that waits on Gus hand and foot.

As Gus handed the coffee to the fella, they both started to walk up a side street heading straight for the park. I thought I could easily get away with following them, after all I was just out shopping, it was pure coincidence. It wasn't deliberate or sneaky or anything.

Gus looked his usual smart self, he is lovely looking but God does he know it. His dark hair was spiked up and I could almost smell the aftershave Gus always plastered on himself – even from the distance I was keeping. The other fella didn't look that special. Nowhere near as good looking as Oli.

I was like Colombo. I sneaked as close as I could without risking them seeing me. I was desperate to hear some of their convo. Town was busy and they both seemed engrossed so they didn't seem to notice me lurking behind.

"So how was the trip?" The bit on the side asked.

"Oh you know, ok I suppose. Would have preferred it if you could have come," Gus answered.

"Sorry, it's a shame I had to work last minute. I was really looking forward to it. Was your brother able to take my place?"

Some woman pushed in front of me, then, so I didn't get to hear the bastard's answer. Gus had even been lying to his bit on the side. I couldn't believe it.

I managed to catch up with them in the park. It was a much better place for them to get away from prying eyes, snuggling up together like they were right love-birds in the safety of the park.

I was like David Bailey on speed. I used the whole film on them snoggin' and canoodling. The shits!

I took the camera to the one-hour place and have

just looked through them all. Poor Oli, I don't know how I'll tell him.

The time was as right as it was ever going to be. Shirley had sufficient evidence of Gus's infidelity. She could prove it one hundred per cent.

Pulling up outside Oli's house with a knotted nervous feeling in her stomach, Shirley hoped that Gus wasn't in. He usually played a game of football on a Monday. That's if he really ever was in football – it could have been another of his excuses. Oli answered the door with a huge smile on his face, pleased to see Shirley he hugged her and pulled her over the threshold like a long-lost sister.

<u>8pm</u>
Just come back from Oli's. He took it quite well really. All of Gus's clothes are now out on the road out front – all the kecks minus their crotch! Good for Oli, he did scream and shout and blow his friggin' top but as he said, "No one treats me this way and gets away with it."

I then had to drive him round while he put up the picture of Gus and the fella on walls and lamp posts and wrote on them LYING CHEATS.

Apparently the other fella is Matt, the landlord of Frankie's.

So it went well then!

<u>Tuesday, January 15</u>
<u>1pm</u>
Oli's been acting really strangely today. It's like he doesn't really care. We went to Barbara and co. today.

I really felt for Oli cos they were all waiting for all the Paris details, but he was fine.

"So girls, thanks to Miss Marple over there, I've found out in time what a little shit he really was. Thank God for Shirley. She did a great bit of the old detective work there, didn't you babes?" Oli said smiling.

Barbara looked on as if in deep thought.

"Well at least you had a bit of a holiday out of it, Oli, love," Joan said.

"Aye Joan, girl, so if I get a bit desperate can I borrow your little pal?" Oli said laughing.

Shirley's house was never short on friends calling round. Shirley revelled in the fact that her kids brought friends round. It made her feel that her home was a welcoming place. Tonight Jason was treating Digo his best mate to tea at Shirley's.

Digo was a lad some might describe as 'the lights are on but nobody's home'. Not the smartest kid in the world, but Jason and Digo had been friends since primary school. Shaz had a crush on Digo but he wasn't interested. Digo was more into cars, motorbikes and hanging around with Jason.

8pm

Jason bought Digo over for tea.

"How's it going, Digo, your mum all right?" I asked.

"Oh, aye, yeah, she's sound. She's gorra job now, so she's made up. She works on the market, on the shoes and that," Digo answered.

"Oh, nice, I bet she can get you a good deal eh?"

"Na, Shirley, I wouldn't wear them, they're all plastic crap."

Well I know a girl who would... It looked like the plastic-coated Shaz might be in for a disappointment on the Digo front...

THREE

<u>Wednesday, January 16</u>
<u>5pm</u>
Well, an eventful day! Oli keeps getting text messages from pond-life Gus. He even had a text message from Matt, threatening to do him over for splashing photies of the pair of them over town. Oli wasn't bothered.

The big news of the day is I'M GOING ON A DATE! With Charlie from the wholesale. We went in today. He said the same thing as usual and I said YES. He said he would treat me, cos I give him a treat every time I go in! So we're meeting in town, Friday night. Well, I didn't want him to come to the house. It is only a casual date after all. I don't want to start bringing fellas to the house. It's not fair on the kids. When I meet Mr Right then maybe, but until then our house is a private place just for me and the kids. I'll get a taxi, we'll have a few drinks and go on for something to eat.

I am a bit nervous but in a way I'm looking forward to it. I'm looking forward to being taken out really. I know I go out with me mates and all that but this is a chance for someone to take me out, treat me, and hopefully spoil me a bit. I miss that side of a relationship. Mind you the spoiling doesn't last that long does it, eh? Before you know it you're paying half on nights out, then paying the lot and it's onto washing his socks and undies in no time!

Oli was made up, bless him.

What the frig' am I going to wear?

Shirley's wardrobe bulged with clothes, but like many women she never seemed to have anything to wear. She always bought stuff she liked without stopping to consider whether or not she had anything that it would look good with. Her wardrobe was full of lovely things but only a few actual 'outfits' that went well together.

Oli, however, had a great sense of style. No, there was no alternative, he would have to sort Shirley out, so they took advantage of their lunch break and went into town to have a look for something suitable for a casual first night out.

Oli picked up dresses and skirts for Shirley to try on and found the most beautiful high-heeled strappy sandals Shirley had ever seen. Much to the young sales assistant's horror, Oli pushed his way into the changing room with Shirley.

"I'm her personal shopper so I have to go in. Plus I'm no threat to anyone, in fact I'll offer a bit of advice," he said barging past the taken aback teenager.

Shirley tried Oli's choices on and together they decided on the perfect outfit for a first date.

Oli offered a few women who were trying on their choices a bit of advice too and as usual was a huge hit with them all. He was even offered a job by the manager, who'd returned from her lunch break to find Oli had encouraged three women to spend more than they had bargained for.

"I'll bear you in mind," Oli said to the manager, as they were leaving. "I've had a few offers from London fashion houses... If they don't work out I'll be back in touch."

<u>Thursday, 17 January</u>
<u>2pm</u>
Had quick look in town for something to wear tomorrow night. With Oli's advice I decided on a midnight blue straight skirt just on the knee, nice three quarter-sleeved cardigan with velvet trim to match and a gorgeous pair of really high, patent leather, strappy sandals, they are fan-bloody-tastic and they cost a fortune. I hope the outfit isn't too much for a quick drink and something to eat...

"You look fab, babes. I could almost shag you meself," Oli'd said when I tried the lot on in the shop.

"I'm not looking for a shag, just a nice night out, a bit of pampering and being made to feel special."

"Well you are more than special to me, babes," Oli replied, giving me a kiss on the cheek.

I love that man. I hope he will get over that shit Gus soon. I know he is hurt and trying to be brave.

11pm
Jason and Fi are ok about this meal thing tomorrow. Well, it is only a meal and a few drinks, hardly the date of the year is it?

Before Shirley went down to breakfast on Friday, she pulled the little pink diary from its drawer. Shirley smiled and then gulped, the butterflies started to build up in her stomach as she thought about the date that night.

Friday, 18 January
8am
I didn't sleep that well last night; I kept waking up thinking about this date. Maybe I should cancel. I think I will. It's been so long since I went on a proper date and the thing is if it all goes wrong I'll have to face him again. Why am I putting myself through this?

The working day lay ahead for Shirley and she really hoped this would take her mind off the date – otherwise she might well lose her bottle before the off. And that wouldn't half be a shame given the effort Oli had put into getting her to look the part – he was looking forward to it more than she was!

"How you feeling about tonight, babe?" Oli asked as they drove away from the first job of the day.

"Me nerves are shattered. I don't know if I can go through with it," Shirley answered taking a deep breath.

"Behave, you daft cow. It's only Charlie. Just be

yourself and have fun."

Luckily, they were just turning into Henshaw's and the girls were on them before Shirley had time to respond.

They were all delighted to see Oli and upset for him when they found out about Gus and his cheating.

Susan put Oli in full charge of Angie's hen night, to keep his mind off his own disaster. He was over the moon, this was going to be even more fun than kitting Shirley out for a date, and ran around the place as excited as a kid on Christmas morning. He promised Angie a night never to be forgotten.

The busy afternoon (five blow dries and four restyles) did take Shirley's mind off her anxieties and listening to the girls recount the week's jollies she even started to relax and look forward to an evening out.

Back home there were still the kids to sort out prior to the big glam up, though. She wasn't quite sure what to say to them about where she was going and, more importantly, who with.

"What's for tea, Mum?" Jason asked.

"Hey, I'm off out tonight, can't you get your own?" Shirley replied.

The last thing she wanted to do was start preparing food, she had herself to prepare.

"Oh, aye, yeah, the big date, can't you give us some money and I'll go the chippy for me and Fi?"

"I suppose. More bloody money!" Shirley said.

Shirley gave Jason the money and headed upstairs to the seclusion of her pink fluffy bedroom to start the task of getting ready.

<u>7pm</u>
Text message from Oli. "Have a gd 1 babes, U deserve it. Luv ya xxxxx."

Ah he's so sweet. Better get me skates on. I'm meeting Charlie in town at eight. God I hope he turns up.

With her diary safely back in her drawer and her make-up and hair looking the best she had ever managed it Shirley set off downstairs to parade herself in front of the kids before her taxi arrived.

"Oh my God, Mum, you look lovely," Fiona said going over to Shirley for a closer inspection.

"Very nice, Mum.' Was all Jason could muster.

Shirley felt good. The outfit was perfect although she did wonder how her feet would feel by the end of the evening.

Just on eight o'clock, Shirley arrived in town and made her way up the stairs to the bar. It wasn't too crowded and Charlie sat waiting for her.

Charlie had obviously made an effort: he was wearing even more gold than usual and his eyes near popped out of his head when he clocked Shirley. Within seconds there was plenty of conversation, no awkward silences, and the drinks were certainly helping to settle Shirley's nerves and it all seemed to be going well. By the time they left the bar and headed for the Indian restaurant down the road, Shirley felt almost relaxed.

Once inside the restaurant, they were ushered to a table for two by the door. It was a little draughty, but the place was crowded so Shirley thought she would soon warm up.

The food arrived and Charlie appeared to have romance on his mind... The more he drank, the more he complimented Shirley. Though it was flattering, she felt a bit embarrassed. She wasn't used to so many compliments and tried to change the subject every time. She hadn't envisaged this when she confided in her little pink friend, nor what was to come...

Saturday, 19 January
1.30am

Just got in. What a night, what a friggin' night!

Met Charlie in town, we had a few drinks in the bar, first. I must say, even before a few vodkas, Charlie looked pretty good. We had a right laugh, and got on really well. The drinks were flowing and so was the conversation.

"Let's go the Indian," Charlie said, about nine-ish.

"Aye, ok, I fancy a curry."

"Even if we will be shittin' through the eye of a needle tomorrow, eh girl?" Charlie said. I should've known then it was about to go downhill.

"I've fancied you for ages, Shirl', and tonight you look amazing," he said, clutching a piece of limp naan bread in his hand.

"Oh ta, this is lovely this," I said, feeling a little embarrassed. Hoping to change the subject I went on about work.

We finished our food and sat and chatted over coffee. We did seem to get on ok. I had enjoyed meself, despite worrying about it.

"I'm just going to nip to the loo," I said.

"It's not working already is it?" Charlie asked laughing.

"Oh, no. I just need to powder me nose," I said feeling a bit uncomfortable.

I was just coming out the ladies when Charlie came to meet me.

"Ok then, girl, off we go."

"I haven't finished me coffee yet," I said.

"Never mind that, I'll get you another one later. Come head, let's go," he said hurrying me out the door.

Thinking nothing of it, I followed him out. I did wonder what the rush was, though.

"Quick, run. Run," he said grabbing me elbow as I struggled to get me coat on.

He grabbed me arm and started pulling me along the road.

"What you doing, you mad bastard? Are you round the friggin' pipe?"

Then I looked behind me and saw three Indian fellas running after us, shouting and bawling. Obviously waltzing bollocks had done a runner without paying.

Me new sandals were getting the run-in of their lives. They'd ruined. We must've run half a friggin' mile along the street, looking like complete loons.

Somehow we managed to outrun the restaurant staff, though God only knows how.

"Soz about that, Shirl, but when I looked in me wallet I was spent up. You like a few drinks you, don't yer?

"I haven't been out for ages. I didn't realise how dear thing are now. Oh eh, and yer Jesus boots are knackered. I am sorry love," he said looking down sheepishly at the remains of me beautiful sandals.

I looked down. Seventy-five quid's worth... One strap held the left one and the right one had only half a heel.

"You're all right, Charlie love, it can't be helped. I would've paid if you'd said."

"No way. I'd never be able to look you in the face again. I'd be so ashamed."

And you're not now I thought?!!

"Maybe we can do it again some time? Eh, Shirley?"

"Aye, maybe," I said. Thinking, you must be friggin' joking.

"Great, but wear yer trainees next time, eh?"

Poor old Charlie. I can't help feeling sorry for him. I know I shouldn't. I won't be able to go to that restaurant again ever and I am friggin' mad about the sandals, but the look on his face... I think he got out of his depth going out on a proper dinner date. I don't think he's used to it. Maybe Oli was right and he's dead lonely really.

A lie in was definitely in order for Shirley, she needed to recover big time from the night before. She arrived home in tears about the beautiful sandals. How was she going to explain to everyone? She would have to lie about the whole thing. There was no way she could admit to doing a runner she thought, as she lay shell-shocked in bed.

But it was too late to suddenly dream up some great excuse, the evidence had already been found...

"Hey, what's going on?" Shirley asked feeling the cold on her feet as the duvet cover lifted.

"Friggin' 'ell, Mum. I was just checking your feet. I saw the state of your sandals and thought you'd been run over or summat. I was panicking there for a minute. What the bleeding 'ell happened?" Fiona asked, looking very concerned.

"Hey, language... I don't want to talk about it now," Shirley said pretending to go back to sleep.

"Did he see you and do one, and you had to run after him?" Jason asked.

Shirley hadn't even heard him come in.

"Jason, don't be tight." Fi said.

"Only jokin', Ma. What happened?" He said trying not to laugh.

Shirley refused to tell them. She couldn't think of any excuse at such short notice – how could she say that their mum had done a runner from the Indian without paying and completely knackered a pair of expensive sandals in the process?

She spent the rest of the morning in bed, going over what had happened in her head. Her diary entry was certainly entertaining if nothing else!

Oli was due over later and Shirley knew then she could bare her soul to him, safe in the knowledge he wouldn't laugh – at least at her – or spread the story of her humiliation. The fewer people that knew, the better, as far as Shirley was concerned.

Oli turned up eager for the lowdown. Jason was out with Digo, and Fiona was at Shaz's house, so Shirley knew they had the house to themselves for a few hours at least. She put the kettle on, made a coffee and they both sat down with a pack of biscuits at the ready for a post-mortem on the previous night's activities.

Shirley started from the beginning, from getting ready to the meeting in the bar and the debacle at the Indian and its aftermath – Oli thought they should get seventy-five quid's worth of free hair products as compensation.

"Tight bastard, wait till I see him. Short arms, long pockets that's his trouble," Oli said disgusted.

"Nah, Oli, leave it. He was sorry."

"I bet you looked a right couple of arseholes running up the road. Oh my God, I would've paid good money meself to see the state on you. He's never asked you out again has he?"

"Yeah, he has," Shirley laughed.

"Well put yer granny shoes on next time!"

Shirley and Oli said their goodbyes and she invited him round for Sunday dinner the following day. Sunday was one of the rare days Shirley cooked. She was very good at cooking roast dinners, one useful thing she had been taught by her mother and she used her foolproof guide every time. Shirley thought it made her look as if she could cook everything if she was able to do a roast. No doubt by the end of Sunday evening there would be a house full with Shaz and Digo along for the ride.

Sunday, 20 January
9pm

Oli came round for Sunday dinner. All seems quiet now on the Gus front. He's had no more messages or threats about photies. All the lads that usually hang around in their gang think Gus is a scum-bum now and have changed their drinking gaff from Frankie's,too.

So at least Oli doesn't have to look at Gus and Matt all the time while he's out on the town.

He's had a few offers, an' all, now that people know he's back on the market!

Shaz, Fi's mate came over after tea, Digo turned up as well. Apparently Shaz fancies Digo and wants Fi and Jason to get them together. Oli was still over so we all sat down to watch a DVD.

Everyone had made themselves comfortable to watch the film, when Oli thought it would be fun to have a little laugh at Shirley's expense. He knew he could get away with it if it was done in good heart.

"Hey, did you see 'Crimewatch' last night?" Oli asked, looking over at Fi and Jason.

"I never watch it me," Shaz said.

"Oh, you missed a treat there, girl, all forces have been called in..." Oli continued.

Everyone looked over at Oli eager for more information.

"Oh, aye, yeah; big hunt on. The bizzies are looking for a couple last seen pegging it from the Indian on Hope Street. The only evidence is half a heel left from the woman's shoe." Oli said, by now a big smile was slapped wide across his and the kids' faces.

"Bloody 'ell, it's like Cinderella that is. I wonder who she is. I think that's dead romantic that me," Shaz said.

"What, doing a runner, romantic? It's breaking the law that, don't you think, Mum?" Fiona said looking straight at Shirley.

Everyone laughed, including Shaz, though they were all sure she didn't have a clue what was going on.

While everyone sat glued to the television, Shaz was glued to Digo. Shirley smiled as she looked at Digo and Shaz. Someone would have to tell Shaz that Digo thought shoes from the market were crap... If she's to be in with a chance with Digo, Shaz will have to ditch those plazzy boots, Shirley thought to herself.

"Who's farted? Smelly gits..." Fi said looking over at Jason.

"It's a poor arse that doesn't rejoice," he laughed, along with Digo who thought it was hilarious.

"Minger," Fi said, disgusted with Jason and Digo.

Just before a riot was about to break out Shaz stopped the whole thing with her screeching.

"What the friggin' 'ell's this?" Shaz screamed, pulling something grey from the side of the sofa.

"Pass it here, Shaz," Shirley said, going to switch the big light on.

The material came at Shirley flying through the air.

"Oh my God, it's a pair of undies!" Shirley said shocked.

There were aargh's and urrgh's from everywhere. Shirley held them up. Originally white, now grey, M&S Y-fronts.

"Hey, where have they come from? Hey, are you sure you didn't bring that old cheapskate fella back here Shirley?" Digo said.

Shirley looked at him horrified – how did he know about Cheap Charlie?

"Hey, you cheeky... Are you sure they aren't yours, Jason?" Shirley asked looking over at him.

"No way, I only wear boxies me. Look they've even got a big on 'em," Jason said looking disgusted.

"Well I thought maybe your nanna had bought you

some once. I'm sure she did. Yeah, one Christmas," Shirley said determined to identify the owner of the mysterious undergarment.

"Behave, Mum. Maybe when I was about five," Jason responded, looking embarrassed as every one laughed.

"Well they're not mine. Only the finest quality thongs for me," said Oli.

Digo looked at him and squirmed! Shaz on the other hand looked on eager for more info', which needless to say she didn't get.

"Are you a boxie or a thong fella, Digo? I'm definitely a thong girl. Oh yeah, none of your belly warmers for me," Shaz said, looking over longingly at Digo.

"Me dad says you used to 'ave to open a girl's knickers to see her arse, now you 'ave to open her arse to see her knickers."

"You askin? " Shaz shot back at poor Digo, trying to look all sexy.

"You're all right," he muttered, looking terrified, as the rest of them tried to cover their giggles with cushions or papers.

"I know, they must be Frank's – from New Year's Eve. When he did the full Monty, someone must of shoved them down the back of the sofa. Dirty gits..." Shirley said, glad to have solved the mystery.

"Ah, shame. To leave a skid like that poor old Frank must've really been shitting himself," Oli said looking – fairly – serious.

"My God, Mum, I've eaten loads of dinners on this sofa since then and those skiddy undies have been right next to me. I feel sick. I really do," Fiona groaned, pulling a face.

"Let's chuck 'em away, he can't have missed them."

"He's probably too ashamed to ask for them back. I would be, wouldn't you?' Fiona said.

Next minute, Shaz was on her feet, through to the kitchen and grabbing a carrier bag. She threw the undies in and went out the door and put them through Shirley's neighbour's letterbox. The only thing is she posted them to the wrong house. Now they are lying on Ted and Pam's hall floor, not Frank's. Pam, the peroxide loving blonde; Ted, the women's-knicker-wearing perv'...

Monday, January 21
6pm
Made a mad dash for the car this morning. Shitting meself in case Ted or Pam see me and ask if I know any thing about the mystery under cracks.

Spent the morning with Barbara and co. "So Oli love, Shirley did a good job finding out about your fella then?" Barbara asked.

"Oh, aye, yeah Barb. Right little Sherlock this one. Photies the lot. Didn't you babe?"

"Oh yeah. I had me suspicions, but you can't do anything till you've got concrete evidence can ya?" I answered.

Barbara looked deep in thought.

"Come and look at me new kitchen tiles," Barbara said, all officious like, looking at me and Oli.

We both went through, a bit puzzled really.

"Oh, aye, yeah: very nice Barb. I looked at these when I was doing up my place," Oli said inspecting the tiles.

"Oh sod the tiles, Oli," Barb said quickly, closing the kitchen door.

We both looked at her wondering what the hell was going on.

"Now listen, Oli, you said Shirl did a good job of finding out about your fella?" Barb said.

"Yeah, but what's that got to do with your tiles, love?" Oli asked all confused.

"Nothing, I just didn't want that lot to hear, not yet anyway, not till it's all sorted out. Me mother would only worry," Barb whispered, starting to get a little bit annoyed that we were both being so thick I think.

"So?" I asked her.

"I think my hubbie's up to no good. He's never in, always working, well so he says. When I ring up work they say he's out or working from home." Barb told us sticking the kettle on again.

She only wants us to find out, get all the evidence and stuff. All top secret. Only her, me and Oli must know, and she'll pay us and all!

Me and Oli looked at each other.

It was all well and good me doing the digging for Oli. He's a mate. I wanted to help him out. This was gonna be a bit different. It was quite exciting though, sneaking around after Gus. I did really enjoy nailing him. It was horrible having to tell Oli after, though, but it wouldn't be the same telling someone not so close, I suppose.

Oli was made up. He thought it was a fantastic idea and told her we were up for it.

"It's great isn't it, providing an extra service to our client," he said, all excited, as Barb went through with the pot of tea for everyone and a plate of biccies.

"Well, it's certainly different," I told him, as we both took a few minutes in the kitchen to think about the offer.

"Hey we'll be like Dempsey and Makepeace," he said seriously. "Or Starsky and Hutch, I used to love that when I was younger. Saturday nights were never the same when that finished. I watched all the detective and police stuff when I was little. I was well into all of them. Me dad had hoped I'd join the police."

"Yeah, saw yourself as Starsky did ya?'

"No I always wanted to be Makepeace. She had lovely hair, didn't she?"

"Typical. Well, like you say we have got the perfect cover in our line of work and she's paying us an' all. That will come in handy for me anyway, the kids are always needing stuff. It'll be a laugh an' all eh?"

9pm

Well, it would be quite an adventure, now I've had time to think about it a bit, especially as Oli has already taken on the role of Inspector Clouseau!

So now it's Operation Dave and Mave, I suppose, or D + M for short. We have to find the concrete evidence so that Barbara can take him to the cleaners.

Barbara knows where this woman Mave lives, so I thought we could go round an' offer a free hairdo or something, say she's won it or it's a promotion... Hey, I'm dead chuffed cos I'm getting good ideas. We can get some info from her then. I'll see what my partner!! Oli thinks tomoz.

Shirley spoke to Oli about her plan for Operation D & M over lunch on Tuesday and he thought it was a great idea. They got Mave's address from Barbara and a useful tip – apparently Mave the homewrecker works a half-day on Wednesdays, so they decided to pay her a visit the next day. The game was on!

Tuesday afternoon, however, was something Shirley was not looking forward to that much. It was her stock-up day at the wholesaler and she would have to face up to Charlie for the first time since the Indian incident.

"All right Shirley, love? I've been trying to get hold of you all weekend but you're mobie must be off," Charlie said.

"Oh, aye, yeah – flat battery," she lied.

"Hey, we had a boss night didn't we, girl…" he went on, oblivious to the fact that anything had gone amiss.

"Yeah, apart from wrecking me new shoes," Shirley pointed out.

"Oh, aye, yeah. Sorry about that, Shirley love," Charlie smirked, pulling a bit of a guilty face.

"Oh, aye, yeah, I heard about that Charlie mate. Come on then Rockefeller, I think Shirley deserves a good deal on her stuff today. They cost a load them you know. Call it a bit of compo," Oli butted in.

"Don't worry, you're all right."

"No, he's right. Stock up love, today it's all half price, honest."

So they took him at his word and piled the stuff in. The trolley was loaded high with products they didn't need for ages.

"Make the most of it girl. Call it compo for the insult to your dignity, having to do a runner the other night like some old scally. Cheap old git," Oli told Shirley.

So they carried on loading up and it ended up costing Shirley a fortune, but as it was buy one get one free, as Oli kept reminding her, she got her money's worth out of Charlie all the same.

"It was great to see the look on Charlie's face. I don't think he'll ask me out again, not in a hurry anyway. Thank God...' Shirley said to Oli as they loaded up the car.

Oli laughed.

"Well I'm back on the market, just like you. What do I mean back on the market I was never friggin' off was I?' Shirley said flatly.

"Not for long babe, not for long. The right fella will come along for us both, you mark my words," Oli said.

Shirley wasn't so sure, not on her account anyway, but for now she had other things to occupy her mind... Sorting out Barbara: the start of Operation Dave and Mave.

Shirley woke up early knowing that today, Wednesday, she would have to make a start on her new part-time career. She did feel a bit strange and so, as usual at such times, leaned over to pick up her little pink diary and put her thoughts down on paper, to see if she could make any sense of them.

<u>Wednesday, January 23</u>
<u>8.30am</u>
I feel a bit weird about going to spy on this Mave woman today. It doesn't seem right. I know I did it for Oli, but I know him, and I was only doing it cos I love him. I don't know these pair at all. Anyway I'll see how it goes. Bloody 'ell, am I getting a conscience? Na!

The morning was to be spent in West Haven nursing home where Oli was as usual a great hit with the old folks and the staff, and then onto Mave for the start of their first official snooping mission.

5pm
We spent the morning in West Haven. Mavis's ginger pubic-looking hair looked little less pubic now and a bit more like she had just been sat too near the fire.

"Hey, Mavis, your perm has held well," Oli said as he passed her.

I pulled a face at him, and one of the young carers turned away laughing.

"Thanks love, I can't see that well, you know, but me grandson came at the weekend and said I looked like Ronald McDonald. I don't know who that is, do you, love?" Mavis said.

"Oh, aye, yeah, Mavis, one of them dead famous people off the telly. Famous all over the world, worth millions."

"Ooo, really? You've made me day, love," Mavis smiled.

"Oh, Oli." I said, when we were out of the room.

"What? I never lied, did I? He is famous and loaded and I don't think there are many countries – if any – that haven't heard of him. Well it made her day, eh?"

We went to see the homewrecker Mave next. I told Oli I'd been feeling weird about the spying thing...

"Listen, girl, if he is a lying shit, well we'll've helped to catch him and we will've saved Barb years of hell and lies."

The plan was to call at Mavis the homewrecker's and say we were new to the area and offering the first hairdo free. Barbara is paying all the expenses, or should I say Dave is really, so we wouldn't be out of pocket.

"Hi, we're Cuts and Curls mobile hair salon. You are the lucky winner of our free hairstyle," I said, all professional like, when Mavis's front door opened.

She was onto us like a rash. Shows she must be a grabber. We didn't have time to explain it all properly even. As soon as I said 'free', we were in.

"Oh great, I've just finished work and I could do with a hairdo cos I'm off out tonight," the grabber said.

"Oh, anywhere nice?" Oli enquired politely.

I looked at him. Talk about making it obvious. Mind you she probably thought he was a typical nosy hairdresser.

"Yeah, I'm out with me fella. It's a birthday meal. A bit late like. It was his birthday the other day," she said.

"Oh couldn't make it on the day then?" I said. Well, I thought in for the kill. She was obviously too thick to notice anything.

We were by this time in full swing of a cut and blow.

"Well ya see, 'es only married, isn't 'e? " she went on.

"Oh no, who is he, not your boss?" Oli blurted.

I held me breath.

"Aye, yeah, it is. I shouldn't say anything, but you don't know him do ya?" she went on.

Anyway we got the lot. She was full of info. A right bragger. To make matters worse she loved the hairdo and wants us to go there regular. Well, as I said to Oli, for the time being it will be good, cos if Barbara wants to nail Dave for every penny, and he's got a fair few, she needs concrete evidence like photies.

Mave said they have a business night away planned next Monday. Apparently Dave hasn't told his wife he's going away yet. He's gonna say it's a last minute meeting. She said they were off to this really posh hotel in Manchester, showed us the brochure thing and all. It looked fantastic.

Thursday, 24 January
1pm
I phoned Barb this morning.

"Oh hiya, Shirley, love."

"How's it going, Barb?' I asked her.

"Well, he came home and told me he's got a last minute meeting on Monday," she said. "I did try and get him to take me along an' all. Said I could do a bit of shopping while he's in the meeting.'

"What did he say to that?' I asked.

"Said there was no point cos he couldn't spend the evening with me, he had to network over dinner with colleagues. Network indeed!"

Well he wasn't lying there was he? The little shit. Well big shit actually, he's like a sumo poo, I thought. I didn't say it to Barb, though. I was going to, but thought better of it. Mavis the homewrecker is probably after his dosh. Mind you she's a minger. Common as muck and a face like a smacked arse.

"So, Shirley, are you and Oli up for going to Manchester to keep an eye? All expenses paid...' Barb asked.

"Are you serious, Barb?" I felt really shocked. "I mean we're happy to do it for ya, but the all expenses paid bit I mean, it'll cost a fair bit to stay in the hotel."

"Course I am, he'll be paying in the long run. All expenses paid and a couple of hundred quid each for you and Oli for your trouble,' Barbara continued.

"We'll do you proud, Barb love. We'll get the photos an' all."

"Well if you get photos and I can nail him I'll give you five hundred quid each. It'll be worth it believe you me.

"No one makes a fool out of Barbara," she finished.

I put the phone down and phoned Oli straight away. I couldn't wait to tell him, especially about the money side of it. All expenses paid plus a couple of hundred quid each for our trouble and if we nail him five hundred. That's loads to a single mum like me. Tax free an' all. I could definitely make a career out of this detective work if the money is always this good.

"Oh great, we'll have a right laugh," Oli said, when I explained the crack.

"Yeah, but the best is yet to come, it's worth two hundred quid or five hundred a piece if we nail him," I said all excited.

"Bloody hell, we could do with another one of these babe. That Gus took me for a few bob you know."

"Well this'll help pay some of that back, Oli," I suggested.

Shirley decided to ask her mum to stay and keep an eye on the kids while she went to Manchester. They were old enough to be left alone, but Shirley wanted to make sure they got to school and her mother was sure to make sure they went.

She told her mum and the kids that she and Oli were off for a few days training in Manchester on some new colouring products.

"Bloody 'ell, Mum I didn't think any of your clients were into top fashion colours. More the blue rinses." Fi said when Shirley told her.

"Hey, cheeky, we're branching out. We wanna get some new clients," Shirley said. She didn't feel she was lying exactly, when she'd said they were branching out. They were...only more on the detective than the hair-dyeing side!

FOUR

<u>Friday, 25 January</u>
<u>12pm</u>

We're all sorted now for Monday. We're gonna work till dinner then get off to Manchester. We've booked into the same hotel, so we've really got to blend in so they don't see us. A hard thing to do when you're going with Oli the drama queen!

We'll come back Tuesday some time, it depends what the cheats are up to. I'd only booked Barbara and co. and the two misses for Tuesday, but Barbara is going to cancel her mum and that and I went to the two misses today instead. They were great. I told them Oli and I were off on a course and they said they will both try a new colour when we get back. Well let's hope a slightly lighter shade of blue tint will impress!

As it was Friday afternoon it was on to the factory girls after the two misses. What with plans for their new career in full swing, Oli had forgotten to make plans for Angie's hen night.

"Come on Oli, they gave you this to help you take your mind off Gus, so you've got to get cracking," Shirley said in the car on the way over.

"Gus who? I'm having a whale of a time. No babe, I will sort something out for her. I've got a few ideas already. Never fear, party animal Oli's here. It's next Saturday, isn't it?"

Luckily Angie was off.

"What's up with her?" Shirley asked the girls.

"The wild shites," one of them said.

"Been out on the ale again?" Oli said.

"Aye, yeah. Legless she was. Apparently the beer was so flat it could 'ave been sold in envelopes. Mind you twelve pints is enough to make even Angie ill, eh?" Gail said.

As Angie wasn't in they all started to plan a few things for her. Oli was put in charge of the dare list!

Susan's sister Tracey turned up for a quick trim. She used to work in the factory with her sis, but finished to have a baby last year. She used to be a regular so Shirley and Oli didn't mind doing her once in a while if she popped in. She'd brought the baby with her...Wesley!

"Hiya, Trace love, how yer doing?" Oli said.

"Aye great, ta, glad to be away from this place..." she said looking round in disgust.

"Aw in't he lovely, little Wesley. He looks just like his dad," Shirley said looking down at the baby all covered in melted chocolate. He didn't look a bit like Tracey so Shirley thought he must look like his dad.

"Hey Shirl, do you know something we don't know?" Susan said all excited.

"What d'yer mean?" Shirley asked looking confused.

"Well she doesn't know who his dad is, do you, Trace love? So who do you think 'e looks like?" Susan said all serious.

"Na, could be one of five – don't think Shirley knows any of 'em, though. I'm gonna have to get one of them DNA thingies cos I need to go after the CSA to get some money from one of 'em. I'm dead skint, even with me benefits." Tracey looked as confused as Shirley felt embarrassed.

Oli and Shirley looked at Susan and Tracey with a mixture of horror and pity.

"If you've got any ideas, though, Shirl, we could narrow it down a bit so as not to involve all of them at first. I mean you don't want to get a bit of a reputation do you Trace? I mean if they all know at the same time it could be a bit dicey for yer girl," Susan said, looking seriously at her befuddled sister.

"Gail thinks it could be Kev who works behind the bar in the Dragon, Steve who works behind the bar in the Albert, or Mike, Tina's boyfriend," Susan said looking over at Gail who stood on nodding her head.

"Na, it can't be Steve cos I never shagged him, well not that month anyway," Tracey said, seemingly not caring a damn.

"You'd best get it sorted properly girl, you don't want to blame the wrong fella do yer?" Oli said, trying to haul his chin back up off the floor.

"Aye I know, I'll go for those five one at a time then if it's not them I'll keep on going. It was the time those lads from that Welsh darts team were over for the week.

They're due back again in the summer. I'll sort these five out first and if I've had no joy by then I can start on the Welsh darts fellas." Tracey looked quite pleased at her ingenuity.

"Hey, I thought you said it was one of five not twenty-five!" Susan shouted at her.

"Aye, I thought it was, but I forgot about the darts team though," Tracey said, trying to defend herself.

"Bloody hell how does she sleep at night. Well I suppose the answer is that she's not sleeping is she, that's the problem!" Shirley whispered to Oli.

All the girls booked their hairdos for the following week and Angie had left a message saying she wanted a colour before her big night out, so they booked that in too.

"No probs we're going on a course on colour on Tuesday so we'll be bob on for yer, next week, girls," Oli said.

There were excited oohs and aahs from the girls.

"Friggin' 'ell, Oli, we're not actually going on a colouring course yer know," Shirley said when they left the factory.

"Oh no, we're not are we? Bloody 'ell I'm beginning to believe it meself. Well isn't that the sign of a true professional, believing in the role. Making it seem real..."

Saturday was all arranged. Shirley was due to pick her mum up and take her into town with Fiona. Shirley wanted to keep on her mother's good side because she wanted to keep her happy before her Manchester weekend. She needn't have bothered though, her mother adored the kids and was excited by the prospect of spending the weekend with them. Her mum felt a bit neglected now

Jason and Fiona were older. She realised they had things to do, friends to see, just like Shirley had at their age, but she missed them so much. She was really looking forward to a weekend in charge...

Shirley's mum was after a few things for Auntie Dilys who, surprise, surprise, was feeling a bit under the weather. Again! Shirley herself bought a new pair of shoes, similar to the strappy pair but cheaper, and a few bits for her overnight stay. She picked up a pack of batteries for the camera for Monday, too. They were going to take Oli's fantastic new camera. The latest digital model. Shirley hoped they could figure out how to use it when the time came.

"So you're on your own in the bingo tonight then, Mum?" Shirley asked.

"No love, why?"

"Well what with Auntie Dilys being not well."

"Oh no she'll be all right to go the bingo."

"So, too ill to lug her shopping round town. Resting ready for the bingo, eh!" Shirley whispered to Fiona.

Fiona got a pair of boots. She tried for the plastic pair like Shaz from the market. They had a new line in pink ready for the summer!

"It's still bloody January. No way," Shirley said.

"No one cares about the month now, Mum. People wear boots in August. It's all about the fashion ya know. You'd better get to know that before you go on that colouring course with all those trendy hair stylists," Fi whined.

"Am I more the blue tint and perm brigade than the trendy haircuts and new look hair colour? Imagine all the clients in West Haven with the latest shades and new chic styles! Like they would give a shit," Shirley threw back.

"So why you going on a colouring course then?"

"Erm, well, to encourage new clients," she lied.

Shirley was just waiting for her mum to ask her to give them a lift to the bingo when she said, "Fiona says you've got a house full tonight so I'll book a taxi for me and Auntie Dilys, you're all right."

"Shaz is sleeping over. You said she could last week."

Oh no, not Shaz. Shirley had forgotten...

"We're meeting her in town. She's got a job on the market on a Saturday, selling fruit and veg," Fiona told her gran.

"Oh that's handy for her," Shirley's mum replied.

"Yeah, she only started last week. I'm surprised she's stuck it this long."

"Stuck it this long? It's only been two weeks!" Shirley couldn't help laughing.

They picked Shaz up from the market about half-five. She looked shattered, and cold.

"I brought you some apples and a few spuds, Shirley. The apples are a bit bruised, though. They're the ones I kept dropping and Carlos, the fella who runs the market, said I couldn't sell them. So I put them to one side and thought I'll keep 'em, they'll do for you. The spuds are the same. I had to run for ages to fetch some of 'em. They were off down the street."

"Oh ta, Shaz. But why don't you take them for your mum?" Shirley said hoping...

"Na, you're all right I nicked a few for her when Carlos went for a bacon buttie. I stuffed 'em in me bag." No shame that girl...

Shirley dropped her mum off – who took a few spuds

and apples, having told Shaz it was good of her to think of them! They had a Chinese takeaway for tea. Surprise, surprise. It's takeaways most nights thanks to Shirley's aversion to the kitchen (Sunday roasts aside, of course).

Shaz and Fiona spent the rest of the night trying out new make-up techniques, so Shirley went up to write a bit more in her little pink diary.

<u>Saturday, January 26</u>
<u>8pm</u>
Left Shaz and Fi trying out new make-up techniques. Shaz wanted to have a go on me but I said I was allergic to that brand of make-up. She was dead proud of her bulging make-up bag, full of stuff from the quid shop. I tried to signal to Fi not to put it on but it was too late.

Fi's got lovely skin, she doesn't need all that crap, and so has Shaz really if she would only leave off it for a bit. But to ask Shaz to leave off the slap would be like asking Auntie Dilys to do her own shopping. Unheard of!

<u>Sunday, 27 January</u>
<u>11am</u>
Woke up to screams of horror from the bathroom. Fiona's face looked like the arse of one of them monkeys in the zoo. It was red and swollen from all that cheap crap she'd put on it last night.

It was the wailing that got Shirley out of bed – she rushed through to the bathroom to find Fiona in tears and her face shining like a beacon through the steam.

"I can't understand it, I've always been fine with it," Shaz said.

"Well we're not all the same," said Shirley, annoyed with Shaz for inflicting such rubbish on Fi.

She had to send Jason down to the chemist. They were open for a couple of hours on a Sunday morning, and he came back pronto with some allergy cream.

"Here ya go. Bloody 'ell you're scary," he said.

"Oh piss off," Fi spluttered, by now in tears.

Fiona said she wasn't going to school tomorrow if her face was still like a monkey's arse. Shirley didn't blame her.

2pm

Phoned Oli. He was still in bed, suffering from a hangover. He'd been out clubbing with a mate who'd come over from somewhere. I can't remember where exactly.

"Oh aye, what's this then?" I said.

"Behave, he's only a mate. Anyway he picked up some fella so he went back with him."

"Ah, you missed out there, love." I said feeling genuinely sorry.

"No way he was minging. I'm not that desperate. Yet, anyway."

I made arrangements with him for Monday's job reminding him to look at the camera instructions, and let him get back to bed.

11 pm

Fiona's face is getting less monkey arse-like now. I

think she'll be ok for school tomorrow after all.

I've got all me stuff ready for this little trip. I'm feeling dead excited now.

Shirley looked over to her little pink suitcase on wheels, all packed up ready for their trip. She felt really excited, it had been ages since she last went away. She was really looking forward to it, so much so she almost forgot that she'd be there to do a job not just to enjoy herself.

Shirley put her little pink diary in one of the pockets of the suitcase, she was sure she would need it if she were going to remember every detail of the trip.

Monday, 28 January
9am
Thank God I am no longer the mother of a girl with a monkey's arse for a face. Fi is back to her beautiful self.

I felt a bit sad saying goodbye to the kids. I'll miss them like mad but I am looking forward to the break.

1pm
We had a busy morning. Oli went to see Marsha and was given a good groping. He's getting used to her now. She's determined, I'll give her that.

I went to pick me mum up so she's ready in ours to keep an eye on the kids. They're great kids and both of them dead clever, but I couldn't trust them to get off to school; they might just decide to skive off for the day while I'm away, or end up having wild parties. Trouble is I remember what I got up to at their age!

So they can't be trusted. Imagine Shaz and Digo over an' all with the place to themselves, well I'd have no home to come back to.

Oli sorted out me best mate Maxie, so the cat will be all right till tomorrow night!

Oli has started on the dare list for Angie, too, so we're well away for Saturday.

They arrived in the 'conference' hotel in a taxi from the station. The hotel was beautiful, four star luxury. Shirley had never stayed in such a lovely place.

They made their way to reception, on the lookout at all times for Mavis; they didn't want to blow their cover having just arrived.

They were given their room key and made their way to the lifts. Their room was on the fourth floor. Excitedly Oli opened the door. A huge king-sized bed stood magnificent in the middle of the room. There was cream and deep red bedding covering it. On either side of the bed stood mahogany bedside cabinets and across from them a huge mahogany wardrobe. The room was massive with an inviting cushion-covered cream sofa under the window, just the place to sit and watch the wide-screen TV.

<u>3pm</u>
Just booked in at the hotel. It is fantastic and the room…! We've got a double room so for one night only me and Oli are a couple! Marsha would be pig sick! We've got a luxury suite. It's bloody fantastic. No expense spared. Well let's face it; it is a lying cheat

that's paying for it, so I don't feel too guilty.

4pm.
Oli's halfway through the mini bar!

6pm.
Just been for a little look round the hotel and who did I see at reception but Dave and Mave looking all lovey dovey. I hid behind a marble pillar.

The porter was with them ready to take their stuff up. I wondered if I could get him to tell me their room number. Probably not...

"This way, sir, madam," the porter said.

It was music to me ears. I couldn't get the porter to reveal all but I knew a man that would. The porter's voice was nearly as camp as me mate Oli's. Hurray, fanbloodytastic! Sorted.

Double time back up to our room: "Oli, quick, get up you lazy bastard. Quick. You've got some serious flirting to do."

Oli was flat out after drinking half the minibar. Tough I thought. We had a job to do and that's what we were gonna do. Ten minutes later Oli was fully informed of the situation and in the reception flirting with Jonny the Porter.

7pm
"Well?" I asked him.

"Room 112. They've booked dinner in the restaurant for eight," Oli said with a big grin on his face, and holding up a spare set of keys with 112 on the fob.

"Result. What did you have to do to get them?" I asked.

"More like what did he have to do?" Oli laughed.

We are miles from them, in room 445, so there should be no chance of bumping into them by accident and giving ourselves away. **Brilliant.**

They had their plan mapped out all they needed now was for it to work. But sometimes even the best made plans don't always go accordingly...

<u>11pm (back in the hotel room)</u>
Thank God we're back in the room. Safe from view.

We went into room 112, just after eight, armed with the digital camera. Oli took a picture of some of their stuff in the room. I stood outside along the corridor keeping Dixie, one eye on the lift the other on the stairs. The next thing I knew, not even ten past eight, Dave 'n' Mave were on their way back.

I pranked Oli on his mobie and luckily he hid himself in time. Apparently Dave had left his mobie in the room and Mavis the silly cow had gone up with him to touch up her make-up.

The loved-up pair only decided it would be exciting to have a quickie while they were waiting for their meal...

Poor Oli, who was in the closet, had to listen to it all. He got a load of photies though, even if he felt like throwing up after his ringside seat at the performance!

"Friggin' 'ell Shirl. I don't think I'll ever recover. I mean I know I've got a weak stomach but that just takes the biscuit. I have never been able to look at any naked woman without feeling sick. I used to throw up nearly if I accidentally saw a Page Three girl over me dad's shoulder of a morning. It was curtains if I'd already eaten me cornflakes. They'd weigh on me till after first break. I'll have to have a drink babe." He was still shaking.

"You're all right now, Oli, love. Well done. It was for a good cause."

Thank God it was Oli and not me.

Well we should have enough evidence with all those photies so now we can sit back and enjoy the pampering.

"I think we deserve room service and a bottle of champers," I said.

"Nice one," said Oli picking up the phone.

The champagne arrived on ice. "Bottoms up," I said.

"Oh friggin' 'ell, Shirl, you've gone and reminded me of them again."

"Don't forget we'll have to look at the photies tomorrow," I laughed.

Tuesday, 29 January
10am

We had room service for breckie. We don't want to run the risk of being caught at this late stage do we?

I've been thinking about it. We're lucky old bushy Mave came back to the room with Dave, if she hadn't we'd have had to work much harder for the evidence. We had quite a nice night really. Getting pissed on champagne and lazing about in a fab hotel, watching telly in bed.

We went shopping for the refills for the mini bar. Well there's no way we were gonna pay them prices.

(Even if it is Barbara's money.) I mean five quid a short, and one quid fifty for a tiny bag of nuts, it's friggin' ridiculous, especially the way Oli goes through them. Well, we don't want to take the piss do we?

I do feel for Barbara. How will she manage looking at them photies? She'll be gutted. It's one thing suspecting something, it's quite another thing staring it in the how's yer father.

<u>11am</u>
We had a near miss just then. Bushy Mave (as Oli now called her...) was in reception drinking coffee and reading some mags when we came in.

The photies are mint. Poor Oli, it was bad enough having to look at them in the photies, but in the flesh... No wonder he was shaking.

Oli went missing for about an hour. He only went to say goodbye and thanks to Jonny. He was a help. We couldn't've done it without him really. I'm sure Oli will have made it worth his while!

The taxi picked the intrepid duo up from the hotel and delivered them to the station on time. During their train trip Oli and Shirley recounted the events of the last 24 hours and Oli even managed to scan the photographs again. They decided that it would be best to report back to Barbara as soon as they got home, so Shirley phoned and arranged to call in straight from the station.

<u>4pm</u>
Just come back from Barbara's. I feel dead tight

really, but she was ok about it and even laughed at some of the photies of bushy Mave.

Me 'n' Oli were both feeling dead nervous about telling her; we really didn't know what to say.

In the end Oli said, "Sorry Barb love," and just handed over the photies. There was no need to say anything else after that.

"Oh my God. Is this her? I haven't really seen her properly before, only from a distance. She's no oil painting is she kids?" Barb said sitting down and looking at the photies. Oli had downloaded them from his camera and printed them off in a shop just round the corner from Lime Street.

"You're right there Barb, she's a minger, not a patch on you love," Oli told her.

"Oh, ta love," Barb said. "You're not the only one that thinks so though, I've got someone who's interested in me already. He's only been a friend up till now. Met him in this creative writing group I've started to go to. Dave thinks it's a waste of time, of course, but I really enjoy it and this fella who lost his wife three years ago has shown an interest. We've only been for a coffee so far, but now I know how this one has been behaving I think it's time to clear out the joint account and send him packing. She can put him up. Let's see how he likes roughing it in her place."

Barb was still flicking through the photos.

I'm glad she's found someone else, and she's done the decent thing and not got involved till she's got shot of her hubbie. It looks like it's all turned well in the end. Everyone was gonna be happy, except Dave of course...

Barbara paid us as well. We got the five hundred

apiece, all in cash so it can't be traced. Listen to me again. I'm starting to talk like a PI. It's all still top secret who got the info for her, but she said she is sure that we could go into business full time doing this kind of work!

"Oh, it's like living a secret life, babes," Oli said when we left Barbara's.

"Aye, yeah. I knew I was destined to be more than just a hairdresser," I said proudly.

"We've still got one problem though; bushy Mave wants us to do her hair again. She's booked in on Wednesday afternoon."

"Oh frig'; we'll have to cancel her. It'd be so two-faced."

"I don't think I could anyway babes, knowing what I know about her. I think I'd be sick!" Oli said, pulling a face.

9pm
We spent the rest of the evening gossiping and telling me mum and Fiona all about the new colouring techniques we had learnt!!!

We were dead lucky: the mags in the hotel were doing a special on hair and the latest colours and techniques. We're getting quite good at lying... We both decided we're too chicken to confront Mave, though, so we're gonna stick a note through the door saying "no can do" and just hope for the best.

Wednesday, January 30
5pm
We put note through bushy Mae's door saying that there had been a mistake and she hadn't really won

the hairdo, and that really she owes us twenty quid. We'll forget it this time, but due to illness we were unable to do her hair today. We hoped that that would put her off trying to find us.

Oli spent most of the day dreaming up a load of dares for Angie's hen night, while I slaved away on the old biddies at the home. So far he has come up with:

1. Snog a fella called Kevin.
2. Show her tits (no problem, she does that every weekend anyway).
3. Show her arse (same as tits, a regular thing).
4. Get ten fellas to give her their undies (easy!).
5. Drink ten pints (again, for Angie, easy!).
6. Snog an ugly fella (does she ever do anything else?).
7. Do a sexy dance on the podium in the club (why not?).
8. Have a quickie with a fella she's only just said hiya to – with a condom of course!
9. Make sure she goes home without her bra and knickers! (A usual Friday night then.)
10. Get the fellas to buy her drinks all night.

Oli's booked a stripper, an' all. He's a big black fella that Oli's seen before. He'll get her to burst balloons with her teeth and all that.

We've bought the usual toys, vibrator and stuff. One of the girls got us some photies of Angie's fella and Oli's cut the face out and stuck it on a pack of fellas-in-the-buff playing cards. It looks well good. I can't wait, it should be a laugh.

<u>Thursday, 31 January</u>
<u>6pm</u>
Oli's on a roll now with this hen night. There's no work in him, he's too busy planning. He's onto his outfit now! Friggin' 'ell.

Fair do's though, he's planned it all, what pubs and clubs and mini bus an' all.

He's gonna sleep over in mine. He was gonna bring that flaming Maxie, till I said me mum was over and she's allergic. Well anything to avoid that cat!

As usual Friday was Cuts 'n' Curls' day for the factory girls and major work would be needed to get them all up to scratch for the hen night. Gail was first up and then she would keep Dixie. Angie would be next because she wanted a lot doing. She wanted a special colour ready for her big night out.

Shirley and Oli set up shop as usual getting their equipment out and ready for action. Angie settled into an office chair ready for the big make-over and eager to hear any gossip Shirley or Oli had.

"Friggin' 'ell hurry up, Comb-over is on his way back. His car's just pulled up outside," Gail shouted in a mad panic.

By this time Angie had a head full of tint. The girls threw Shirley and Oli's stuff in the store room and poor old Angie grabbed her paper hat, stuck it on her head and all the girls were back out on the shopfloor by the time old Comb-over walked back in.

Comb-over had gone and left his briefcase behind. To make matters worse the phone rang while he was there and he was chatting away for nearly an hour. Shirley was really worried because Angie had no choice but to leave the tint on her head for the whole time.

"As soon as he's gone, we'll be out and onto Angie like flies round shit," Oli said trying to comfort Shirley.

Shirley just looked at him mortified.

Suddenly the door flew open and the girls dragged them from the storeroom. Comb-over had gone.

"Are you all right, girl? Mind you, I don't know why I'm asking you, I thought I was gonna pass out in that two be two!" Oli said to Shirley, worried that her head was in a hell of a state about the state Angie's head would be in, but also trying to recover from a nightmare of being buried alive beneath stacks of boxes of God knew what.

"Oh, aye, yeah, I'm ok. Typical, the bastard never usually does that, does he?" Shirley said.

"Hey, Shirl, we're lucky you didn't let one go in there eh?" Oli said all dead serious. Shirley just looked at him daggers.

"It's me who has to put up with his smelly farts, especially after he's had curried beans, his fave!" Shirley shouted across to the girls, who all giggled.

Oli washed Angie's tint off.

"It's a bit on the orange side, love," Oli said getting a mirror.

"I look like I've been friggin' Tango-ed. I quite like it though. It's a change, Oli. Yeah, I like it."

"You're right, babes. It's good to have a change, ya know. Friggin' 'ell don't go out in the dark, though, girl. You'll light up the whole flaming street."

"I'd rather have Tango hair than have me cards, though, eh?" Angie said patting her new 'do.

"Oh, aye, yeah. He's a right bastard, old Comb-over," Shirley said.

"Tight as a crab's arse him," Gail agreed.

"I bet you didn't learn that colour on your course, eh?" Angie said.

Oli and Shirley just laughed. They hadn't learnt a thing about colouring, but little did the girls know…

All hairdos done, they all said their goodbyes and made arrangements to meet up on Saturday.

Saturday, February 2
11am

I had a bit of a lie in ready for the night of the year! Into town later for a few more things for tonight. Oli wants me to pick up some badges that he's had made for us for the hen night. Probably something really tacky… Hopefully!

5pm

Just got back in from town. What a friggin' performance that was! I was happily doing me shopping when me mobie rang – I shouldn't have picked it up! The things I get roped into.

Shirley had been busy doing her food shopping when the theme tune from Charlie's Angels echoed along the aisle.

"Shirley, love, is that you?" her mum's voice shouted from Shirley's mobile phone. Her mother hadn't quite got the hang of mobile phones yet, bless her. She always spoke as though she thought she was talking to some one in another country.

"Yes, Mum; don't shout," Shirley shouted back without

realising.

"Shirley, love, Auntie Dilys has been on the phone. Apparently there's a special offer on toilet roll at the moment. She's just seen it on the telly. It's that nice new soft stuff. We were wondering if you could pick up some for us. It's a good offer and it'll last us, love. It's buy one pack of six and get another pack of six free. That's brilliant isn't it? So get me a set and Auntie Dilys a set will you. That should see us both through till about March."

"Bloody marvellous! As if I haven't got enough to carry," Shirley muttered under her breath.

"What, love? I can't hear you," her mother shouted.

"Nothing, Mum, just the loud speaker here," Shirley lied.

To cut a long story short, word had got out in Grannyville, as Fiona liked to call Auntie Dilys' estate of oldies, about the offer of the century on toilet roll and now three more of Auntie Dilys' friends wanted to cash in on the deal. Shirley's mother phoned twice more. Now she needed to get five sets!

So there she was with sixty toilet rolls and nothing else in her trolley when the Charlie's Angels theme tune went off for the fourth time. She was poised to reject the call (not more orders for toilet roll) when she saw it was Oli.

"Hiya babe, where are you?" he said all excited.

"Up to me neck in bog roll."

Shirley told him the story and he asked for a set as well! She had toilet roll for so many people there wasn't enough room for her own bog roll 'bog-off'.

"Oh and while you're there babe, you couldn't put in a couple of packs of condoms could yer. I'm feeling lucky."

Shirley walked over to the condoms while she was still on the phone to Oli. Surprise, surprise, they were buy-one-get-one-free too.

"Great, babe, put two sets of the twelve in will yer, ta."

"Variety packs, ordinary, ribbed or a mixture?" Shirley asked, starting to feel like the home help. Except of course the home help wouldn't be buying condoms. Well maybe for sex mad Joan, if she has a home help that is, Shirley thought.

"Oh... A mixture. And while you're there, seeing as they are buy-one-get-one-free, put a few sets in for the hen night. We'll need them, won't we, to blow up and stick 'em on Angie an' that?" He said with great enthusiasm.

Half an hour after entering the supermarket, Shirley set off for the tills with a trolley load of seventy two toilet rolls and ninety six condoms when who should loom into view, but David Wilmore, Fiona's dishy form teacher.

He just looked in Shirley's trolley and said, "Mmm, bulk buying," with a mischievous smile.

"Err, none of it's for me," Shirley said pathetically. "It's my mum's..."

Still smiling, Mr Wilmore sauntered off down the aisle.

"What the hell's he going to think of me, eh? From going out in me slippers to shopping for millions of bog rolls and condoms," Shirley said out loud, prompting some very odd looks from her fellow shoppers – as if the sight of her trolley-load wasn't bad enough.

Shirley dropped Fiona and Jason off following her afternoon of bog roll hell. She didn't dare tell Fi about bumping into Mr Wilmore again. She'd kill her.

Not particular in the party mood, Shirley made her way upstairs to start on her preparations for "Friday night is hen night".

<u>6pm.</u>
Fi is sleeping over in Shaz's house...I know! Jason is sleeping over in Digo's house. Better! Well I think so. They're looking forward to tonight cos Digo's dad's got one of them radio scanner thingies. Got it from a mate of his, who said it's great. This mate knows all the carryings-on on their estate, where all the police raids and that are and what's going off. He gets all the info then goes down himself to have a Dixie. He's got a dog now, so he doesn't look too suspicious, just a fella doing walkies! But a fella that turns up to all kinds nevertheless. If he carries on, I'm sure the bizzies 'll recognize him. If you want to know anything, though, then he's your man. He's not into anything dodgy like, just one hell of a nosy bastard. He even knows who's off out of an evening and where they're off to cos you can hear all the taxis and stuff.

Anyway, Jason and Digo are going to try to help Digo's dad set this thingy up. They might find out a bit of juicy gossip, with a bit of luck, but knowing those pair will probably draw attention to themselves and be asked to move on!

Better start getting ready cos the taxi's coming for six. I'll be on me back from the booze by eight!

FIVE

<u>Sunday, 3 February</u>
<u>2pm</u>
Woke up to Oli's special hangover cure of fried egg, fried bread and fried something else. God knows what it was...

"I think we had a good time, but I'll have to wait for the photies to give me all the info," Oli said.

"Ta for the brekkie, but I don't know if I can eat it all," I said.

"You'd better, any way I'm off to see Mixie, and I'll ring you later babe," he said and left, frying pan still smoking.

So back to last night. It was even better than we planned. We started off going round a few bars, getting into the spirit with the games and playing with the toys Oli had got. He'd made us all badges with 'Angie's hen night' on them. She was dressed like a bride, with a veil an' all. She looked like the sugar plum fairy. The cards with the naked fellas and Angie's fella's face stuck onto their bods were ace.

"If only girls, if only," she'd laughed.

Fair do's to Oli he had gone all out with the party games and toys. You could see and hear us coming for miles. What a night – it was brilliant.

Shirley lay back in bed and, still clutching her beloved diary, closed her eyes as she drifted off, reliving the wild hen night.

They'd been a sight to behold: a gang of 'girls' plus Oli walking down the high street in the best clubbing gear Comb-over's wages could buy.

"Hey I'm starving; I could do with a curry," Angie said after they had all had a few drinks.

Luckily Oli had booked them all in for a Chinese, so that saved Shirley any embarrassment in the Indian. She didn't want to be made to cough up for Charlie's night.

They were all getting into the spirit of the modern hen night, maybe a bit too much for some of them. Shirley had thought maybe Angie took it a bit far when she started harassing the men in the Chinese for their undies. The women diners didn't look too impressed and in the end they all got thrown out. Luckily they'd eaten most of their food by then and no one made them pay!

Result.

"God, if I carry on like this there won't be many places I can go out for a meal in town. I'm getting to be a right rebel me," Shirley said to Oli as they staggered away from the restaurant.

Then it was on to the bar where Oli had booked the stripper. Angie was in full swing and some of the girls had thought the poor bloke was a bit scared of her!

"Come on big boy, where's the baby oil and whipped cream?" She shouted, needing no encouragement at all. At one point she stripped off and did her back in jumping legs akimbo to wrap herself around him!

Then all the factory girls were all wanting a bit of the action. The stripper had to call for security to get them all off. Susan was the worst. Tonight instead of the 'Gorgeous' top, she was wearing one with 'Fancy a Shag' in gold glitter on it. It looked as if she'd even been down to the dentist specially as she had a tooth on a plate in her mouth at the start of the night.

At one point in the increasingly lively evening, Oli noticed Susan take the tooth out of her mouth and wrap it in a tissue. He gave Shirley a nudge for her to see what was happening.

"She didn't wear it for long though, did she? She told me it made her gag, so that's probably why she's taking it out."

"Said she nearly swallowed it loads of times trying to have her ale," Gail added, noticing their interest in Susan's dental work. "I told her it would be a waste of money taking it out, but she said she hadn't paid for it. It was her old gran's and she'd found it in the drawer at her mum's. It didn't even fit properly but she thought she'd give it a go!

"Her gran's been dead ten years. I did wonder why her mum was keeping a manky old tooth but I didn't like to ask. Funny keepsake that though, eh?" Gail continued. Oli and Shirley looked more horrified by the second.

Even Ali, one of the less fashion conscious girls, was

all glammed up.

"Hey I like yer gear, Ali love," Oli said, admiring her new rig-out as she sat watching the other girl's manhandle the stripper. She obviously wasn't so keen to get with all the baby oil.

"Ta love. I hope I don't spill anything on it though, it's gorra go back tomorrow," Ali said looking really worried.

"What d'yer mean, Ali?" Shirley asked her.

"I've only borrowed it for the night. It's from me sister."

"Oh it must be great that having a sister the same size, so yer can borrow each others clothes," Shirley smiled. She was having a bit of a rest from all the pushing and shoving.

"We're not the same size love. No. Me sister does them clothes parties an' this was ordered from one of her parties last week. She's gorra deliver it tomorrow to the woman."

"Oh my god, you're never wearing someone else's clothes that they've never worn yet?" Oli sounded disgusted.

"I had no choice, did I, cos all the clothes she's got just for show were all too small for me, kid. It was pure luck that another big girl had ordered this and it came yesterday."

"I wonder who she is," Shirley thought.

"Hey remind me never to go to one of them clothes parties, Oli," she whispered and he just nodded, looking as mortified as Shirley. Was there nothing these girls wouldn't do...

Their attention wandered back to the stripper. He was so terrified of Comb-over's production line he'd done a runner without getting paid, so Oli put the money into the kitty and it was cocktails all round!

"Let's see that dare list again," Angie shouted.

She had completed most of them by ten o' clock. She'd done 1 to 6 easily, as helpfully, the stripper had been called Kevin, and she'd got most of her kit off. So, next on the list was doing a sexy dance on the podium.

"She's the star performer," the club's owner, a slimy looking man of about sixty, said to Oli. "If she wasn't so pissed I would think of giving her a permanent spot," he went on.

There was only one other dancer, a woman of about seventy-three, presumably the owner's wife.

"Look at the competition though, eh, girl?" Oli said to Shirley.

"Aye, I know, where are the sexy young things?" Shirley asked looking around to see if they had missed them.

"Probably avoiding this dump like the plague, I mean, would you want him leering all over you?" Oli ventured.

"Friggin' 'ell what would old Comb-over say? Me handing in me notice to be a sexy dancer. Well if he gives me hassle again I'll tell him to piss off and come down here. Mind you I couldn't exactly get me hairdone at work then could I?" Angie guffawed.

The girls cracked open a bottle of homemade punch they had bought with them. They were sitting around a table in the corner away from view of the bar staff.

"Come on, get it down your neck," Angie shouted to Oli.

"Where did yer hide this, babe?" Oli asked.

"Why do yer think I'd bring such a big one?" Angie said holding up an enormous handbag. "You can't get pissed on drinking out. Not the friggin' prices they charge here anyway. It'd cost a fortune! I always bring me own with me."

"Well, me fella spends a fortune when he comes out. They've nowhere to hide it have they, fellas?" Susan said dead serious.

Everyone nodded in agreement.

"Mind you it's great when they come home, isn't it, and you can raid their pockets eh girls?" She said laughing.

Every one nodded again in agreement.

"What d'yer mean babe?" Oli asked looking confused.

"Well, when they come in they're that legless they haven't a clue what time of day it is never mind how much they spent, so us girls go through our fellas' pockets taking what's left for extra housekeeping. Eh girls?

"Gail was the one who first started it. She'd been doing it for years, so now we all do. Hey, it can be a great little earner, especially if he's really gone, which, let's face it girls, is every weekend, eh?"

"Poor bastards, living with you lot. I bet they don't get any extra grub with the money you rob off them. Sort yourselves out more like," Oli teased.

"Where d'yer think the dosh came for this new top?" Susan squealed in hysterics, flashing her new top.

"Hey, well that's one good reason to get hitched then," Angie said all excited.

"You're all right Susan, your fella doesn't notice a thing when you 'ave a new top. I 'ave to hide me stuff for ages in case me fella notices anything. I've only just started this lark, so I don't want him to get suspicious like. He thinks he keeps getting the wrong change and stuff in pubs. He threatened to do one of the barmen over last week when he went back, so I'll 'ave to take it easy," Kelly the youngest of the factory girls said, looking fed up.

"Hey you lot, teaching Kelly your old tricks..." Shirley

said laughing.

"Hey she'll be a real professional when we've done with her, eh, girls?" Susan went on holding Kelly's hand. Shirley had noticed that Susan had taken Kelly under her wing since her sister Trace had left the factory. Pity poor Kelly!

"Oh hiya, how are you? Nice to see you've remembered your shoes tonight," a voice said from behind Shirley.

It was David Wilmore, Fiona's teacher. The last two times Shirley had seen him she'd made a total fool of herself. Meeting him again tonight, in full hen night regalia wasn't promising much better.

"Oh, hi, yeah. Well I don't normally go out in me slippers, it was a sort of emergency," she said nervously.

He just smiled nodding. "Now I get it," he said looking over at Angie who was covered head-to-toe in blown up condoms.

"Oh, yes, I'm not some sort of sex maniac," Shirley muttered.

They got chatting after that, and Shirley thought he was lovely. They even had a bit of dance, with Angie doing a turn in the background. Given that sight it was a miracle that David asked Shirley if she'd like to go out for a drink sometime and took her number.

"He's even better looking close up. In fact he's well fit. I hope I didn't show meself up. I was well gone on the homemade punch!" Shirley said to Oli when David had gone.

"He's not bad babe. Not the type you usually go for, though, is he?"

"How d'ya mean?" Shirley asked.

"Well, he's got hair for a start, quite a lot of it come to

think of it, and he's tall and thin. The total opposite of what you go for in fact. I like his clothes, got a good sense of fashion from what I could see. Mind you I couldn't really see him that well." Oli went on.

"I know, I don't know why, maybe my tastes are changing. I think he's gorgeous. He looks a bit like that Ioan Griffith fella, you know that Welsh actor, the 'Hornblower' fella."

"Bloody hell, does he? Get in there, kid." Oli said excitedly.

So with number seven on the list done and dusted, and given the fact that Angie didn't buy a drink all night, it was time for the quickie and home with no undies.

They left the club and made their way to the taxi.

"So how many actually copped off tonight? You Shirl. Who else?" Oli asked the assembled company.

"Oh did ya babe? Nice one." Angie said to Shirley. All the rest of the group aired their congratulations, too, as no one else had managed it.

"Oh shame, queen, you never got the quickie and home with no undies," Oli said all serious.

"There's still time, babe."

"I'm starving again now after those tight sods chucked us out before me banana fritter. Let's get some chips," Angie suggested.

They got their chips and next thing they saw Angie disappearing behind the chippy with the greasiest man from the back of the queue, a great big grin on her face, and a bag of chips in her hand.

About five minutes later she reappeared, and the greasy bloke walked past the girls and Oli on up the street, looking as if he'd been dragged through a bush backwards.

"All me dares done, now, you bastards," Angie crowed, demonstrating that she now had neither knickers nor bra on.

"Bloody 'ell. You didn't shag him?" Oli asked her.

"Oh, aye, yeah, I did. It was flaming good too, considering. I nearly dropped me chips!"

"Just call her 'any time Annie'." Oli said looking shocked.

"You're only jealous," Angie laughed.

"Bloody 'ell. So he had been dragged through a bush backwards!" Shirley giggled.

<u>8pm</u>
Oli phoned earlier and we jangled about the hen night. Apparently, he'd copped off with some Australian who is over here working while we were all having a good old boogie, though he didn't want to say so in front of the girls. He's got his number and has been texting him today. They're meeting up in the week. I filled him in on David Wilmore. So, by the end of our chat we both felt quite excited. He did catch a quick glimpse of David, but not a proper look.

Fiona and Jason came home later. She wanted to know all the gossip. I told her most of it, but left out the obvious, and the quickie. I don't want to let me kids think I approve of casual sex now, do I?

<u>11pm</u>
I wonder if David Wilmore will ring me. I bloody hope so. I can't remember much of what I said to him.

<u>Monday, 4 February</u>
<u>1pm</u>
Went to do Barbara and co. Barb really seemed to be all right. She's chucked old waltzing bollocks out and apparently he's moved in with bushy Mave. Not before Barbara cleared their savings account, though, and transferred a load of shares and stuff into her name only. Nice one, Barb!

She was great. We had a bit of a laugh at Oli's tales of bushy Mave. Joan has offered Barbara her little pal, now that she's husbandless, but Barbara told her she's got her eye on someone else so she doesn't need it... yet, anyway!

<u>8pm</u>
Busy afternoon. Dropped Oli off and went round me mum's cos it's her birthday today. Met Jason and Fi there and we all went out for tea. We had to go and pick up Auntie Dilys, an' all, who by some miracle had sod all wrong with her today!

Shirley hooted the horn and out of the tiny bungalow came Auntie Dilys. The front seat was saved for her. Shirley's mum, Jason and Fiona were all squashed together in the back. Auntie Dilys didn't seem to notice they were so tightly packed, she just got to the car oblivious to the fact that anyone was suffering for her comfort.

"How you doing, Auntie Dilys?" Shirley asked.

"Oh great, girl. I'm fit as a fiddle me. Mind you, I never complain do I, love?" she said, turning round to look over at Shirley's mum who smiled and shook her head smiling.

They decided on the Italian, cos that was Shirley's mum's favourite.

Shirley had to pull up right outside the restaurant even though it was on double yellow lines and a very busy road.

"Ta, Shirley love, it'll save me legs," Auntie Dilys said waiting for someone to go round and open the car door for her.

They all piled out, leaving Shirley to park down the road and make her own way back to the restaurant.

Once inside, Shirley was ushered to a table in the back. There was the usual Italian restaurant décor with pictures of Sicily, Rome and various Italian beach resorts. The typical red and white gingham tablecloths covered the round tables and a wax-ridden wine bottle took centre stage holding a short red candle. They all settled down in their seats, Shirley opposite Auntie Dilys.

"How's that mate of yours, Shirley love, that nice looking feminine boy?" Auntie Dilys asked.

"Who d'yer mean?" Shirley said, knowing full well.

"That fella who works for you. A bit light on his feet," she went on, slightly annoyed that Shirley hadn't answered her question with the requisite details.

"Oh, Oli you mean."

"Is he a bit 'that way', or has he got a girlfriend?" Auntie Dilys said determined on getting the gory details.

"Oh, he only shags fellas," Shirley replied in a loud and slightly miffed way.

"Shirley, shame on you. Especially in front of Fiona and Jason," her mother said.

"We've heard worse than that at home, Nan. We're scarred for life, us, eh Sis?" Jason laughed.

After similar bits of jolly banter, they all settled back

to spaghetti carbonara. Jason looked over at Shirley laughing; Shirley smiled and winked at him.

The meal carried on and the conversation turned to what the kids had been up to. It was a birthday party after all, and Shirley wanted her mother to enjoy it. Talking about the kids activities would fit the bill.

On to the puddings and Shirley had arranged for her mum to have a pudding with a sparkler in it seeing as it was her birthday. She knew that would please her.

The Italian ice cream with bananas and fresh cream all topped off with lashings of chocolate sauce arrived.

"Ah, that's lovely that is. Get one for your Auntie Dilys as well, will you love?"

"Typical," Shirley whispered to Fiona who was sitting by her side.

Good old Auntie Dilys enjoyed the lot.

They left the restaurant, Shirley having picked up the tab. She didn't want anyone to say she didn't treat her family, plus she thought she would never hear the end of it if her mum had had to pay for her own birthday tea.

Shirley dropped off her mother and Auntie Dilys. They both claimed to have had a wonderful time, although as she left the car Auntie Dilys did start to complain that she had a bit of a pain in her stomach.

As Shirley lay in bed with the page open in her little pink book her thoughts drifted to David Wilmore, Fiona's hunky form master...

<u>11.30pm, in bed</u>
No news from David Wilmore. Perhaps he was all talk! Or maybe I was too pissed and didn't hear him properly. Bloody typical and he was dead fit an' all.

Shirley's ponderings regarding David Wilmore were soon to be answered.

<u>Tuesday, 5 February</u>
<u>2pm</u>
I can't believe it. I've had a phone call on me mobie from David Wilmore. He was on his dinner in school. Fancy him ringing me from work. We're going for a drink to town on Thursday. Yes!

Oli was dead made up for me. Things are looking up on the fella front anyway.

Me mum phoned this morning, too, to say thanks for the birthday meal. She really enjoyed it. So did Auntie Dilys, but she was up all night with an upset tummy from the rich food. Apparently foreign food doesn't agree with her! She ate enough of it, mind.

Oli had an appointment with Marsha. Another near miss, but she said she's got a new mate who wants us to do her hair. Oli's shitting himself in case she's just like Marsha – an old tart. Her name's Sapphire. I know, it doesn't sound too good, does it? Oli said there's no way he's going on his tod so we'll go together, on Friday.

<u>6pm</u>
I wonder what Fiona would say if she knew I'd got a date with her teacher. He's a history teacher, too, so he must be dead clever. It'll make a nice change from the usual scallies and cheapskates!

Having spent the night worrying about her outfit for her

date with David Wilmore, Shirley decided she needed yet more clothes, so decided a trip to town was in order.

She looked at her hair in the mirror. Luckily, having fair hair, the first signs of aging were disguised but she felt that her hair could do with a boost so she would ask Oli to work his colour magic later.

She watched Jason and Fiona, while they were all in the kitchen eating breakfast, and wondered what they would say if they knew who she was going on a date with.

"What's up, Mum?" Fiona said in the middle of eating her cereal.

"Nothing. Why?"

"You keep looking at us dead weird."

Jason looked up at Shirley and Fiona. He hadn't noticed anything.

"I'm just looking at you both and wondering how come I got so lucky to have you two." Shirley smiled, kissed them both on the head and took a sip out of her mug of tea.

"Aw, ta, Mum," Fiona said, getting up and kissing her mum back.

Jason just looked over at Shirley, raised an eyebrow and shook his head.

That would keep them off the case Shirley thought. She cleared up the kitchen as best she could. She would be back at lunch time so she could finish clearing up then. She sent the kids on their way and dashed out to work. Oli needed picking up and she had things to do before she could spend her money on glamming herself up for that date.

<u>Wednesday, 6 February</u>
<u>1pm</u>
Only worked this morning. I just dropped Oli off in the old folk's home to do the afternoon there. After me dinner I'm off into town to get something new for tomorrow! Bloody 'ell I hope it won't be a repeat performance of the last flamin' date I had!

<u>6pm</u>
Thought I'd go a bit smart but casual. I don't really know him that well and I don't want to look a bit of a tit on the first date, turning up like I'm off to a dead posh do or something. So I got a new top, more like a blouse really, in like a baby pink, cos I read a thing on colour therapy once in a mag' that said you should go for that colour if you want to impress in a romantic sort of way. Well, I'll give it a go. I'll wear it with jeans and boots.

It didn't say what blue and black mean. So long as it doesn't mean running along the road like a blue-arsed fly again I don't give a shit!

Oli's coming over later, to put a bit of colour through me hair and give it a bit of a trim. I'll stick a bottle of plonk in the fridge I think. Just in case...

<u>11.30pm</u>
Two bottles of wine later and I'm in me bed. Happily pissed, with a boss hairdo, thinking of me date with Mr Wilmore tomorrow. Best be on me best behaviour. I don't want to be sent to his office for a spanking now do I? Or do I?

<u>Thursday, 7 February</u>

9am

God, I'm starting to get a bit panicky about this date tonight. I mean he's dead clever and all that and I'm, well, I'm not thick or anything, I got a few CSE's and, of course, got me hairdressing apprentice certificate and that was quite hard. It's just I don't want to show meself up, or our Fi for that matter.

I've told the kids I'm off out with Oli tonight, so they won't get any mad ideas. I probably won't ever see him again any way. Except, of course, in the parents' evenings. Oh shit! How embarrassing will that be when I have to see him again at one of those?

5pm

Today flew by. I had booked loads of people in just to keep me busy and me mind off tonight.

"Bloody 'ell, babe, are you trying to friggin' kill me?" Oli said when he saw the client list for today.

"I just want to be busy and make the time pass quick. Remember I'm meant to be out with you tonight. We're off for a few drinks, ok?" I said.

"Oh, aye, yeah. Fine by me. Just calm down, will you girl. Enjoy the night."

Shirley decided a nice long soak might be the way to calm her nerves before the big night out. She filled the bath with warm water and added some of her Christmas bubble bath. She got in carefully – she didn't want to damage her hairdo with having the water too hot and end up with a frizzy wild look. The bath didn't turn out too relaxing, though, as she sat so upright and stiff because she didn't want her hair to get wet.

Once out of the bath, Shirley laid out the clothes she was going to wear on the bed.

"Hey, what's all this?" Fiona asked. She was standing in the doorway.

"Oh, hiya, love. I didn't see you there," Shirley said surprised.

"Where you off to? New gear?" Fiona asked, taking a closer look at the new clothes neatly laid out on the bed.

"Oh just a drink with Oli. Thought I'd treat myself. They still have the odd sale on you know," Shirley lied.

Fiona raised her eyebrows, knowing Shirley wasn't being totally honest with her and walked away grinning to herself.

Shirley let out a huge sigh and made a start on her make-up.

With full make-up, hair and dressed to kill, Shirley was ready to go, with plenty of time to spare.

<u>7pm</u>
One hour to go!

<u>8pm</u>
Half an hour to go!

<u>11.45pm</u>
Just got back. David dropped me off. Friggin' 'ell a few weeks ago he was Mr Wilmore, Fiona's teacher, now he's David, my sexy fella!

We had a boss night out. Nothing fancy, just a few drinks and a chat. Found out loads about him. He's originally from Manchester, but he's been in Liverpool for about five years (since his divorce!!!). Said he wanted to get away from his ex, she was teaching in the same school as him, so it would have been awkward to work with her. She's a history teacher an' all. He's got two kids, boys, sixteen and eighteen, and he sees them regular which I think is dead nice.

He's dead easy to talk to and he wants to see me again!!! A walk down the docks on Sunday. He said he loves it there! Wait till I tell Oli. I think I'll send him a text.

<u>Friday, 8 February</u>
<u>8am</u>
I felt a bit sly, this morning, when Fi asked if I'd had a good time last night. I don't want to say anything yet, do I, or she'll get all edgy and stuff – it's best to keep quiet for now.

God knows what I'll say about Sunday's walk down the docks. Anyway I'd best get on with getting ready for work. We've got that new client today, that Sapphire one. What kind of a name's that?

Still glowing from the previous night, getting the breakfast and kids off to school was a breeze for Shirley and this time it was the kids who kept giving Shirley funny looks.

"So Mum, good night last night?" Fiona asked.

"Oh lovely," Shirley said recalling the date.

"Oli ok?" Fiona asked.

"Fine, fine," Shirley said in a dream.

Fiona gave up, finished her breakfast, grabbed her bag and made her way out of the door. Jason still not sure what he was missing out on, grabbed another piece of toast, his bag and made his way out. Shirley didn't even notice that they had left the house.

"Oh..." she said looking around the kitchen, and still in her own little world made her way to work.

6pm

Spent the morning with the old biddies. Old Mavis in the home now looks a bit like Cilla Black rather than Ronald MacDonald. Oli told her and she was made up.

'He's such a lovely boy, Oli. I love Cilla Black me," she kept saying, much to Oli's amusement.

We went to the factory girls, on dinner. Not many of them today. A load had phoned in sick, cos they couldn't be arsed going in. They'd been on a bender the night before!

Angie was first to phone in sick, of course. She's been getting cold feet about the wedding, according to Gail, Susan and Jacqui who were full of goss' with the others off sick! Well, to be honest I don't think she's ready for the commitment. Jacqui said she's off shagging all sorts of a weekend. Let's face it she was well up for it on her hen night.

Jacqui was saying that it was only few months ago Angie had to make up all sorts of excuses to her fella why she wouldn't shag him. She'd only got the clap from some old scally she'd met on the same night. She's the only woman in history to have a month-long period and he's thick enough to believe her.

The factory was always a hive of gossip for Shirley and

Oli, and today they weren't disappointed. With a head each Shirley and Oli got down to business...

"So what's Angie's fella like, then?" Oli asked the girls.

"He looks like a sausage that's been pricked and burst," Gail said seriously.

"Nice."

"She's only got a week to go so she'll have to let us know what's going on, we're down to do her wedding hairdo on the day," Shirley joined in, concerned.

"Hey you'll never guess who joined the slimming club last night," Susan said all excited.

"Who, kid?" Oli asked eager for any goss'.

"Fat Sandra. Remember she worked here for a few months," Susan announced. 'She didn't last long. Couldn't stand the pace, the lazy cow.'

All the other girls nodded in agreement and sat down to listen to the gossip.

"Oh my God, you should 'ave seen the state of her. She must be at least nineteen stone by now. Absolutely massive," Susan went on.

There were ooh's and aah's and looks of disgust from all the girls.

"She had that much hard skin on her trotters she could 'ave sanded down five bookshelves and a dining room table with them!"

More ooh's and aah's. All the girls were horrified!

"I bet all that hard skin must weigh something," Gail said grimly. More nods from the girls.

"Where's she working now, babe?" Oli inquired as he snipped away at the head in front of him.

"She's not. She said she did do a stint in the bookies but apparently she caused a right to do there. She paid out some old fella a load of dosh and the horse he backed came last. She didn't understand the set up," Susan told him, eager to dish the dirt.

"I wondered what happened to her. I haven't seen her for ages," Shirley murmured.

"Shame for her really that she gave this up... I mean this is a cushy number. You girls sit on your arses all day. Getting your hairdone, more jangling than work half the time," Oli said teasingly.

"Hey you. It's not many that would work in these conditions is it girls? She was a right pain anyway, that fat Sandra, going on about her fella and farting all day," Susan protested. "And she wanted to know the ins and outs of the cat's arse, the nosy cow," she added.

"You know he's winding you up, Susan love. Don't fall for it," Shirley said looking over at Oli and shaking her head, but thinking he might have a point.

"Hey, are you still going to that slimming club queen?" Oli asked obviously in a teasing mood.

"Aye, yeah, I am. I know it doesn't look much like it does it? D'yer know I weigh more now than when I started six months ago. I can't understand it," Susan moaned.

"Flamin' 'ell it costs a bit that love doesn't it?" Shirley said, wondering why Susan was wasting her money.

"Let's face it, it obviously isn't working," Gail whispered to Oli.

"Aye Shirl it does. Nearly a fiver for the slimming, then on the way home we stop at the chippy and I have either fish and chips or I may have a battered sausage, chips and curry sauce. Always with a Diet Coke, you know, cos I'm slimming like.

"I suppose it's a tenner a night, really. So this slimming lark isn't cheap, plus the fact it's not really working. I can't understand it..." she went on.

"No wonder it's not working, you daft cow. I bet the chippy isn't on your slimming plan is it?" Oli said shaking his head.

"What d'yer mean. I'm friggin' starving after slimming. I leave here after I've been slaving all day, go home, I have no tea, just to make sure that doesn't weigh in any extra pounds. By the time slimming is over and that wafer thin Lindsey has finished talking about flamin' food, I'm that starving I could eat a weightlifter's jockstrap!" Susan yelped in self defence.

By this time they were all in fits of laughter.

"There's no hope for yer, queen. Sit at home and stuff your face," Oli said warmly.

"No way. It's a night out. We have a right laugh. There's a load of us big girls that aren't doing that well at the moment. We all sit together in the back. One of them, Jan, she's waiting to have her stomach stapled. She's been on the waiting list for three years yer know. Criminal isn't it eh?

"Then some of these skinny girls come in and sit right in the front, nodding and smiling at wafer-thin Lindsey's every word. Best of it is they want to lose half a friggin' stone. Flamin' 'ell I could eat half a stone's worth of food in one go after one of them meetin's.

"Mind you I can't see fat Sandra sticking to it. She was sneaking sweets in her gob in the middle of the class. You could hear the sweet wrappers going ten to the dozen. If she loses a pound I'll give up me chippy dinner after slimming for a couple of weeks!"

"Give up her chippy dinner! I bet you won't," Gail said raising her eyebrows.

They finished off in the factory and then it was on to

do Sapphire!

They parked up outside a high-rise block of flats. A young boy of about eight rode past on his bike. "Wankers," he shouted throwing a bag of half-eaten chips at the windscreen.

Oli looked over at Shirley and raised an eyebrow.

Shirley stormed out of the car. "Oi you little sod," she shouted to the boy, who by now had ridden off to join his group of friends – most of them looked about six.

"Don't you shout at my lad, you cow," a woman shouted down to Shirley over the balcony.

"What? Did you see what he did to me windscreen?" Shirley said pointing.

The woman looked over.

"I'll bloody kill him when I see him, that was his bloody tea I paid for," the woman complained.

Oli sat in the car watching all the action. Once the woman had disappeared from the balcony he got out of the car.

"Nice neighbourhood," he said nervously looking around.

"Ta for that, a little bit of support wouldn't have gone amiss like," Shirley said annoyed with him for his lack of assistance.

They made their way though the rusty old bikes, supermarket shopping trolleys, car tyres and bin bags up the staircase and followed their directions to Sapphire's flat.

Oli kept jumping from side to side convinced someone was going to jump out on him.

"I really don't think we should be coming to places like this, Shirley, we could catch anything here," he said with a mixture of fear and disgust.

"Behave, soft lad. It maybe a bit rough looking but I'm sure they're a harmless lot," Shirley said unconvincingly.

From where they stood outside the blue painted door, a net curtain covering the glazed panel, Sapphire's flat looked half decent. It certainly didn't look like the next door flat, which had packing tape holding a piece of cardboard in place of the glazed panel.

Oli raised his eyebrows and said, "Could be worse I suppose."

Shirley knocked on the door and they both waited anxiously for the reply, keeping one eye out for scallys.

"Oh hiya, Sapphire is it?" Shirley asked as a pretty but wild looking girl answered the door.

"Oh, aye, yeah. You must be Shirley – and this must be the super sexy Oli..."

Oli's eyes rolled.

"You look about ready to leg it. Don't be worrying there, babe, I'm not into trying to convert ya. Not like that Marsha one, eh? Too much like hard work for me, that. I like 'em ready, willing and very able, if you know what I mean..." Sapphire had a very impressive laugh, which she used to great effect, putting Oli a little bit more at ease.

They walked through a tiny pink floral hallway into the living room, and putting their bags of tricks down, Shirley and Oli did a sweep of their surroundings. Better than expected, although the décor was far too old-fashioned for Oli's taste, way too 1980s. Oli relaxed in the apparent safety of the flat and was soon back to himself.

Sapphire's hair was peroxide blonde with black roots and as wiry as a yard brush. She told the intrepid duo that she wanted colour, cut and blow dry and straightening. It was certainly going to take both of them to sort out her current excuse for a 'do.

"Don't mind the knickers drying on the radiator... They're me good ones like. Not the ones I keep, you know, for me monthly's," Sapphire announced whispering the last bit.

Oli and Shirley raised their eyebrows. "No you're all right, love," Shirley said carrying on regardless. Bless him, Oli only faltered slightly and tried to keep his eyes on the job in hand.

"Your hair's a bit out of condition love, what you been doing to it, eh?" he sighed, looking at her way past its prime, almost matted hair as he tried to brush it out.

"Been bleaching it since I was nine, ya know, and all the smoke at work doesn't help."

"Oh right, what d'yer do?" Shirley asked with interest.

"I'm a singer and a PA," Sapphire responded happily.

"Sounds dead posh and glamorous, that, girl. That why you've got such a smart name?" Oli said looking over at Shirley and pulling a face.

"Well, yeah, Sapphire's me stage name. Me real name's Lyn. Not quite so glam that is it?" she cackled.

Oli looked over at Shirley – they'd got a right one on their hands.

"So tell us more about your singing career, babe. Sung with anyone famous?" Oli asked, egging Sapphire on.

"Na, not yet, love. Well to be honest with ya, it's not like professional or anything. I sing karaoke down the Black Dog twice a week, Friday and Saturday. The landlord Stan says I bring in all the punters. I get me drinks free all night for doing it, so that's like over fifty quid's worth for the two nights."

Oli and Shirley were trying not to laugh.

"Oh nice one. What about the PA? Sounds dead important that..." Oli inquired.

"Yeah, very impressive. What's that all about?" Shirley asked brightly.

"Well that's a bit more like hard work that."

"Oh right, a bit more to it is there, babe?" Oli said teasing out a particularly matted section of hair with the point of a comb.

"Oh, aye, yeah. I help people fill out their benefit forms so they're guaranteed of getting a good benefit. Charge them about ten to twenty quid, depending, ya know. Sometimes I do about ten a week. So with me own benefit – cos ya see I'm on income support, since I don't actually go out to work – I do all right.

"All me ale money's covered from me singing, the rest just goes. Mind you I think I'll have to up me prices soon. These forms aren't half getting longer and harder to fill in."

"Bloody 'ell babe, how d'yer learn how to fill all them forms in?" Oli asked, gobsmacked.

"I had a good teacher; me old man showed me how to get the most from me benefits, so I thought why not turn it into me own little business. Bit of a gold mine really."

"Well you've got balls, I'll give you that, girl," Oli said.

Sapphire just smiled, looking well pleased with herself.

"Me brother tries to get me to do bit of work for him every now and then, mind. I do it when I'm bit slow on the old PA front which to be honest isn't very often. Thank God," she said with relief.

"Oh, right what does your brother do?" Shirley asked, eager to know more, she wouldn't be surprised by anything this particular client got up to, what with benefit fraud and knickers out for all to see!

"He's a chef, got his own business. I take over when he wants a break or I fancy it," Sapphire explained cheerfully.

"Bloody 'ell girl, you've got it good eh? Where's that then, a coffee shop in town or summat?" Oli asked.

"It's called A Coffee Break, but it's not in town. It's a catering caravan on the motorway. He does lovely stuff. Bacon butties, egg butties, or you can have 'em both if you like. All top quality stuff ya know."

By this time Oli and Shirley were really struggling to keep a straight face.

Over an hour later, the revamped hairstyle was almost complete and Sapphire was transformed. Delighted with the new look, Sapphire walked out of the living room and a few moments later appeared carefully holding three mugs of tea.

She handed the mugs of tea to Shirley and Oli.

"Oh you didn't have to, babe," Oli said stretching a distinctly reluctant hand out for the tea.

Shirley thought the mugs looked clean enough, so she took hers happily. Having inspected his mug and realising that all was well with the tea Oli said, "You haven't got any bikkies have you babe? I could do with something sweet."

"Oh nah sorry kid, I never buy bikkies, I think I may have a mint in me handbag though, shall I have a look for ya?"

"Friggin' 'ell that Sapphire's got more front than the pier head," Oli said when they were safely back in the car, which seemed to have survived its visit unscathed by small boys, and they both sat there laughing. And to think they thought the factory girls were pushing it...

"She'll be a good client that one. Mind you her and the factory girls on the same day, we'll need the Monday off to recover."

"Talking of the pier head, what d'yer think of me date down the dock?" Shirley asked Oli smugly.

"Oh, aye, yeah. With Sir? Very nice, but why down there? You'll freeze your tits off, girl."

"Aye I know, I thought that, but he says he likes to walk round there. He's dead brainy and that, likes all the history stuff.

"What shall I say to Fi about where I'm going? I thought I might tell Jason the truth, I'm not sure though."

"Tell her you're coming over to bleach me hair, or give her a few quid to go the flicks with that mad Shaz. That'll keep her off your case."

"Nice one, I will," Shirley said feeling a lot better about it. "I love you, Oli. You always know the right thing to say. Well, most of the time." She gave him a big hug.

With her alibi sorted, Shirley could relax and look forward to the weekend. She didn't really know what her kids thought of David, after all she maybe pleasantly surprised, they might like him too if they got to know him outside school.

"I hate that flaming Wilmore. He's a right knobhead," Fi shouted throwing her school bag across the room. She was back home and judging from the noise the whole street would know it.

"Hey – you watch your mouth young lady and watch where you're throwing that bloody bag," Shirley objected. "I hate it when you kids swear."

"Well he is. He's only give us loads of boring homework about the Vikings. It'll take me ages to do it. It's not fair. What do I want to know about some boring old fellas running round the place in skirts? Dickhead." Her voice lowered to a mumble.

"Listen, love, do it tonight and tomorrow and I'll treat you and Shaz to the pictures on Sunday for all your hard work, eh? Now lift that chin before you trip on it," Shirley said, trying to butter her up.

"What's up with you?" Fi asked suspiciously.

"Nothing, just trying to encourage you to work hard by giving you a treat when you've put the effort in that's all. You're in an important year now, love. You've got to try your best in school. It's very important you do well," Shirley said trying not to sound too guilty at her subterfuge.

With the situation calmer, Shirley went up to her room to finish off her diary entry for the day. Given what had come to light with regard Gus and Barbara and the new Cuts 'n' Curls sideline, who knows what else she would be called to record.

8pm

Jason came in on the tail end of the conversation I was having with Fi, so I ended up promising to treat him and Digo the same. I must be one huge mug to do this and all just so I can go out with David. Looks like I'm gonna have to find a whole load of excuses if I do get asked out again, cos I can't see Fi being over the moon if she found out. Not given what she called him – twice...

<u>Saturday, 9 February</u>
<u>2pm</u>
MAJOR GOSSIP! Oli's just phoned from his mobie in town. He's bumped into Angie looking all bronzed up from the sunbed. The wedding's all off and she's away on honeymoon to Falaraki with her sister. She told Oli that the pair of them had bought a couple of Viagra each from some fella in the pub and they're off to have a shagging good time!

Apparently Angie told her fella she was having second thoughts about the whole wedding thing, and he said so was he, so they decided to call it all off and just ring each other up if they ever fancy a shag!

Bloody 'ell, some people eh?

<u>6pm</u>
Just been informed that Shaz and Digo are coming over to sleep tonight, so they can be ready for their day at the flicks. Shaz has planned it so they can all go together in the hope she'll cop with Digo. Poor lad.

Jason and Digo have got some party to go to in another mate's house tonight but Shaz and Fi thought I might like to have a takeaway and a DVD with them. My treat, of course! At least Jason's gonna get a taxi back; so I'll have a few wines tonight, well it is Saturday after all.

I hope Shaz doesn't bring me any more cast-offs from the stall. She's working today.

Shirley dropped Jason and Digo off at the party and picked up a Chinese on her way home. Shaz's mum had put in a box of Bacardi Breezers for the girls.

"Talk about encouragement," Shirley moaned to Fiona.

Fiona just laughed, pleased to have them.

They all settled down to the DVD and food. Shaz was wearing a red top that clashed with her orangey fake tan, a denim mini skirt and the infamous white plastic boots. Her knees were all streaky.

"I would have got you a bit of stuff from the stall, but I must be getting better at it cos I didn't drop anything today, Shirley," Shaz said tucking into her chow mein.

"Oh you're all right, Shaz, love," Shirley replied relieved.

"I'd got a load of stuff already in me bag, so I couldn't fit any more in," she went on.

"What sort of stuff?" Fi asked.

"Fruit and veg, of course; I've got a bit of a sideline going selling it cheap on the estate to the neighbours. I made fifteen quid last week," Shaz said proudly.

"You'd better watch you don't get caught. You'll get the sack, love." Shirley was concerned for her, she didn't want Shaz arrested, daft cow she might be, but she wasn't all bad.

"Well with the crappy wages that Carlos pays me I've gotta do something. He's loaded, raking it in. Slave labour that's what it is."

"You could do with another little job, Fi love. I know you help me out and all that, but that's only in the holidays isn't it?" Shirley said hoping. At least Jason had a job in the caff down the road.

"Yeah, yeah," Fi said, unconvincingly.

"What time you lot off tomorrow?" Shirley said changing the subject, no point flogging a dead horse. Fi couldn't be bothered and the less Shirley knew about

Shaz's goings on the better.

"The film starts at two, so could you drop us off at about half one?"

"We can have a bit of a lie-in in the morning, but don't forget I need a bit of pulling time with Digo. I've got to try and nail him. I can't believe he's playing so hard to get," said Shaz shaking her head.

"I don't know what the hell you see in him. I mean he's a minger and he's an idiot," Fi said, looking over at her mate.

"No way. He's easy meat. Let's face it there's no competition for him. He'll get fed up soon then I'll be in," Shaz protested as if she'd got it all planned.

"Hey, you should raise your standards, Shaz. Don't go for any old minger," Fi pleaded. "I know I won't."

"Standards, what d'yer mean? I only want some one to buy me chips on the way home from school," Shaz assured her.

Fiona looked at her and shook her head.

"Poor old Shaz. Maybe I should say poor old Digo," Shirley teased.

Shaz looked over at Shirley and giggled.

With the DVD over Shirley left the girls to it and made her way up to her bedroom. She was delighted that arrangements had been made for tomorrow. If she had to go to great lengths in order to see Dave, so be it.

She just hoped it would be worth it and not a disaster.

<u>11.30pm (in bed)</u>
That Shaz is mad. Mind you she's had a good teacher; you only want to look at her mother. Hardly a role

model. Back to tomorrow, though, it's all sorted then, I'm meeting lover boy at two by the pier head! And I just can't wait.

<u>Sunday, February 10</u>
<u>1pm</u>
No one seems to suspect a thing, thank God, so I can relax and enjoy the day.

<u>6pm</u>
I nearly died of shame... It all started out so well, we were chatting away walking along the river walk, round the docks. It was freezing like, but I was happy enough. I'd put on a thermal vest I found in me drawer that me mum had got me one Christmas. I knew it would come in handy if I kept it long enough.

David was all wrapped up an' all. He had a really thick red coat and black jeans on. A long black scarf covered his neck and dangled down to his waist. His black curly hair was covered with a black beanie hat. His hair is that thick and curly that a few curls had escaped in the back. There was an overwhelming smell of aftershave, my favourite, the same one Oli always wears. I'd gone and forgotten me gloves, though, so he took his off and gave me them to put on.

While we were walking along he grabbed me arm and linked it through his. I'm not sure if he did it so he could still keep his hands in his pockets but I like to think that it was cos he wanted me to hold onto him.

It started pissing down with rain so David being David dived into the nearest building, which was the Maritime Museum! All very interesting if you're on a school trip but not really the place to go on a date, is it? But with the weather being so shitty we had no choice.

"Look at the size of that tornado," I said looking round the war section trying to get into it.

David looked at me smiling, and a little lad of about eight walked passed. "It's a torpedo, you silly cow," the lad said.

I nearly died of shame. I was as red as a beetroot. It put me off saying anything after. Then to make things worse I missed the last step on the way down from the top floor and went arse over tit!

I don't know what the hell he must think of me. Me hair was dripping wet and me make-up had run all over me face by the end of the date, cos it was still pissing down by the time we got out of the museum.

I thought that would be the last I'd see of him, but he said he'd had a great time and would ring me in the week. We'll see... I won't hold me breath, I don't think he'll want to know especially after me making a tit of meself.

Monday, February 11
1pm

Went to see Barbara and co. today. She was like a new woman, all glammed up, and says she's madly in love with this new fella, the one from the creative writing group. They've started salsa dancing classes now. She said he brings out the best in her. Anyway, Oli and me have only got another private detective job from her!

Some woman she knows has asked if we'll do a bit of the old snooping for her cos her fella's kecks are up and down like a fart in a bottle. I'm gonna go over to see her this afternoon. Oli's made up. He's been calling me Sherlock all morning. Same financial set up as for Barb. I can't believe it, we could be sitting on a little gold mine here.

With the morning's work under their belts it was time to head over to investigate Barbara's contact.

"Should we be wearing sunglasses or something?" Oli asked when they arrived at the address.

"What? And a big mac' and hat? Yeah, right, sure-fire way to get arrested, babe," Shirley said.

With a mix of excitement and nerves they rang the doorbell and were greeted by Silvia.

Once she'd dragged them inside the house, Silvia was keen to pour it all out. Convinced Franco, her man, was up to all sorts and had been for years, she hooked Oli and Shirley into gaining as much information on her cheating husband as they could.

"I'm sick of it, now, but I need the photies to prove it cos he's always denying it. It's no one in particular, not like Barb, it's whoever's up for it on the night," Silvia said grimly.

"Well we can follow him one night, see what he's up to and try for the photies," Shirley suggested.

"Nice one. He goes out every Friday with the lads same old routine, same old clubs," Silvia said.

"We'll go in for the kill this Friday, then. Come on David Bailey," Shirley said to Oli and off they went.

<u>9pm</u>
I've heard nothing from David yet. I wonder if he does think I'm a clumsy old cow. Probably!

11pm

Just had a lovely phone call from David. I think I'm in love! "I thought you wouldn't ring after yesterday. You must think I'm just a mad Scouser." I told him.

"I think Scousers are great, especially mad ones," he said.

Bloody 'ell. We're off out again on Saturday night, to see a film and for something to eat! Yes!

Tuesday, 12 February
8pm

I've just had this woman Mrs. Smith on the phone playing hell about Fiona. Apparently Fiona has only been piercing kids' ears and noses in school and charging them for the pleasure. Now her kid's ear is all red and she's worried it'll turn gangrenous and drop off.

"You were the one who told me to get a job. I made a fortune today. Trust that silly cow Melissa to spoil it. I knew I shouldn't of done her," said the guilty Fi.

"You could get expelled for this, you silly cow. That Mrs. Smith one's a parent governor and she's gonna take it further," I told her.

"Old Wilmi will see his arse tomorrow," Fi said.

I reckon we'll all see our arse tomorrow!

Wednesday, 13 February
8am

Waiting for the phone call from school today. I think I might turn me mobie off.

1pm

Just turned me mobie back on and sure enough a message from David Wilmore, my sexy fella, asking me

144 - 144 -

to ring school to arrange to go in and see him. Shame it wasn't about our date.

<u>5pm</u>
Left Oli to it after dinner and went over to the school. Thought I may as well get it over and done with.

"Hello, Mrs Cartwright, please do come in," he said to me, all official. He looked up and down the corridor as I passed him and went into the room.

I was shitting meself. It was like being back in school meself.

"Look, she's not really a bad kid. It was my fault, I told her she needed to get a job, make some extra cash for herself. I didn't expect her to turn to this kind of thing though." I babbled like a mad thing.

"The woman who phoned is a right whinger anyway. She complains about something every other week. Anyway I thought it was very entrepreneurial of Fiona," he said smiling.

The glorious smell of his aftershave filled the room. He dresses lovely for work an' all. Dead trendy but very smart too.

He smiled over at me, "I will have to be seen to be doing something, though, maybe if you could give her one of these books and she could do one of the exercises in it, nothing too much or she'll hate me. I don't want to make it too obvious by keeping her in. If you take the book home it will keep the whinging woman happy and Fiona won't have to feel embarrassed as none of her mates will find out," he said walking into the tiny storeroom at the front of his classroom.

I followed him in to collect the book. "Of course I will. Ta."

He closed the door of the tiny storeroom behind me and leaned forward to kiss me. It seemed to go on for ages and it took me breath away. I thought he was meant to be a history teacher not geography, his hands certainly were able to find their way around a fair bit. I wasn't complaining mind.

Then from nowhere, breaking up our special moment, we heard laughing and shouting coming from the classroom. It sounded like Fi and Shaz.

"I wonder if your mum has been in yet to see old Wilmi." Shaz's voice could be heard clearly from our vantage point behind the storeroom door.

"I thought she'd be here now, late as usual. Come on Shaz, quick, get your bag I don't want to bump into her," Fi answered.

I held me breath, and so did David.

"What are you pair doing in here?" A loud voice of authority shouted.

"Oh I forgot me bag, we're going now, miss," Shaz said to the woman, who sounded very much like the deputy head according to David. He had his hand over his mouth; I thought he was going to get a fit of the giggles.

"Out," we heard her shout, then silence. The coast was clear.

"That was a close shave, I'd best be off," I said to David, sorting meself out.

"Here you go," he said, handing me the book and kissing me again, this time on the cheek.

Thankfully I didn't see Shaz, Fi or Jason for that matter on the way back to the car. I sat in the driving seat and dialled Oli's mobile number.

"So it was a near miss, eh? Hey, you lucky cow, did

you have a chance at a shag in the cupboard, Boris Becker stylie?" he asked me.

"Behave… No," I said, but maybe next time…

SIX

<u>Thursday, February 14</u>
<u>9am</u>
I can't believe it. First time in years I got a Valentine's card. At first I thought it was Oli messing around, but I've just phoned him and he said it wasn't. It's signed with a great bid D and a load of kisses. Well, it must be David.

I never thought to send him one. Maybe I should go round the school and give him one...and a Valentine as well! I'm due to see him on Saturday, but it can't wait till then. I think I will.

<u>2pm</u>
Popped into town with Oli, to choose a card. He'd had three. He says he doesn't know who they're from but I bet he does!

Got a bit of a jokey one for Dave and signed it

Sxxxxxxx. I put it in a brown envelope and gave it to a right sourpuss secretary at the school. She obviously never got one, the gob on her.

<u>4pm</u>
Just got a text from David, he loved the card!

<u>6pm</u>
The kids came home. Jason got five cards in school. Fi got two. Well they obviously take after their mum. Good looking, the pair of them.

So it turned out to be a good year for Valentine's Day cards in the Cartwright household.

"So, five cards eh, Jason, love? That's a bit of all right," Shirley said brightly.

"Oh, eh, yeah, they were all from his little year seven fan club," Fi said laughing.

"No way! Well, all right four of them were, maybe, but one I'm sure was from that new girl in year ten, from down south somewhere. She's dead fit her," Jason protested.

"Yeah, right. She's well out of your league."

"Hey, Mum, Shaz sent ten cards and got one back," Fi announced.

"No way. Shame. Who off?" Shirley asked.

"Don't know, but she hopes it was Digo," Fiona said cheerfully.

Jason walked out laughing.

"Don't say anything, Mum, but I sent Shaz that card just to make her feel better. I knew she was sending ten and that she'd be gutted if a load of us got one and she didn't, so I put one on her desk in reg'. No one saw and no one knows, only you. Don't say anything, will ya?"

"'Course I won't, Fi, love," Shirley promised.

<u>11pm</u>
My daughter, the kind, caring girl. Sparing her bessie mate the shame of having no card on Valentine's Day. I'm dead proud of her. I only wish I'd had a mate like her in school. I was four years with no card and that cow Sarah Moore had about a hundred, and she used to rub me nose in it.

Well not this year, I've got one from sex on legs and I'm over the friggin' moon!

It's a shame I can't show off me card, I've put it in the drawer but I keep getting it out and looking at it. I feel like a schoolgirl meself. I'm so chuffed.

We're back to work tomorrow on our secret job. I've been that busy with all the other stuff I'd forgotten about our detective work. We've called this one the Italian Job, for the obvious: Franco's Italian!

<u>Friday, February 15</u>
<u>9am</u>
Day of code name the Italian Job. I've sent Oli a text so he knows we're knocking off handy today so we can have a bit of a chat later about the details. We've still got a day and a half, what with the factory girls and our new mate Sapphire.

The highlight of the week for Cuts 'n' Curls, the factory girls, and once again Shirley and Oli weren't disappointed.

"Anyone heard from Angie, then, from her hols?" Oli asked while they were busy cutting and blowing.

"Oh, aye, yeah. I had a phone call yesterday. She's having a whale of a time with her sister. They've shagged a load of fellas and got pissed every day and night. Sounds like a great place. She wants us all to go with them next time. A load of us could go. It'd be boss," Ali said excitedly.

"She used that Viagra yet?" Shirley asked, eager to get all the info.

"Aye, yeah, she has. She said she needn't have bought it though, cos the fellas are all well up for it anyway, lucky cow. Better than those lazy sods in the pub over the road. They've all let themselves go."

Shirley and Oli looked over at Ali in amazement; she sat there in navy leggings, white ankle socks, sandals and floral silk blouse. All twenty stone of her. Talk about the pot calling the kettle...

"So when she comes back she wants us to get together and start to arrange it for the summer," Ali went on.

"Bloody 'ell old Comb-over will have heart failure if you lot all desert him at the same time," Shirley protested.

"Serve him right, tight old bastard. We've got rights yer know. He's even been keeping count on when we all go the khazi. Poor old Vera had a right rollicking last week cos she was in and out of there like a fart in a colander. She had the wild shites, poor cow, from a dodgy curry the night before. She let one go in the morning and it nearly set off the sprinkler system, didn't it girls? So I knew she was desperate. It was gas masks at the ready all morning," Ali said sympathetically, shaking her head.

"John says it puts him right off me when I let one go," Gail carried on with the fart conversation.

"So, if I'm not in the mood for any action, like, I just let one go. If I am in the mood for action and I let one go by accident I blame the dog. He never realises. Works every time," she said dead serious.

The girls all looked on as if Gail had given them the best tip they'd ever heard. Amazing what they talk about in that factory, thought Shirley.

She looked over at Oli wanting to laugh but he looked on all serious and sympathetic. She tried to change the subject in case they roped her and Oli in on the holiday. Now that would be a holiday and a half.

"Hey, Susan, love, how did Fat Sandra get on with her diet this week; did she do any better than you kid?" Shirley asked smiling.

"The jammy cow. D'yer know she lost ten pound in her first week. I don't know how she did it. I bet it's all water," Susan said disgusted.

"Aye, aye, Susan, did you go without your chips then?" Oli asked teasing her.

"I did, yeah, not one to go back on me word, me. I went to the Chinese instead."

"Bloody 'ell..." Oli shouted.

Next it was on to Sapphire. They weren't bombarded with chips this time.

"How's it going, babe?" Oli asked her as he tried to comb through her hair, which she'd somehow managed to return almost to last week's state. He didn't know how she did it.

"Great. Sorry about me hair. I haven't brushed it since you did it last week. I have put a bit of lacquer on it, though," she said proudly.

"Not brushed it. Why not, babe?" Oli said looking

horrified.

"Well that's what I pay you for isn't it, to do me hair."

"Yeah, but you've got to friggin' brush it, love," Oli said still in shock.

"What you been up to anyway?" Shirley asked.

"Been busy you know with all these forms. Got a load of new customers, now. The words got out. I'll have to cool it a bit. Don't want a knock from the Social do I, saying I'm getting paid for it? Done me usual singing and I met up with Marsha. She's really got the hots for you, Oli babe."

"Don't remind me. She's a right one her," Oli said shivering.

"Well I'm trying to fix her up with the landlord from the pub I sing at. He stinks a bit, but he's up for it. I'm not sure about her though. She's a bit fussy, isn't she? Let's face it, what else is she gonna get the state of her. She may as well go for him than wait for something that isn't gonna happen."

Shirley got the mirrors out, and showed Sapphire the repaired do and she was delighted with the results.

"Now make sure you comb that friggin' hair this week and lay off the lacquer. You're lucky you've been nowwhere near a naked flame. You'd've needed a wig for the rest of your days, not a hairdresser," Oli warned.

"Aye, but look at the money I'd of saved," Sapphire said, laughing.

They clambered over the rusty old bikes and prams, struggled down the concrete steps, made their way to the car and went on to have a coffee in town to put the finishing touches on the Italian Job.

"Hey, it's dead exciting this, isn't it, eh? You and me," Oli said warmly tapping her hand while they were waiting for their coffees.

"So what's the plan then, babe, let's go through it?" Shirley said. "Just so's we know what we're doing."

"You pick me up at about seven; we'll pretend we're out as a couple," Oli went on. "We know where he hangs out, and that will give us plenty of time to get to the places we need to be."

"Ok, maybe we could try and get chatting to them, make friends sort of thing. We must remember the camera. We could get them to take photos of us together and then suggest we had a pic of all of us, and then maybe one of just the two of them. If we did it that way, well it wouldn't look so obvious us taking photos of them," Shirley suggested.

"We could pretend it's our anniversary and we're out celebrating, everyone in a happy mood," Oli said getting carried away with the story.

"Sounds like a good idea," Shirley said brightly. "We're leading secret lives. Ordinary hairdressers by day, detectives by night."

"So we're all set for tonight then?" Oli asked.

"Aye, yeah, I'll have to think of something to tell the kids. They'll start to get suspicious you know, all these fibs."

"Tell them we've been picked for the pub darts team," Oli said, chuffed that he had thought of an excuse.

"Forget it, they'd never fall for that one. I'm gonna tell them you need some advice about your love life cos you haven't got one," Shirley announced.

"Oh they will fall for that one, though, well ta a friggin' bunch."

<u>11.30pm</u>
The Italian Job has gone tits up!

We got to the pub and Franco was there sure enough, in full swing with some blonde. We followed him around a bit as he went from one woman to another. I couldn't flaming believe it, we'd only gone and left the friggin' camera at home!

"I'll go back and get it and you stay here keeping an eye out," I said to Oli.

"Hurry up, babes, he might go on somewhere else and what do I do then?" He said to me dead worried.

"Follow him: we've got to give the photies to Silvia on Monday. We'll be knackered if we don't get them. Ring me if you've gone on somewhere else," I told him.

"Right you are," Oli said looking really stressed out. Poor sod.

I got a taxi home, picked up the camera and taxied it back to find Oli.

No sign of him or Franco in the pub. I couldn't believe me eyes when I looked at me mobie. It was dead. No battery at all. They had obviously moved on and Oli couldn't get hold of me. I couldn't even ring him cos his number is only in me mobie. Friggin' 'ell.

I got another taxi back home and Oli's just phoned to say they went on to another club and it was so packed that he lost him.

"We're gonna have to get our act together if we wanna do this properly," Oli said grimly.

"I know. I'm well pissed off now," I said.

<u>Saturday, 16 February</u>
<u>10am</u>
I had a brainwave in the night. Franco runs a printing

shop in town. Maybe we could get him today. I'll phone Oli to tell him.

Armed with a notebook and pen Shirley dialled Oli's number and began to reveal her plan.

"That's all well and good, babes, but he's hardy gonna shag someone in his work, is he?" Oli said.

"I know that, soft lad. We could catch him out. If a young woman was to go into the shop, do a bit of flirting... Hey presto, we've got him."

"What are the chances of that?" Oli asked.

"Oli, you daft pillock, we could arrange for someone to do it."

"Shirley, love, I think that's called entrapment."

"Entrapment, my arse. It's only entrapment if he hasn't done it before and he has. We've seen him with our own eyes."

"Aye, I suppose. But who, surely not you?"

"No way, not me. But we know a girl who would if there's a few quid in it for her."

The next phone call was to their would-be accomplice.

"So you want me to do a bit of flirting, no questions asked, and you'll give us a few quid for it?" Sapphire said.

"That's right, love. Are you up for it?"

"Too bloody right I am."

"I tell you what, I'll call for yer at about twelve and I'll do your hair first as well," Shirley encouraged.

Although Shirley and Oli had been to Sapphire's only the previous day, Shirley felt if yesterday's hairdo was anything to go by Sapphire couldn't be trusted to keep it presentable for the next day, especially if she was going to seduce the Italian stallion. A touch up hairdo would definitely be in order.

Everything was all set up, this time they wouldn't forget the camera!

<u>6pm</u>

Good old Sapphire. She was fab.

We went over beforehand to do her hair and get all the details sorted.

"Now you make sure you keep your gob shut," Oli said to her sternly putting the final touches to her hair.

"Ask no questions, me. So long as I get me money that's all that matters to me. I don't care what's what," she said.

Sapphire went into the shop to get some papers photocopied. The plan was for her to get Franco to shut up shop and take her out for a few drinks and a bit of a walk. We would follow as a couple and take the photies.

"Sapphire, love, we'll make sure that your face can't be seen in any of these photies, it'll only be his mug and the back of your hair," I told her before she went off.

"Aye, ok, love that's fine by me," she said and she did us proud. We got the photies all sorted and printed off ready for Silvia on Monday.

"That's another one in the bag, babes. I think this calls for a bit of a celebration," Oli said, cracking open a bottle of bubbly when we got back to his house.

To be honest I feel a bit pissed now and could do with bit of a kip, but I've got a hot date tonight with

David. The thought of him in his nicely-fitting black jeans is enough to get me raring to go.

Sitting down to a cup of tea with Fiona, Shirley looked at her watch.

"You off out again tonight, Mum?" Fi asked.

"Yeah, I'm going to the pictures with Oli," Shirley lied, hoping that Fiona wouldn't push for any more information.

"Nice one Mum. I'm glad you're going out a bit more now. You should think about getting a fella, ya know."

"What, and you wouldn't mind?" Shirley asked surprised.

"No way. I think it would be good for you, so long as he's all right."

"How d'yer mean all right?" Shirley enquired.

"Not a dickhead like that Rob one. Someone who'll treat you good."

"So who ever he is, so long as he treats me right, then that's ok?" Shirley asked her; just to make sure she'd got her facts right.

"Yeah," Fiona said smiling. "Mum, you deserve it."

Shirley smiled to herself, wondering if Fiona would still feel the same way if she knew who her mother was going out with tonight...

<u>Sunday, 17 February</u>
<u>10am</u>
Had a lovely night last night with David. He really makes me feel special and he's getting dead romantic with me now. I know it's early days an' all that, but he's

really different. Last night we went for something to eat after the film. It was dead quiet in the restaurant and he just held me hand staring at me with his great big green eyes.

"You're really special, Shirley. You make me feel alive," he said.

Imagine that. I couldn't believe it. I was gobsmacked. No one has ever said anything so beautiful to me ever. I'll never forget it.

"Thanks." I said to him. "No one has ever said anything like that to me before."

Not only is he gorgeous – well to be honest gorgeous is the wrong word to describe him, he's more beautiful really, he's got a very unique look. Maybe that's why I'm so drawn to him cos he's so different. I love his hair an' all. It's a bit mad really; he's got loads of it, all black and curly, it just sort of falls about his face. It's not tight curls or anything like that, just sort of small bouncy ones. He wouldn't look out of place in one of them period drama things. Oli's right, he certainly isn't the type I would normally go for but there is something about him.

I told Oli this morning when he phoned.

"What – you mean after that you still haven't shagged him?"

"He respects me Oli. There's more to a relationship than just sex you know, and that's what it's turning out to be, a relationship. I must admit though I think if he tried to I'd take him up on it.

"To be honest with you, Oli, I don't think I've ever felt this way about a fella. I think I might be in love with him."

"Friggin' 'ell babes. What you gonna tell the kids?"

he asked.

"Nothing yet. Let's just see what happens," I said.

Shirley decided it was about time she played the dutiful daughter again, after all this self-indulgent lovey-dovey gossip, so set about ringing her mum.

"Oh I'm up to me neck in it, love, doing Auntie Dilys' washing. Her washer's broken, so I sent a taxi down to hers to pick up the bin bag of washing and the taxi bought it back up here to me to do it. I'll put it all in the dryer later and taxi it back."

"I can't believe it. Taxis going backwards and forwards with bin bags full of washing and no flamin' people," Shirley said to her mother.

That wasn't a good idea as Shirley then had to listen to her mother go on at her for half an hour about how much she did for Auntie Dilys and all on her own. In the end Shirley made her excuses, saying that there was someone at the door.

Half an hour later the phone rang. It was a very distressed Shirley's mother...

"I don't know what to do, Auntie Dilys has just phoned in a hell of a state. Says her washing has come back and all her knicks and bras are missing. That taxi driver must have gone through it all and pinched them."

Shirley wondered if Ted from next door had got a new job...

Monday, 18 February
6pm
Went to give Silvia the bad news today. It doesn't

seem as hard the second time somehow, I don't know why. I really felt it when I went round to Barbara's. Probably cos it was our first one. Oli's got plans for us now though – bloody hell!!!!

"I've been thinking babe about this little thing we've got going. We have a right laugh, don't we?" Oli said.

"Yeah, we do. I really enjoy it," I told him.

"We help people out and we get a bit extra, don't we, and still keep our usual clients?"

"Your point is Oli?" I asked.

"Well I think we should do a bit more of it. I think we're a great team and we should make it a bit more official like."

"How d'yer mean?"

"We could advertise. Put an ad in the paper, all confidential like. Use a PO box number."

"Sounds like a good idea. We might not get anything but, hell, it's worth a go."

"Nice one. I'll sort it out today," he said.

Bloody 'ell, Christmas time me life was dead boring, now I've got loads going on. Shirley Cartwright, the world is your oyster!

<u>Tuesday 19, February</u>
<u>1pm</u>
Dropped Oli off at one of the homes this morning and then, cos there was only a few that wanted their hairdoing, I came back home to do a bit of cleaning. Oli didn't seem to mind.

I've just finished Fi's room. What a state! I found the floor full of clothes and a wardrobe full of empty coat hangers! As for Jason, I found the remains of last week's tea under his bed. God, I hope we don't get rats.

Shirley finished off her cleaning up routine then went to check her phone. Waiting on the phone screen was a little yellow envelope indicating a text message had arrived. It was from Oli to say he was ready for a lift. He wanted to call and put their advert in the paper on the way back.

Shirley touched up her make-up, brushed her hair and put her coat on. Heading out, she took a quick look at herself in the mirror by the front door. Not bad, she thought to herself and smiled.

Outside the old folks' home, Oli stood eagerly waiting for Shirley. As her car turned into the entrance road he waved frantically, glad to be escaping the freezing cold wind that was picking up. He got into the car and as usual was off detailing the day's events without taking a breath.

"Bloody 'ell, there's this new woman in the home. Came the other day apparently. She wants a regular from us. Nice old girl, but hair like a wire brush, poor cow. I had to put a load of hair lacquer on her just to hold it. She's like Sapphire now," Oli said laughing.

"I hope they don't put the lekkie blanket on for her tonight then," Shirley said and they both erupted into fits of giggles.

"So d'you want to put this ad' in on the way home then, babe?" Shirley asked.

"Oh yeah, kid, I'm dead excited," he said brightly.

<u>Wednesday, 20 February</u>
<u>12 noon</u>
According to Oli our ad' will be in tomorrow and it will be in for six weeks to start with. He's put,

Other half doing the dirty?
Give us a call, no need to get shirty.
If it's evidence you want then we'll give it to you,
What you do with it is up to you.

Then he's got our PO box number! I must admit I'm not too hopeful for a response with that as our ad! I think it will be a case of stick to the day job.

<u>Thursday, 21 February</u>
<u>8am</u>
Got a really busy day today. We're all booked up all day. Well, I thought I'd better, we have been slacking a bit. It's all blue rinses and perms today. We're with the two misses, and then in West Haven the rest of the day. No time to fart today, so I'll have to pick up the local paper on the way to Oli's.

Back in the car, Shirley opened the paper scanning the classified pages eager to find their advertisement.

"Hey, I'm dead excited about this, aren't you, babes?" Oli asked leaning over her shoulder looking for their piece.

"Yeah, Oli, I am, but don't be getting your hopes up. We probably won't hear anything, you know," Shirley said reading an article on hair and make-up.

"Positive thinking, girl, that's what you need. Look

we'll be helping all those women not only to look good but to sort out their lives as well," Oli said, snatching the paper from Shirley, slightly annoyed that she seemed to have forgotten what she was looking for.

"We might get fellas, yer know. It's not only the fellas cheating on the women, it might be the women cheating on the fellas," Shirley informed him.

"Oh, aye, yeah, I hadn't thought of that. What will we do if we need a fella to do that entrapment thingy that we got Sapphire to do? You'd better not look at me, I'd rather shag that Comb-over than some woman. I just couldn't do it, babe. I still haven't really got over bushy Mave. God knows how I'll feel when I see candyfloss the next time." Oli said mortified.

"Well we couldn't use my David that's for sure," Shirley reported, snatching the newspaper from him and folding it before throwing it on the back seat and driving off.

They spent the afternoon working hard on the perm and blue rinse brigade, but Oli kept looking at the newspaper advertisement every chance he could – much to Shirley's amusement. Deep down she didn't really think anything would come of it. On the other hand, Oli was delighted and was convinced that this would be a new adventure.

Digo had been invited over for tea. He had a present from his dad and was eager to show it off.

"Mum, come out and see Digo's scooter. It's boss," Jason said all excited. Digo was sat proudly on the scooter by the front gate with a huge grin on his face.

"Eh, you look dead good on that love. What's Shaz gonna say when she sees you on that, eh?" Shirley asked smiling.

"It does thirty miles an hour on a good run," Digo said proudly patting the side of the scooter.

Jason walked around the scooter scrutinising every part with a huge big grin on his face and rubbing his hands together.

"I know it's not brand new, like, but it'll get me about won't it?" Digo said enthusiastically.

"It's sound, mate. I want one now, give us a go," Jason said eagerly looking over at Shirley.

"No way, you're not insured," Shirley shouted anxiously from the gate.

"Jason looks really pissed off. And look at Digo, he looks glad, I don't think he wants to let it go. Probably doesn't trust our Jay," Fiona said to Shirley, laughing.

"You'll have to get a little job now Digo, to pay for your petrol," Shirley said to him, moving closer to have a better look at the scooter.

"Na, not really. I filled it up before I came out. I went round me Nana's. She cleans for this couple, the Smiths, and me granddad does the garden for them. They've got one of these petrol lawn mowers. Me granddad sorted me out with some petrol from that. Says I can get petrol any time I like. The Smiths are loaded. They won't notice," he went on, unashamed.

"Bloody 'ell are my kids attracted to the rogues or what?" Shirley thought raising her eyebrows.

"I'm gonna go down to Rhyl on it, give it a bit of a spin like. Me dad said he'll follow us down in the car," Digo went on.

"Bloody 'ell it'll take you ages on that at thirty. Won't your dad get a bit miffed having to go that slow all that way?" Shirley asked knowing that she would in similar circumstances.

"Na, he can't go any faster himself, the head gasket's gone on his car anyway so he has to drive dead slow," Digo replied flatly.

"He'll never make it to Rhyl, Digo, love. You'd best wait till the summer; you'll have had a bit more practice by then and maybe your dad will have sorted the car out, eh? It's dead icy on the roads, now, you might do a wheel spin and burn out your tyres." Shirley tried to put him off, because if he was going then she was sure Jason wouldn't be far behind in Digo's dad's clapped-out heap.

"I've been trying me best to do a wheel spin, Shirley, but it won't do it for some reason," Digo said turning the handlebars from side to side in mock wheel spin style.

"It's all in the technique, mate. Here let's show yer?" Jason suggested edging forward, attempting to get Digo off the scooter.

"No, you're all right. I don't want to wreck it on me first day, do I?" Digo said pushing him gently away looking worried.

"Flamin' 'ell something else to worry about now. Jason wanting one of them scooters... Well tough tits, he can forget it. I can't stand the worry of it, so he can whinge as much as he likes, he's not getting one. I can't even see Digo letting him have a go on his," Shirley said to Fiona who pulled a face knowingly.

Next to arrive was the one and only Shaz, in her white plazzy boots. Along the road she sauntered and was delighted with the sight that greeted her.

"Oh my God, it's Barry Sheen," she said at the top of her voice.

Digo looked dead proud of himself striking a biker-style pose as she approached.

"How the hell do you know who Barry Sheen was?

You're too young, love." Shirley was surprised that someone Shaz's age would have heard of the seventies motorcycle ace.

"Me mum used to 'ave a crush on him. We've got a kitchen clock with him in all his gear on it. It's only got one hand, like, so it doesn't work. You 'ave to guess the time. That's why I always miss the bus for school. She can't bear to part with it even though she's had at least five letters from school complaining about me punctuality or something," she said matter of factly.

Well maybe the clock had been the height of fashion in the seventies, but Shirley didn't think she'd be popping round to Shaz's anytime soon for interior design tips!

Poor old Shaz though, she didn't stand a chance with a mum like that. You'd of thought she'd make sure Shaz got to school on time at least. She's probably not up before dinner herself anyway, Shirley thought as she watched Shaz move into action. Poor Digo was about to be terrorised.

"Hey give us seater, Digo," Shaz said walking towards the scooter looking ready for action.

"No way, it's only meant for one, you daft cow," Digo said trying to protect his new toy.

"Come on, soft lad, don't be tight, show us how it's done," Shaz said not taking no for an answer.

"No way. I've got to go down to Rhyl on this, yer know. I'll have no tyres left if you get on it, you mad cow." He was trying to start the engine so he could pull away from her.

"You cheeky git. Go up and down the road on it then. Let's see you in action." Shaz had accepted defeat but wanted to see what she was missing out on.

"Poor old Shaz. 'Daft cow! Silly cow!' Good job she

fancies him," Shirley said to Fiona who was in hysterics by this time.

Managing to get the scooter going, Digo exacted a loud rev from the engine, as loud as is possible on a scooter and off he went. Shaz and Fi were doubled over with laughter as Digo went up and down the street leaning forward for more speed, thinking he was a top racing driver. He went up and down the road twice, eventually coming to a stop right by Shaz, not having achieved more than about 15 miles per hour tops.

"Bloody 'ell there's more oomph in me hairdryer than that thing. I'm sure if you did a fart on it you'd get an extra thirty miles an hour out of it," Shaz said laughing.

Neither Jason nor Digo were at all impressed with the girls, who wasted no time making fun of them for the rest of the night.

11.30pm

Me legs feel like jelly I've worked that hard today. Oli had already been down the paper shop to get the newspaper and check out our ad. We both had a look at it together. He's made up with it. I'm not so sure.

Digo turned up after tea, it's his birthday today and he wanted to show off his new scooter that he got from his dad. We all had a look at it. Bless him he was dead chuffed with the old heap.

Just phoned David. In secret from my bedroom, of course. I've arranged to go out with him tomorrow. We're gonna meet in town. I'm gonna make sure we accidentally on purpose bump into Oli. I really want Oli to meet him, see what he thinks of David.

Friday was the usual great day for Oli and Shirley and not only because it was the start of the weekend...

Once inside Comb-over's factory they were all-out setting up the treatment area. No work got done on the production line as the girls all sat about watching each other have their hairdone. Mug of tea, a few biscuits and a good old natter, what could be nicer?

"Come on then, queen, tell us all about your conquests," Oli said to Angie who was back from Falaraki, looking all tanned.

"Oh we had a fab' time. We're definitely gonna go again. I had the time of me life," Angie said, sitting in the chair ready to be pampered.

All the factory girls looked on having heard the stories loads of times already, but eager to see Shirley and Oli's reaction.

"Didn't you feel a bit upset, Angie love, you know, it was supposed to be your honeymoon and all that?" Shirley asked slightly concerned.

"No, couldn't give a shit, Shirley love. We had such a boss time there was no time to be moping. This one fella asked me and me sis' for a threesome yer know," Angie said proudly.

"Bloody 'ell, what was his name, Stevie Wonder?" Oli asked laughing.

"Behave, soft lad. He was quite nice really, but we didn't go through with it. I've got standards, yer know."

"Have yer, babe," Oli said winking at Shirley. "What about the Viagra, girl? Heard you gave it a go..."

"Aye, yeah, I did but there was no need, they were all up for it, yer know," Angie assured them all.

"Tell them about you farting on the job, Angie," Susan said all excited.

"What...you never?" Oli said looking horrified.

"Oh, aye, yeah, I did. I couldn't help meself. We were in full swing and he just sort of grabbed me arse and out it came," Angie said laughing. "It must 'ave been the dodgy foreign food."

"More like all the ale," Gail said sarcastically, listening to the conversation even though she had heard the story before and she was meant to be on lookout duty.

"Oh my God, I'd've died of shame," Shirley said really feeling embarrassed for her.

"I couldn't give a shit. I'll never see him again, will I?" Angie said matter of factly.

"I suppose you're right, but still..." Shirley replied pulling a face at Oli who pulled a face back, all behind Angie's back of course.

Tiring of the poolside antics, Susan went on a bit about fat Sandra.

"It seems she's doing really well with her slimming and, surprise, surprise, Susan hasn't lost a pound," Gail said to Shirley, her voice lowered to a discreet mumble.

"Fat Sandra even received an award for the biggest weight loss. Apparently she asked Susan if there was a job going in the factory cos she could do with the extra cash to buy some new gear, because she's already dropped nearly two dress sizes," Gail went on.

Oli picked up on the tail end of the conversation.

"Hey, what's all this about Fat Sandra, Susan, girl?" Oli called out.

"Oh, aye, yeah, only wants to come back here to work, the cheeky cow," Susan moaned.

"Never, she must be desperate to want to come back here with you lot."

"I told her old Comb-over has got even worse, that we

have to work through our dinner and the wages are going down, to try and put her off."

"Why queen? You could all do with a bit of help here, what with you lot being rushed off your feet," Oli said, winding her up.

"What, Fat Sandra working here on that slimming diet. Friggin' 'ell she used to fart a lot before. I bet she lets off some right stinkers, now, if she eats all the veg that skinny Lindsey tells you to. No way am I encouraging that."

"Not the fact that she is losing all that weight and starting to look good then?" Oli asked.

Susan ignored Oli and while the girls continued chatting, he and Shirley finished up their latest attempt at trying to make the factory girls beautiful.

Next it was onto Sapphire who was in full swing...

"Hey, girl, had that call from the West End yet?" Oli said teasing her about her singing career.

"Aye, aye, comedian... Listen, I've got a new sideline now with the pair of you, haven't I, and it's a bit more exciting than singing for a load of old drunks," she replied seriously.

"Aye, queen, you're right there; did a good job, girl, ta for that," Oli said, meaning it for once.

"Now any time the pair of you want me services again, don't be afraid to ask. I enjoyed meself. Ask no questions me, so long as I get paid that's all that bothers me. In cash an' all, I don't want the Social after me do I?"

"Well we'll definitely keep you in mind, love. Cash in hand every time," Shirley said trying to brush Sapphire's hair without pulling it out by what was left of the roots.

"Did you forget that we told you to lay off the lacquer?" Oli asked her, looking quite fed up.

"I know, I know, but at least I brushed it this week, eh?" she said laughing.

Walking back down to the car, Shirley made arrangements with Oli about where they were to accidentally on purpose meet up later. She was anxious not to mess things up.

"I'll tone me dress sense down a bit tonight, babe," he said sincerely.

"You wear what you like, Oli love. I want David to see you just like you are. I love you whatever you wear and so will he," Shirley said honestly holding his arm.

There was just enough time for Shirley to fill in her diary entry for the day before she made her way out to meet up with David, and, accidentally on purpose, Oli. At least this time she wouldn't be lying to the kids, not totally anyway.

<u>Friday, 22 February</u>
<u>7pm</u>
Had a great laugh as usual. I love work on a Friday. Those factory girls and Sapphire are fab. It was the usual wonderful gossip.

It's all gone a bit quiet on the love life front for Oli. He hasn't mentioned anyone for ages now. There was that one fella when I first met up with David but he didn't last. I hope he finds someone soon. To be honest though he doesn't seem that bothered. I think he's enjoying being single.

Off out tonight with David and I'm gonna accidentally on purpose meet up with Oli. I can't wait to find out if they both get on. That would be the best!!!

<u>Saturday, 23 February</u>
<u>10am</u>
It's official David is sex on legs and Oli is the best
bessie mate in the world. They loved each other and
got on like a house on fire. I'm so chuffed. They were
chatting away as if they'd known each other for years.
I'm so happy. I've only got to convince the kids now.

Delighted as she was that Oli and David Wilmore had got
on so well, Shirley was convinced that the only way she
stood a chance of the kids liking him was to do a bit of
crawling to them. Let them get their own way a bit for a
while, not too much, but not complain that their music
was too loud, that they were watching rubbish on the
TV, that sort of thing. Another way was to tolerate their
friends more. Shirley didn't mind them having their
friends over, in fact she enjoyed their company and was
always guaranteed a bit of fun with them, so that was
at least one thing she could succeed at on the crawling
stakes.

Barry Sheen – as Digo was now known – called round
on his 'Harley'.

"How you getting on with yer wheels?" Shirley asked
him.

"Sound, Shirley. I'm a free agent now. I can go where I
like, do what I want. It's great."

"Been down Shaz's street yet?" Fi asked giggling.

"Oh, she told you then, the sad cow..." Digo said
looking sheepish.

"What happened?" Jason asked, wanting to be
supportive of his mate but trying not to laugh.

"Shaz got a load of the kids to chuck her manky old

fruit and veg at him as he went up and down. They'd got a bit of a skittles-type of game going. She said it was boss. You nearly fell off a few times though, didn't you Digo?" Fi said laughing.

Digo looked both embarrassed and annoyed.

"Why did you keep going up and down?" Jason asked looking confused.

"Well, it's on a bit of a hill and what with dodging the flying fruit and veg, I was getting good practice manoeuvring and that. I thought it would be good experience for riding down to Rhyl," Digo said looking wounded but trying to defend himself.

What kind of mates have me kids got? thought Shirley, but she didn't say anything and tried not to laugh in front of them, remembering she was trying to keep them on her good side before dropping the bombshell that their mother was dating Fiona's form teacher.

<u>Sunday, 24 February</u>
<u>9am</u>
Up early today for a bit of a tidy up. Oli's coming over for dinner. He's bringing the wine!

<u>3pm</u>
Oli and I had a bit of a heart-to-heart after dinner when the kids had gone out.

"So where do you see this going with David, then?" he asked me.

"I don't know. I think he's great and all that and I want to get more serious but I'm not too sure if he feels the same way."

"Seems to me like he wants to take it slow. I mean,

how long's it been now and still no sign of a shag?" Oli was trying his best to be tactful, but the thought had occurred to me, too.

"I know, but I think this weekend I'm gonna try and go for it. Bloody 'ell it's been that long..."

"Let's hope you don't fart on the job like Angie, eh, babe?" he giggled, which didn't make me feel any better about the prospect! Friggin' 'ell the thought of it. I'd die of shame.

Monday, 25 February
12 noon
Spent all morning thinking about it, and I'm ready to take things up a gear with David. I'm gonna ask him over Thursday for a meal. The kids are going to sleep over with Digo and Shaz, cos there's no school on Friday. That means no school for David, well, only a course and I'm sure he can be a bit late for that. With what I've got planned he'll be in no rush to get off in the morning.

6pm
Sent text to David about Thursday night. He's up for it. I didn't mention I was gonna seduce him though!

Tuesday, 26 February
8am
I woke up in a cold sweat. I had a nightmare that David was over at ours. We had a lovely meal and then it was upstairs for a bit of you know what and I did an Angie on him. I'm shitting meself now in case it happens. I'm gonna do some bum squeezing exercises from today onwards. I'm gonna get one of them tummy

roller thingies as well. They're only four quid off the market. I know I've only got two days but it's better than nothing.

Wait till I tell Oli, I bet he'll wet himself!

During their lunch break Shirley and Oli set off for town. Shirley was determined to buy an exercise roller.

"Are you all right today, babes?" Oli asked looking all concerned.

"Aye, yeah, why?" Shirley replied.

"You've been looking dead serious, like you're concentrating or in pain or something."

Shirley told him about her nightmare and how she'd been practising clenching her bottom all morning in case she did an Angie. Shirley was right, Oli did nearly wet himself, it took him a good five minutes to catch his breath.

"And is this why you're getting this roller thing as well? You silly cow. Sorry to break it to you, but you're not gonna get a supermodel look in two days, babe."

"I know, but it's a start," she said, feeling a bit hurt but determined not to let him put her off. With the roller under her arm Shirley vowed to get started on the exercises asap.

<u>11pm</u>
I'm knackered. I've done two hundred of them rollers and I've been squeezing me bum cheeks twenty times every hour nearly all day. I'll be able to crack nuts between me cheeks by Thursday, but I may not be able to sit down!

<u>Wednesday, 27 February</u>
<u>6pm</u>
I could hardly move this morning, I feel like I've been in a fight, I can't even bend forward. I think I've overdone it a bit with the roller, but as they say, no pain no gain. I'm still squeezing as well!

<u>11pm</u>
I've upped it to four hundred rolls. I'm as stiff as a board. I hope I'll loosen up a bit by tomorrow.

<u>Thursday, 28 February</u>
<u>9am</u>
Oh my God. I can't bend in the middle today. I had to sort of fall out of bed. I don't know how the hell I'm gonna manage tonight...

<u>1pm</u>
I had a hell of a job driving this morning and I can't laugh. It hurts too much.

"You silly cow," said Oli when I picked him up. "That's what you get for trying to be something you're not. You're no keep fit queen are ya, babe? I mean when was the last time you did any exercise? In PE in school I suppose, when you were running round the yard in your navy knickers."

I just looked at him in agony.

"Well it's all gone tits up for you tonight now, hasn't it?" he said, all miffed. I don't know why he's getting so miffed, it's me who's in need not him.

"Well, how about if I drop you off in the old folks' and get meself off home. Have a bit of a soak and take a couple of painkillers, eh?" I said to him.

"Aye, go on then. Good job I love yer. Let's hope it's all worth it, eh? Hey, we haven't heard anything from our ad, have we babe?"

"I wouldn't hold your breath, Oli, love. We probably never will."

"Don't be such a pessimist. You never know."

Well, pardon me, but with that ad I think I do know!

<u>6pm</u>
Called in town on the way home to get some muscle-ache relaxation stuff for the bath, and I took a couple of painkillers. I feel so much better now. I think that it did the trick, although I still can't laugh that easily.

Bought the food as well for tonight. I'm a crap cook but I don't want him to know that so I decided to bugger the expense and buy one of them supermarket premium ready meals and a ready-made pud along with two bottles of wine.

I saw Fat Sandra in town, she's looking well good now, lost a load of weight and she's now thinking of being one of them slimming consultants, so I don't think she'll be wanting to go back to the factory. I told her how well she looked and she was dead chuffed. She was asking for Susan, said she hadn't been near slimming for a while! I wonder why?

David's due over at seven and the kids have already gone, so it's time to set the scene with me candles and music.

Shirley dimmed the lights and put a few scented candles

around the room. She had gone to the expense of buying two bunches of fresh flowers and put them together to make one huge bunch in a vase on the dining table. In the background Barry White's Greatest Love Songs played quietly, just enough for effect and she turned the central heating up to twenty two degrees, warm enough for as few clothes as possible.

The food was all prepared, a ready meal that she could just put in the oven and forget about for half an hour, the supermarket's 'best' range, so she hoped he wouldn't be too put off. She couldn't cook, but at least this way David would think she could, a bit anyway, she'd done the veg herself. The wine was chilling in the fridge and the table was set. She had even bought napkins. The scene was ready for seduction. All she needed now was the man.

11pm (in bed alone!!!)

This was not meant to happen! I am not destined to shag ever again.

It all started out well; even though I was in agony again .The bath and painkillers had obviously worn off. Just before the meal David went into the bathroom and all I heard was an almighty bang, I went in and there he was flat on his back on the floor.

I'd given the laminate floor a bit of a clean, hadn't I, after I felt a bit better after me bath. I didn't want David to think I live in a pigsty. It said on the bottle no need to rinse, so I didn't! I didn't see the bit about not suitable for laminate floors, though! Poor fella couldn't move and I couldn't bend to help him. We were in a right state the pair of us.

In the end I had to call on Ted from next door to

get him up. Ted wasn't that impressed. He said he was in the middle of a film, but I'd seen Pam go out earlier, and when he answered the door he was in his dressing gown, which I thought was a bit suspect! I told him it was an emergency and he had no time to change.

What with all the struggling to get David in the car, Ted's dressing gown flapped open and he stood there in the street in Pam's knickers and her bra as well. Poor bastard, he was horrified. I pretended I hadn't seen and David was screaming out in agony that much I don't think he even noticed. In the end I stuck me hand over his gob to try and shut him up. I didn't want any more of me neighbours more involved than was absolutely necessary.

I've just spent the last three hours in casualty, and left David still there waiting on a trolley to see another doctor. He was dosed up with painkillers so I left him to it.

So I'm sat here in bed thinking of what I should have been up to now, instead of lying here in agony alone! Oli will definitely piss himself this time. Who could blame him? David was a sight, but not as much of a one as old knicker and bra wearing Ted!

SEVEN

<u>Friday, 1 March</u>
<u>11am</u>
Had a lie in today. I hadn't arranged any work for this morning cos I was still meant to be living it up with sex on legs. At least me bum and tummy feel as though they belong to me again this morning.

Thought I'd better phone to see how David was, though he'll probably never want to hear from me again. Apparently he had a very painful night and the nurse said he was lucky he didn't do serious damage to himself. Shittin' hell, I hope he doesn't sue!

What the hell will Oli say when I tell him...

Shirley picked up Oli on the way to the factory girls and gave him the low-down on the previous night's antics.

"Oh my God. I don't friggin' believe it. You don't have

much luck you, do ya? Hey, d'ya want me to ask old Joan for her little pal to keep you going? He might be laid up for months now, babe," Oli said seriously.

"Look, don't say anything, especially to the girls this afternoon. I'd die of shame and I'd never hear the end of it," Shirley pleaded.

"No worries, queen. Mum's the word. What about that dark horse Ted though, eh?"

Shirley managed to get through the day. Not even the factory girls or Sapphire could keep her mind off poor old David, flat on his back down at the hospital, though. She wondered when he would be able to go home. And what he'd said to the school when he didn't go in for the course…

Back home it was obvious to Shirley's kids that something was wrong. She hadn't given them the usual grilling about their stay at Digo's and Shaz's. She normally wanted to know every detail.

"You ok, Mum?" Jason asked.

"Yeah? No questions about us staying over last night?" Fiona probed.

"Oh sorry, loves, I'm not feeling meself today that's all. Think I maybe starting with a bug or something," Shirley lied, anxious not to let even a peep of what had gone on get out in front of her kids – she knew what teenagers were like. She'd never hear the last of it, and they might ask who the fella was and that would be even worse…

With that and the recurrence of her stiffness, Shirley decided the best place for her was bed, so she could sleep and wake up the next day hoping it had all been a terrible nightmare. But she couldn't sleep; it was too early so she decided a bit of watching telly in bed might help and of course a flick through her little pink diary, if she could bear to reread the latest entry.

<u>8pm</u>
Got a phone call from David on me mobie. He's gonna be discharged tomorrow, he said the hospital have said if he takes it easy at home he's ok to go so could I pick him up. Apparently he's gonna be ok after a bit of physio. Oh I'm so relieved.

Get the old roller out and restart the bum clenching – a shag may still be on the cards!

<u>Saturday, 2 March</u>
<u>12 noon</u>
Told the kids I was off to do the food shop. I knew if I said that Fi wouldn't want to come, but really I'm off to pick up David.

Feeling very guilty Shirley arrived on the ward. Sheepishly she asked one of the nurses where Mr Wilmore was and was directed to a sitting room where David was waiting.

"How you doing, you poor thing?" Shirley asked guiltily.

"Much better for seeing you, Shirley," he said looking at her, genuinely pleased to see her.

"Really? I thought I'd blown it after the other night. I mean it's not often you ask your fella round and you end up sending him to hospital is it, eh?" she blushed.

"It was a shame; especially because I have the feeling I was in for a treat," David said, eyes twinkling.

Shirley just looked at him and smiled. He was, he

really was, she thought.

"Maybe next time, eh?"

"Are you gonna be off work for a bit now then?" Shirley asked, helping him up and supporting him as they walked out of the ward.

"Yeah, a week or two, so you know where to come if you want to skive off work for a bit, as you Scousers say," he winked.

Things are really starting to look up, Shirley thought to herself.

<u>Sunday, 2 March</u>
<u>12 noon</u>
I've just seen Ted from next door. I'm sure he saw me but he did a runner into the house before I could thank him for rescuing us the other day. Maybe I should leave it, especially if he's with Pam. I still laugh to meself the state of him in that bra and knickers set. I wonder if he washed them before putting them back in Pam's drawer?

Feeling in a much more upbeat mood Shirley and the kids settled down to some family time together. She really would need them on her side given things seemed to be looking up on the David front.

"How's Barry Sheen doing?" Shirley asked Jason over tea.

"Oh, it's dead tight. Everyone's heard about the veg throwing thing. They've all started calling him skittles now," Jason said sympathetically.

"Poor Digo, that Shaz is a case, isn't she?" Shirley said

smiling.

"She's given up on the fruit and veg now, yer know," Fi said.

"Oh that didn't last long, did it? Why's that then love?"

"She couldn't be arsed, and she said it was too cold on the stall," Fiona went on.

"Why, what did she wear?" Shirley asked.

"Well her mini skirt, cropped top and her boots, of course. She said just cos she worked on a fruit and veg stall it didn't mean she didn't care about fashion."

Jason and Shirley just looked at each other and smiled.

<u>Monday, 3 March</u>
<u>6pm</u>
Back to work today. I did the roller and the bum squeezing over the weekend cos I really feel me luck is in. Oli and I were really busy. I packed load of clients in cos I feel I've been slacking again.

"You're a right slave driver, you. Ya must be feeling better," Oli told me.

"Aye, I am. Things are looking up, matie."

It's been a mad few months, I've really enjoyed it like, but I'm looking forward to a bit of normality. Just work, the kids and getting to know David a bit better. No more excitement for a bit now.

<u>8pm</u>
Oli's just phoned. I could hardly understand a word he said at first cos he was that excited.

"Oh my God. Guess what, babe? We've got our

work cut out now hon'. We've only gone and got an answer to our ad. Dempsey and Makepeace are back in business!"

Oh my God, here we go again!

EIGHT

Shirley's hopes for a little bit of peace and calm were destined to disappointment. Unexpected events were on the cards and her life was about to liven up again before she'd even had a chance to get her breath.

Tuesday, 4 March
10pm
What have I let meself in for? I wanted a bit of peace for a bit and all hell has broken loose. I found out that David had signed himself out the hossie cos one of the old girls on the ward kept trying to get in his bed. I thought he'd been discharged, that's what he told me but he let it slip. I wondered why the nurse had looked at me in a funny way. I thought it was just because she blamed me for David's back injury, obviously not

though.

The old girl wasn't after him or anything just a bit confused bless her and thought David was her old fella. Mind you she was a bit frisky for an old girl especially as she'd had her hip done an' all. So now David needs nursing at home for a week or so cos really he wasn't ready to come home. They wanted him to stay in for another three days for complete bed rest. Now who would be willing to nurse old David, I wonder? Well I'll have to, won't I? Can't be letting any of them proper nurses in their cutesy old uniforms get a look in.

The other exciting thing is Oli's got us another job, which in itself is unbelievable given the ad, but what's worse is the client is old Comb-over's missus! I can't believe it. Who on this earth would want to shag Comb-over? His missus doesn't know who we are, thank God; mind you, come to that, Comb-over has never seen us either cos we're always in the factory when he's out. I wonder if that's what he's been up to on a Friday afternoon. I've warned Oli not to blow our cover with the factory girls. They must never know what we're up to on the Comb-over front. Loose lips sinks ships an all that...

Shaz has had a fall out with her mum and Fi has asked if she can stay over for a few days till things calm down. Apparently Shaz is well pissed off – her mum keeps wearing all her clothes cos she said they're good copping off gear! I bet she's bursting out of them. That's the idea, I suppose. Her mum's already been on the phone telling me it has to be temporary like, cos if the Social find out Shaz's moved out they'll stop her mum's benefits! Maybe she'll get in touch with Sapphire to sort them out for her, eh? Upshot is we've got Shaz staying, but only for a few days.

So, I've got to look after David and start digging the dirt on Comb-over, all in secret, plus look after work, the kids, oh, and me mum phoned to say that next time I'm in town could I pick up a new toilet seat for Auntie Dilys cos hers has a big crack in it. Well it'll go well with her arse then, won't it?

I think having a bit of peace will have to take the knock for a bit.

On top of everything else, on Wednesday, Shirley was given the unenviable job of lottery manager by the factory girls. It was pushed on Shirley as everyone thought she'd be the most reliable.

Wednesday, 5 March
10am
We've started a syndicate in the factory for the Saturday lottery. It's my job to do it every week. I'm shitting meself in case I forget or do it wrong one week and we miss out. I've tried to pass it on to Oli but he said his nerves couldn't stand it and that I have to cos he doesn't trust any of the girls in the factory to do it. He reckons they'd rob it! Mind you, one Christmas Angie did do a charity collection for the local hossie, a raffle. The prize was a video recorder her brother had nicked from the warehouse he worked in. Rumour has it they went halves on the proceeds and their Christmas pressies were all bought and paid for plus all their ale money. We're not sure if it's true but I never buy a raffle ticket from her now.

We all decided to put in a pound a week and we could choose three numbers each. I chose Jason's, Fi's and my birthdays. Oli chose his birthday, Mixie's birthday and Mixie's age when he got him! Bloody 'ell. Mind you, better than them girls. At first they had chosen a range of numbers from how many fellas they'd shagged, how many working days till Easter shut down, and how many biscuits left in the tin.

"No friggin' way, you'll have to choose birthdays or some other memorable date," I said when I called in for the money.

"Why, babe?" Angie said looking all confused.

"Cos the numbers'll keep changing, you daft cow," Oli said to her.

"Oh, right," she said, as if someone had just switched the light on for her, bless her.

Now they've come up with, along with birthdays, dates they got back together with their fella's, and a few have added the date their divorces came through. So at least the numbers will be the same every week.

7pm
Called in Dave's on me way home from work to see how the patient was doing. I think he's on the mend. Well he can certainly move a lot quicker now! Chippy on the way home from David's. I can't be arsed to cook for all of us, plus we've still got Shaz.

Thursday, 6 March
Up to our necks in it today. Flat out in one of the homes. You'll never guess who's arrived there. The two old misses. Shame, God love 'em. They can't manage

at home on their own any more. One of 'em fell. They couldn't bear to be parted from one another, so last minute their home help arranged that they go to West Haven.

Oli stood waiting outside his house for Shirley to arrive; he knew he'd have a fairly easy day as it was only one of the nursing homes today, not both.

"Anymore thoughts on the old detective front?" Oli asked when he got in the car.

"I've had no time, babe. I'm up to me neck in it over at ours, we've still got mad Shaz, remember, and what with David..."

"Oh, aye, yeah, I'd forgotten about her. How's it going?" he asked sympathetically.

"Don't ask."

They pulled up outside West Haven; the smell of home cooking filled the hallway as they arrived. It really was a cosy place, not like an institution at all. Over in the corner they spotted two familiar faces, the two misses, who had arrived the previous day.

"Aw, lovely to see the pair of you here. See, you can still get your hairdone here," Shirley said, trying to jolly them along.

"Aye, no getting rid of us that easily, you two," Oli joined in.

"Don't you be worrying over us, love, give us a week to settle in and I'll be top dog in here, and it's a great place to get a fella," Gladys, who always was a bit of a one, said.

"Just cos she's had a bit of a fall, that won't be stopping her, she's like a kid in a sweet shop with all these old fellas..." said her sister, Violet.

"I hope she won't be too graphic, Shirley love. I mean, I know it's our job to chat to these old girls, but remember I've gorra weak stomach; it was bad enough hearing about her younger day conquests. I'm not sure I can handle hearing about her shagathons with these old boys," Oli commented, looking a bit pale.

"So do I. Well maybe they'll have a few vacancies here by Chrimbo. Gladys might 'ave killed a few off by then!"

<u>10pm</u>
Just got a text from David. He's thinking of going back to work on Monday cos he's bored shitless at home. I think it's a bit soon, but if he wants to go... He wants me to go over Saturday for a meal – well a takeaway, he's not quite up for cooking yet. That will be lovely. Texted him back saying I can't wait. Now what excuse can I find for the kids?

<u>Friday, 7 March</u>
<u>7am</u>
Factory girls only today.   Sapphire called her appointment off this week cos she's taking some time to think of a total new look by next week. Apparently she's been into town and bought a load of hair mags. We heard on the grapevine that she went into a salon in town for a chat and an estimate for a new look. The hairdresser said it would take best part of two hundred and fifty quid to sort that wig out. So it looks like she's decided to make do with us.

Shirley and Oli arrived at the factory to find the girls were all counting the days till the Easter shutdown. Comb-over was nowhere to be seen as usual. Shirley had warned Oli not to even mention him. The girls were like radar operators; they would home in on something then they wouldn't let it go. Best not arouse any suspicions Shirley thought. They rarely chatted about him anyway, so it would look suspicious if they started now.

There was a new girl sitting down to her break. Jeanette. Seemed a bit quiet really. Looked taken aback when Shirley and Oli turned up with their bag of tricks. She ended up having her hairdone too, though. Well, Oli could sell ice to an Eskimo. Jeanette didn't give much away at first though. Shirley thought she must be in shock working with that lot.

"Do you want to come in on the syndicate, Jeanette? We've got a space for one more to round up the numbers." Shirley tried to make her feel welcome and to see if she had any gossip.

"Aye, ok then, to be honest with ya, I'm dead lucky me. I always win at the bingo and I've won a few bob on this lottery. I'm sure I'll bring you good luck. I always carry these with me," she said riffling through her bag and bringing out a four-leaf clover, a rabbit's foot, a miniature horse shoe and her lucky gonk.

All the girls looked at her and then at each other. It was the most she'd spoken since she arrived. They had inadvertently found one of her interests. Maybe she was just a bit shy then…

"Choose your numbers wisely, girl, mind you if you're that lucky any old numbers will do, eh," Susan said, all excited.

"Oh no love, I've got me own special lucky numbers,

special to me. A gypsy give me them once. She said if I use all three together then I'll be dead, dead lucky," Jeanette said writing them down.

"Oh my God, and guess how many numbers we want you to choose, girl? Only friggin' three that's all," Oli said – typical drama queen.

"Never? Oh bloody hell this is the first time I've had chance to use just them three all together."

"Hey Shirl', remember to add Lucky Jeanette's numbers when you do it tonight, won't ya?" Gail shouted.

How could she dare not to? If a gypsy had told lucky Jeanette she was gonna win with them numbers well they would all be quid's in.

"Hey Oli, we've got to make a start on the old Comb-over snooping yer know. His missus will be asking for a bit of info' soon. We haven't even started yet," Shirley said as they left the building.

She did still have a very busy time on her hands but going to the factory had reminded her that they really did need to make a start on the case.

"I know, babe. I was thinking maybe Sunday afternoon we could take a walk past his place. Didn't Comb-over's missus Dot say she went to her mother's on a Sunday afternoon with a Sunday dinner for her? Bless," Oli replied.

"Good idea, we'll be a couple going for a Sunday stroll," Shirley said, glad to have made a start on solving the case.

"Hey kid I forgot to ask you, how's them roller and bum squeezing exercises going? Are you still doing them?"

"Well I did 'em for a few days but I couldn't be arsed. The roller's in the shed now. I'll car boot it one day,"

Shirley replied. "David said he likes me just the way I am anyway."

Shirley arrived home exhausted to some very welcome news.

"I'm going back home tomorrow, Shirley. Me and me mum 'ave made up. She's promised never to rob me clothes again. So I've said she can borrow me shoes only – you know show a bit of goodwill like. Thanks very much for letting us stay," Shaz said gratefully.

Shirley was relieved and pleased that Shaz seemed to have appreciated being allowed to stay.

"Me mum said Fi can stay over tomorrow at ours as a way of saying ta for having me like. She's gonna treat us to a Chinese. She's being dead nice to me now. I think she thinks if she is I'll let her wear me new pink leatherette mini skirt and jacket. There's no way like, but I'll egg her on till we've had our Chinese, eh Fi?" Shaz laughed.

Fiona looked over at Shirley longing for her to agree. Shirley wasn't really a hundred per cent sure about it, but with Fiona being almost fifteen she thought it probably was about time she loosened the apron strings. Fiona could almost look after herself, plus Shaz's mum seemed to be being a bit more responsible at the moment, even if it was for her own benefit.

"Aye, go on then. But don't go wondering around the estate after its gone dark," Shirley said, still feeling slightly concerned.

"Nah we won't, Shirley, not that there's any action there at the moment, most of the lads are on tag so they 'ave to be home by seven. Most of them just sit in their gardens of an evening, they're not allowed out the gate."

"Bloody hell. I'm not so sure it's a good idea! Don't

suppose I can go back on me word now, can I?" Shirley asked.

They both shouted no and rushed off out of the kitchen excitedly. So, Shirley only had Jason to sort out. Well he could stay home by himself Shirley thought. She could say she was nipping over to Oli's or something. While she was still deep in thought about what she could do about him, Jason walked in on the tail end of the conversation.

"Ah sorry to see that you're going, Shaz. I'll really miss ya, babe," Jason said sarcastically.

"Oh will yah, hon?" Shaz said thinking he meant it.

Poor old Shaz.

"Tell ya what, you and Digo come over tomorrow for the Chinese, me mum can shell out. She owes me big time for robbing me clothes, then you can sleep over in Digo's, he's only in the next street. In the morning we can take the piss out of him on his Harley," Shaz said, eager for another chance to get her claws into Digo.

So that's sorted then, although I'm not sure if I can relax knowing the pair of them are out with Bonnie and Clyde, thought Shirley anxiously.

Saturday, 8 March
9am
I really can't believe Shaz is going. It will be quieter round here that's for sure. It will be nice to get the place back to ourselves, I suppose, plus the smell of them plazzy boots hasn't half been giving me a headache.

Out and about, Shirley bumped into Karen from the

newsagent at the top of the street.

"Hey Shirl, have ya heard the latest gossip? You know that Ted and Pam from near you, and that Frank and Fay, well the paper boys have said that they are into wife-swapping!" she said all excited.

"Go 'way, never?" Shirley replied really shocked.

"I'm telling ya, the lads have seen 'em, all sorts of strange goings on from those lot, all hours of the night. Other neighbours have seen it all too."

"Well, I've seen nowt," Shirley said honestly.

"Friggin' 'opeless you are, Shirley. Open your eyes and ears, love, and let us know when you hear anything. I've asked the rest of the street to keep an eye out too."

What kind of detective must I be if all this carry on's been going on in front of my eyes and I've seen nothing, Shirley thought to herself.

There was just enough time for a little pink diary entry before her evening with David.

<u>6pm</u>
Made sure I'd done the lottery on the way home. I checked 'em over God knows how many times to make sure I'd got it right. Let's hope Lucky Jeanette brings us some luck any way, eh? Mind you I think I might need a bit of luck tonight. I'm meeting lover boy at eight. This maybe the night. No aching body, no cleaning up gone wrong, no farting on the job, no kids, no work or anything to stand in the way. Yes! Shag city here I come!

<u>7pm</u>
An emergency call-out to the chemist before I go, to

buy a pack of twenty. No, not twenty condoms as I would wish for – oh no, this is me we're on about remember, a pack of twenty friggin' Tampax. Arrrrrrgh!!!

<u>11pm</u>
Just got in. I had a lovely evening with David. I didn't stay too late cos he's still not a hundred per cent yet. He still looked in pain to me, so he wouldn't have been up for any action anyway. Shame!

I wonder how Fi and Jason are getting on in Shaz's house. I had a text earlier from Fi to say that she was ok and for me not to worry, Jason and Digo were staying over as well.

<u>11.30</u>
Just got another text from Fi. Apparently Shaz's mum has taken a shine to our Jason and that's why she said he and Digo could stay. She said I'm not to worry as Jason has barricaded himself and Digo in one of the bedrooms cos Digo is shittin' himself as well cos Shaz is still after him.

Don't worry??!! I'm even more friggin' worried now.

On a brighter note I wonder if Lucky Jeanette bought us any luck tonight. I haven't had chance to check. I'll do it on the way to pick the kids up tomorrow. If there's anything left of them that is.

<u>Sunday, 9 March</u>
<u>9am</u>
Up and out early today. I wanna make sure me kids are still in one piece. That Mo, Shaz's mum, has got a right reputation with the fellas. I don't want our Jason to be the next notch on her bedpost.

On the way to pick up the kids Shirley popped into the newsagent's and was greeted by Karen.

"'Ave you seen anything yet, yer know, with those pervie old crows living by you?" she inquired nosily.

"Nah, love, I haven't, what exactly have you heard?" Shirley asked her.

"Well, there's all sorts going on there Shirley, love. At it night and day, the story goes. Wife swapping, kinky goings-on, the lot. Apparently you can't get a parking space in your street on a Friday with their wild parties. I wouldn't be surprised if they advertise them in the paper. I have been trying to have a look in this week's *Echo* but I haven't found anything yet. You know the type of ads: "Couple, early fifties, looking for other couples for fun nights".

"Are you telling me you can park in your street on a Friday?"

"Well, come to think of it I did have to go to the next street the other week after I'd nipped out to the chippy for our tea. Later on it was an' all. It was ok on the way back from work," Shirley said thoughtfully.

"There ya go. I told ya. Oh we'll have all sorts of perv's around here now, mark my words. They'll be trying to close this place down and open a sex shop here next."

"Get a grip, Karen, love, they'll always need a newsagent here. How else will anyone see their ads? Now check me lottery ticket will ya and see if I'm a millionaire…"

"Aww, Shirley, love, you've gone and won, three numbers, that's a tenner. Well done," Karen said all excited.

Well hardly a fortune, especially in a syndicate, but

the strange thing is the three numbers were the ones lucky Jeanette had chosen.

Shirley received a text from Oli on her way to the car. She had forgotten that they were due to take a walk that afternoon past old Comb-over's place. Shirley texted him back to say it would have to be after three o'clock as she had to save Jason from Mo, Shaz's mum.

Shirley arrived at Shaz's house to find Jason and Digo sat on the wall by the gate looking fed up. There were dozens of children playing out, screaming, laughing, and some running into the road. It was a place where everyone knew everyone else's business. It was just like Sapphire's estate but on a much larger scale.

"Bloody 'ell Mum, where've you been?" Jason said miffed.

"Everything all right?"

"It is now Shirley, just a bit shaken up I think," Digo said making eyes at Jason.

"What's gone on, love?" Shirley asked concerned. She had never seen Jason looking so abashed.

"Nothing, I'm ok, I don't want to talk about it."

Mo and Shaz stood at the front door. Fiona came towards the car rolling a small pink suitcase on wheels. A Christmas gift from Oli that Fiona was determined to use for all occasions.

"Quick Mum, let's go. Mo wants you to go in for a coffee, she wants to know if you want her to give our Jason some lessons in love," Fi whispered stuffing the suitcase in the already packed boot.

"What? I'll kill her!" Shirley said starting to get out of the car, hoping to head for the door.

"No Mum, let's go, I'll tell you all about it in the car," Fi said grabbing her mother by the elbow.

"Oh, you off, no time for a coffee then, Shirley love? Never mind, give us a ring if you want," Mo shouted from the front door.

Fi shook her head and smiled at Mo then pulled Shirley into the car. Jason and Digo were sat in the back, seatbelts on, ready to go.

"Well?" Shirley asked turning around to look at the sheepish Digo and pale Jason.

"That woman is a friggin' loon. Lessons in love, my arse. I don't need any lessons, ta very much, just a fit girl me own age," Jason said.

"Did she try it on with you, Jason?" Shirley asked looking Jason straight in the eye.

Silence.

"We'll have a chat later, Mum," Fi whispered, gently tapping on the steering wheel indicating that she wanted to go.

Shirley looked in the rear view mirror. Jason and Digo both sat in complete silence staring intently out of the windows.

"What the hell happened? I'll have to find out," Shirley muttered at Fiona, who looked at her and raised her eyebrows.

All that would have to wait as Shirley had to meet up with Oli, there was work to do.

After dropping the kids off and not seeing hide nor hair of them as they both immediately disappeared up to their rooms, Shirley managed to escape unnoticed to meet up with Oli. They went for a walk around old Comb-over and Dot's neck of the woods. No sign of anything suspicious, only poor old Dot doing a bit of weeding in the front garden.

"Hiya love, thought you'd gone round your mum's today. Where is he, then?" Oli asked her as they went passed.

"No, she's in hospital this week having her eye done, love, as for him, gone since this morning. Said he had some work to do, God alone knows what cos he does sod all around here," Dot said looking fed up.

"Well we'll find out for you, girl, don't you worry," Shirley said.

"Fancy a cuppa?" Dot asked.

So in they went for a cuppa and a chat. Oli's eyes were all over the grand home Dot and Comb-over had made for themselves. Fine china tea set and biscuits that came on a little plate with a doily were served.

"What we gonna do, Oli? I'll be honest with yer. I don't know where to start with this one. D'yer think we've taken a bit too much on like?" Shirley said as they walked down the long drive way away from the house.

"Behave, queen, it's early days yet. We're just getting started," Oli said giving her a cuddle.

"So, what do you suggest we do next, then?" Shirley asked thinking he had some brilliant idea to get them started.

"No idea," he said, pulling a confused face and laughing.

Arm in arm they carried on walking down the street, when who should they bump into but Lucky Jeanette.

"Hey kid, I didn't know you lived around here, bloody hell a bit posh, innit?" Oli said to her glad to have a bit of information on the new girl.

"Oh, I don't. I do a bit of cleaning for this couple who live here. A bit of extra dosh, you know," she said.

"Talking of dosh, soz Oli, I forgot to tell you an' all. I

went to check our lottery syndicate and we've only gone and won, with your three numbers an' all Jeanette," Shirley said all excited.

"Go 'way. How much?" Jeanette asked excitedly.

"Well only a tenner, all with your numbers though love," Shirley said. "I was wondering if we should put this lot on for Wednesday this week as it's special. It's a fifteen million special draw and it's our first winner. What do you two think?" Shirley went on.

"Hell, yeah, go for it Shirl'. I'll text Angie in the factory for her to get the girls' go ahead tomorrow. You put it on Shirl'. I've got a good feeling about this one," Oli said.

"Anyway we'll let you get on with your cleaning job, Jeanette, love," Shirley said.

"Aye I'd best be off, see you both," she said looking at her watch.

Oli and Shirley watched her sail off down the road.

"Aww, poor cow, having to do a cleaning job on a Sunday an' all," Shirley said feeling sorry for Jeanette, maybe she wasn't that lucky after all.

"Well, she didn't look much like she was cleaning to me Shirl'," Oli said and raised his eyebrows. "She was all dolled up, looked like she was off somewhere, and she had no dusters with her, did she?"

"Well, maybe she uses the boss's stuff. She can hardly carry a Hoover around with her, can she?" Shirley said in Jeanette's defence.

"Suppose," Oli answered flatly.

"You're getting carried away with this PI thing," Shirley informed him. "You'll be saying really she's an escort next."

"What, a Ford Escort? She's got a face like a bashed up one," Oli laughed.

They went for a nice long walk. It was great to catch up and have a proper chat without being at work. Shirley told him all about Karen and the goings on in her street. Well, the alleged goings on.

"I can't see that straight-faced Fay getting up to that kind of thing, can you? The state of her in your New Year's Eve party when her Frank did the full Monty... He'd be up for it no problem, but I can't see her. Can you? Nothing would surprise me with the other pair, Ted and Pam. Does he still wear her knickers?" Oli asked hardly pausing for breath.

"Probably, I don't hang our undies out on the line now yer know. Oh no, I tumble them all, just in case Ted takes a leap for them off me line. I couldn't bear to think of him in me tangas."

"What d'yer reckon went on with your Jason and that double act Shaz and Mo?" Oli asked.

"God knows, but mark my words I intend to find out, Oli. I will get to the bottom of it."

"Hey, and what's the latest with you and David? Still no signs of a shag? Are you sure he's not gay?" Oli asked teasing.

"What, are you mad? No way, the signs are all there, it's just something keeps getting in the way. Any day now babe, any day now," Shirley said rubbing her hands together.

Back home, Shirley was keen to find out what had caused Jason's strange mood.

Still not himself, Jason went up to have an early night. Fiona informed her mother that he'd been quiet all day.

"What happened then, Fi? Come on tell me or I'll go round there and ask that bloody Mo." Shirley was getting increasingly annoyed.

"Look, I'll tell you, but you have to promise not to say a word – especially to Jason, ok?" Fi said, all serious.

"Aye, ok, come on spill the beans…" Shirley said relieved to finally be getting to the bottom of what had happened and they snuggled up on the sofa in their pyjamas to dissect the events that had Jason so unnerved.

11pm (in bed)

Well I've finally found out what happened. It turns out that that mad Mo took a shine to Jason and gave him a few beers. This was to tempt him out of the room, well, what can I say, he is nearly seventeen, I can't stop him having a drink, can I? Jason had his beer goggles on then, didn't he, and thought that Mo was a more mature version of Sophie, a girl he fancies from school. One thing led to another but fortunately Jason fell at the last hurdle and the outsider Digo came up from the rear to take the cup. Poor old Jason. Thank God though, eh?

I did ask Fi what Shaz thought about it cos at one time she was dead keen on Digo. Well one good thing has come out of it for the lad, Shaz said she wouldn't touch him with a barge pole now after he's been with her mum, she said he didn't know where she's been!

Monday, 10 March
8am

Just sent David a text message wishing him luck today in school. It's his first day back. I hope he gets on ok. God love him.

<u>6pm</u>
Got the go ahead from the factory girls to put the lottery on this Wednesday an' all. They were all made up apparently and think that Lucky Jeanette is the bees friggin' knees now.

Saw Pam from next door on my way home from work, I was in the newsagent's putting the lottery on for Wednesday. Pam was buying the paper.

Karen looked over at me, pulled a face and rolled her eyes.

Arrived in from work to find Fi in a hell of a mood, nothing new there then, eh?

Shirley was sure every teenager had strops, worries about friends, boyfriends, school and life in general. It was normal. Shirley's problem was to ensure the strops her teenagers had concerning school were nothing to do with certain teachers, as this would likely have implications that could seriously jeopardise the success of her burgeoning love life.

"That tosspot Wilmore's back. Only gone and done something to his back. He could hardly move when he was writing on the board today. Stiff as the flamin' whiteboard an' all he was," Fiona said storming into the living room throwing her bag on the sofa.

"Why, what's he done to you?" Shirley asked worried about what the answer might be.

"Oh, just a pile of work, plus he wants us all to go on some boring trip for a whole week of the Easter holidays! Can you believe it? Well, no way am I going to look at some environmental crap in the forest in Wales, no way," she went on sulkily flicking through the TV channels with the remote control.

"Well, I'm going, all the sixth form are, it's well good. You ungrateful cow, how come you've been picked out of your year? It was only for the sixth form and twenty others, how come you're so special?" Jason quizzed her.

How come, indeed, thought Shirley. Maybe David wanted them on the trip so he could have her to himself for the whole week. Ah, it must be love, she concluded.

"And that tosser is the group leader," Fi went on.

"What, Mr Wilmore," Shirley asked, her heart sinking.

"Aye, yeah. He's well sound that one," Jason added.

Maybe not, then, thought Shirley.

11pm

Got a text from David about the Wales trip. He wants them both to go cos he feels that it'll be a good bonding experience for the three of them. Bloody hell – bonding! He's probably right. He's even said that Shaz (and lets face it that girl is a liability) can go in the hope that then Fi will be all for it. It's the end of March, the first week of the Easter holidays. A bit of time to get her enthusiastic, then... What the hell will I do for the week with all me loved ones away. Well, except Mum and Oli. Oh shit, I've just remembered I haven't got the toilet seat for Auntie Dilys yet.

NINE

<u>Tuesday, 11 March</u>
<u>8am</u>
Think I'll get that bloody toilet seat out of the way today, show willing an' all that. I'll go on me way home from work and get one.

Still can't get over David wanting bonding time with the kids!

Shirley called into town on her way home from work that afternoon to get the toilet seat for Auntie Dilys, since she wasn't in any hurry, she thought she may as well drop it off too.

"Aww, Shirley love, ta very much. It's been murder trying to go with no seat, but I've no need for that one now. I asked Vernon from over the road to fetch me one next time he was in town so he got one the other day.

You couldn't do me a favour, though, could you love, take these back for me?" she went on, pointing out the eight toilet seats propped up behind her sofa.

"What the hell...?" Shirley murmured looking confused.

"Well, I asked you, Vernon, Dick, May, and a few other neighbours to get me one an' all... just to make sure, yer know. I wasn't to know they all would, was I? Ah, and when they all came and I found out most of 'em had carried them all the way from town on the bus I didn't like to say I'd already got one. Your mum said you wouldn't mind taking them back, love. It shouldn't take you that long Shirley, I think all in all they're from five different shops. Get money back though, eh? I don't want any gift vouchers."

"Well thanks a friggin' lot," Shirley muttered, under her breath of course.

Back in the car, with a passenger footwell full of bog seats, Shirley decided to called in on David quickly before she went home, to see if she could brighten her day at all (and hopefully, his).

"Hey, what a lovely surprise," he said limping his way back down the hallway.

"Aww ta, David. Just thought I'd call in see how things are with you. Fancy a quick drink before I have to get back? Don't want the kids to get suspicious, do I?"

"Nice one, just the thing before an evening of marking."

"I'll drive, you can have a pint then," Shirley announced.

He grabbed his coat and locked the door and squeezed, well eventually, into the passenger seat of Shirley's car.

The front was full of toilet seats, the back full of Shirley's work essentials.

"You can get help for this kind of thing these days, you know," he said laughing.

Here we go again, thought Shirley as she made her way round to the driver's seat, what must he make of me.

David had to travel all the way to the pub with half the toilet seats on his lap and the rest down by his feet. When it was time to get out he couldn't: his back had stiffened up from the awkward position he'd been forced into. The quick drink was abandoned and Shirley dropped him back home to recuperate in a hot bath instead.

Still blushing from the memory of the toilet seat torture, Shirley remembered to stop at Karen's and put the numbers on the lottery. That was one good thing, at least, though she was sure it was a lost cause. They'd had one win, another was surely out of the question.

<u>Wednesday, 12 March</u>
<u>8am</u>
I'm still thinking about David last night. The state of him... I think I've probably set him back about two weeks. Oh friggin' 'ell. Never mind, I can't do anything about it now. I've got work to do.

West Haven was calling and Shirley and Oli arrived tooled up and ready to face the blue rinse and perm brigade.

"Well, Gladys has managed to send one of the old fellas to the hossie already this week and two others were near misses," Shirley informed Oli after she had received all the gory details from one of the nurses.

"Hey, we'll have to sue you if you don't watch out; we'll have no customers left," Oli said, teasing the old girl as they set about her hair.

"The matron has given us a warning Oli, love, any more rowing with these old dames and we're out," Vi said, deadly serious.

"Never... What you rowing about?" Shirley asked.

"Just trying to liven this place up a bit. It's like the living dead half the time in here," Gladys shouted.

"Hey, Oli, there is a nice new nurse here for you, though," Vi whispered.

"I don't think so, girls," Oli said flatly looking around the room.

The place was full of women; neither Shirley nor Oli had never seen a male nurse there, not even once. Then, as if from nowhere, in he came, wheeling a commode, Ricardo, the new Portuguese male nurse. Shirley looked over at Oli, his face said it all. She thought he was going to drop his curlers.

"See, love, what did I tell you? Now if he's not your type, God knows what is," Gladys said sternly.

It turned out to be a pretty successful day... Oli managed to get hold of Ricardo's phone number and Shirley got rid of all the superfluous toilet seats. It turned out the matron was looking to replace a few so she bought the whole lot from Shirley for cash in hand.

Shirley made a mental note to check the lottery. Surely three hits in a row would be too much to hope for.

11pm

Bloody 'ell, I'm in a hell of a state, Oli's just left. I can't believe it. I had to ring Oli to come over and check, and calm me down. We've only gone and won the friggin' lottery. Five friggin' numbers plus the bonus ball.

I was sitting on me own watching the telly, Fi was out with Shaz and Jason was in Digo's. I thought seeing as I'm in charge of the syndicate I'd better take me responsibilities seriously and watch the draw. I'd even poured meself a glass of wine. One by flamin' one our numbers came up. I thought I was seeing things. Five numbers plus the bonus ball.

I've gone through every possible outcome. We could be made for life. I could buy me own salon, get hairdressers in, me and Oli could just do the odd client if and when we felt like it. The kids would be set up. All our money worries over.

"Oh my God, babe, it could be thousands. Thousands, I tell ya. Usually them that win the five numbers plus the bonus get about half a million. Friggin' 'ell with twenty five of us in the syndicate, well, that's about twenty grand apiece, isn't it? Bloody 'ell, girl, we're rich," Oli said all excited.

"Well, we don't know how much for sure, do we. We'll find out properly tomorrow. Hey, text Angie and tell her the good news," I said to him.

Thursday, 13 March
9am
I hardly slept a wink last night I was that excited. The kids are made up and have put in their orders. I've told them it's no good deciding yet till we know for definite how much we've won. I'm gonna ring the lottery people today just to see what happens next.

I'm guarding that ticket with me life. I've hidden it in me money jar in the kitchen.

<u>2pm</u>
Well, there was no work in Oli today. Like a bloody fairy he was, and he kept telling everyone an' all, which I thought was a bad idea.

We got a text from Angie wanting to know when she was gonna get her dosh. She's only gone and walked out of the factory, told old Comb-over to piss off and to stick his job firmly up his arse, she's won the lottery and for all she cares he can burn in hell.

Well, Oli did try telling her that it'll probably only be about twenty grand. I know it sounds like a load of money but hardly enough to retire on, is it? That lottery line has been dead busy all morning, so I haven't been able to get an answer. I'll have to have a go later on.

Having had no success getting through to the permanently engaged lottery claims line, Shirley made arrangements with Oli and the factory girls to meet up in the pub where they could all hear the good news together.

The pub was busy with the usual after work drinkers, a group of old men sat underneath the window staring silently into their pints and a large group of younger men were gathered by the bar sitting with a familiar face that was visibly worse for wear. Sitting opposite Angie and her fan club were the rest of the factory girls all eagerly waiting for Shirley and Oli to make an appearance.

The duo arrived to a fantastic welcome, cheers, party

poppers, silly string; it was like New Year's Eve all over again.

"Get a bag of pork scratchings for me Oli, babe, will ya?" Angie slurred.

"Glad to see you haven't forgotten yourself, Angie, love, now you're in the money," Oli replied winking at her.

Angie waved her arms about in an erratic fashion and tried to wink back at him but ended up looking cross-eyed.

"Apparently she's come straight from telling Comb-over to piss off. She's been here all day celebrating the win," Shirley told Oli after getting the lowdown from the factory girls. "Twenty grand won't last her long will it if she keeps carrying on like this?"

Everyone sat around all excited; Oli had been instructed to get the drinks in and they all waited to find out the results of their win. There were cackles and screams of excitement as Shirley reached for her mobile phone.

"Now shut up the lot of yer. I wanna make sure I can hear them ok in the lottery place," Shirley stood up and shouted over the noise. Silence fell on the crowd. They all sat looking at Shirley, barely breathing, as she dialled the number, her hand shaking.

"Oh, I see, right. So that's eighteen thousand seven hundred and fifty pounds," Shirley said straight-faced, writing the number down on a beer mat.

There were screams and shouts of hurray from the girls, more party poppers and party blowers. Angie had splashed out on a bottle of Babysham to crack open for them all to share; she'd asked the landlord for anything he had with bubbles. It was just as well he didn't have anything better, as the whole lot just got sprayed everywhere.

"Well, I was close, wasn't I? Friggin' 'ell, I knew it," Oli said clapping his hands looking around at all the girls.

"Thank you," Shirley said, putting her mobile phone down on the table.

The place was in uproar.

"A bit disappointing, though, eh? I was expecting twenty grand," Gail said flatly.

"Hey you, it's only just over a grand under, don't be such a scab," Susan said slightly annoyed with Gail.

"Shhh, quiet girls. Now listen," Shirley shouted over all the jollies.

"Shut your gobs you lot, Shirl' wants to tell us when we're getting our dosh," Angie said making a bit of a recovery.

"Yes, you lot shut up so I can tell yer. Our syndicate has won eighteen thousand seven hundred and fifty quid. Apparently this week there was a very high win rate," Shirley went on reading the exact amount from the now slightly soggy beer mat.

"Hang on a min, did you just say *our syndicate* has won that much money?" Oli asked confused.

"Aye, Oli, our syndicate. So as there are twenty five people in our syndicate, that makes individual winnings of..." Shirley said trying to think.

"About seven hundred and fifty quid apiece," Oli said disappointedly.

"You what?" Susan screamed.

"I've just give me job up thinking I was in the money. What the 'ell am I gonna do now," Angie said, mad as hell.

"A bit of grovelling?" Oli suggested raising an

eyebrow.

"Look girls, we were never guaranteed a big win each. Bloody hell, ok, so we're a bit disappointed but it's better than a smacked arse, isn't it?" Shirley ventured gingerly.

"We could still have fun with that kind of money couldn't we girls?" Lucky Jeanette said enthusiastically.

"Well, I've spent friggin' half of that nearly, in here today," Angie said annoyed.

"What?" Oli asked looking horrified.

"Well, the drinks for all these soap dodgers have been on me all today," Angie complained, close to tears by this stage.

"You poor cow," Oli announced, "spent the day buying drinks for all these doleys in the pub. With very little thanks, I bet."

"And now I've got no job to go to tomorrow. What am I gonna do?" she sniffed.

"Can't you say sorry?" Shirley asked her.

"Well, I think that might've worked, Shirley, but to rub salt in the wound she sat on the bonnet of his car and made a big dent in it an' all. He said he was gonna send you the bill for that, by the way, Ange' love," Ali went on.

Angie just burst into tears. The drink was starting to wear off now and she was starting to realise the error of her ways.

"Looks like she won't have much of her dosh left at all," Oli said.

Crushed by disappointment the factory syndicate left the pub, Oli and Susan propping up the distraught Angie. Shirley decided it would be best if she and Oli gave her a lift home, the others made their own way on the bus or by foot.

Shirley waited in the car as Oli dragged Angie up her front steps, opened her front door, pushed her in and shut it quickly behind her.

Back home Shirley had to face telling the kids they were not really in the money after all.

Jason and Fiona were gutted when Shirley told them about the lottery win that almost wasn't, but they did cheer up slightly when she told them she'd give them a hundred and fifty pounds each from the win, to do whatever they wanted with. Well within reason...

They'd brought letters home from school informing everyone that there would be a meeting the following evening at six giving details on the school trip to Wales.

<u>Friday, 14 March.</u>
<u>8am</u>
We've got Sapphire today, and later the factory girls – same old, same old. I wonder how poor Angie's head is today. Poor cow. I can't believe the win. Just our bloody luck. At least I didn't start spending it though, like poor Angie.

The kids were gutted I could tell. I think they were only trying to make me feel better by not making too much fuss over it. I feel a bit responsible, I don't know why. I suppose because I was in charge of the whole thing. Oli did a good job of winding everyone up, making us all think we'd won more, bloody drama queen. Typical of him. He was really gutted. I wonder what he was gonna spend it all on.

Listen to me, talking as if we had it. We never did have it, did we. It's about seven hundred and fifty quid, that's it. So if I give the kids hundred and fifty each I'll hopefully have about five hundred left. Not a bad little amount really. Now what shall I do with it?

Sapphire looked rather sheepish when Oli and Shirley arrived in her flat.

"Oh, wanted us back this week then, eh?" Oli said miffed.

Shirley just looked at him and raised her eyebrows.

"What d'ya mean? I had to cancel ya last week. It was genuine. No need to be funny with me," Sapphire replied in a huff.

"Anyway, let's be having yer," Shirley said trying to change the subject. She didn't want to have an atmosphere, she really couldn't be bothered with it after yesterday's dramas.

"Me hair's in a terrible condition, Shirley, as yer know, so I've been thinking of having a total restyle. Change of colour an' all," Sapphire said, getting out her hair magazines.

"Let's see what you had in mind, babe?" Shirley asked looking over at the glossies.

"She'll need more than a couple of hairdressers to get that look. More like a team of plastic surgeons," Oli whispered, when Shirley went over to him with the styles Sapphire had marked out by turning the corner of the pages over.

"What d'ya say, Oli?" Sapphire sat up suspiciously.

"Me? Nothing, babe."

"Well, we can work wonders, love. Let's have a go. I think you're right to tone down the hair, go for a softer, darker shade," Shirley reassured her, getting to work.

"The fellas are gonna be like flies round shit when they see the new me," Sapphire said proudly.

"Well, there's nothing like blowing your own trumpet, eh kid?" Oli trilled as they finished up. "Bloody marvellous."

Sapphire was transformed. Gone was the dry, brittle, bleached hair and in its place a rich, reddish brown, glossy layered bob.

"You look like one of them women off the shampoo ads. It's done wonders cutting all that dead hair off, babe. Bloody lovely, kid." Oli went on.

"You've done a fantastic job the pair of you, ta very much. I have to say I was wondering about your skills. I'd even thought about giving you the elbow, but then I had second thoughts, thought I'd give you another go, like. By the way, you haven't got any more work lined up for me, have ya? You know the work on the side?" she went on shamelessly.

Shirley thought Oli was going to blow his top, so she made a bit of an excuse that they were a bit quiet on that front at the moment and made a quick exit, pushing Oli out of Sapphire's front door before he could throw a wobbly.

"Well, the neck of some people, eh? You do know she's only using us. Keeping us on to do her hair in case we can get some more work for her. The cheeky cow. I was gonna tell her to stuff her hairbrush up her arse, but I thought better of it. You never know when we'll need her again, eh?" Oli said seriously.

Two peas in a pod, Shirley thought and smiled.

The factory girls as usual were on top form despite last night's disappointment. Shirley had been thinking a lot about how they'd coped with the news of the lottery win.

"Any signs of Angie getting her job back?" Oli asked setting out his brushes neatly in a row.

"Not likely. Comb-over nearly burst a blood vessel this morning when we asked him. Told him the score like. Tight old bastard," Susan said, shaking her head in disgust.

"Aww, shame. Where is he today?" Shirley asked hoping she might get a lead on any extra-marital antics.

"Same as usual, Shirl', off to do some business," Gail said flatly.

"Aye, aye, what kind of business?" Oli said sarcastically.

Shirley looked daggers at him.

"What d'yer mean? No danger of him getting his leg over. If he was the last fella on earth I wouldn't shag him, not even if me life depended on it," Susan went on, disgusted at the thought.

"He's not that bad," Lucky Jeanette said grimly. All the girls just looked at her horrified. "Well not *that* bad," Jeanette went on.

"They've got a special going on down the opticians at the moment, love; I'll take you if you like," Ali said laughing.

"Anyway, you lot, let's tell Shirl' and Oli what we've got planned with the win." Susan was eager to spill the beans.

Gail rushed over to her capacious handbag and produced a fistful of holiday brochures.

"Angie's well up for it too. We've texted her today and she's worked out she's got about three hundred and twenty five quid left if she pays Comb-over for his motor, five hundred and fifty if she doesn't. She's not sure what to do yet. She was thinking of paying him back only if he gives her the job back. I can't see her paying him meself," Jacqui announced.

"Come head, you lot, what you on about?" Oli said dying to find out what was going on.

"Well, we thought it would not only cheer Angie up, but we'd all have a right laugh, if we all went away with our lottery win," Susan said excitedly.

"Oh my God," Shirley muttered under her breath. Fortunately, nobody heard her, Oli just looked over at her horrified.

"We found a well good deal last night on the internet. It's on one of them auction sites. Gail found it. There are ten tickets an all. Guess where to?"

"Surprise me," Shirley said trying to be enthusiastic; they were all obviously well made up at the prospect.

"Fala shaggin raki!" Susan screamed.

"When for, babe?" Oli asked looking shaken at the news.

"A week today! Can you believe it? It'll be boss. Gail's put a bid on, the auction ends at six tonight. Let's hope we get it, eh? Lucky Jeanette's been stroking her furry gonk all morning, sending out the positive vibes, eh, Jeanette? It'll only be one hundred and thirty quid each for flight and bed and breakfast. It's the Easter shutdown from next Friday, the flight is at eight at night. We're sorted here, we only hope that the pair of you are," Susan blurted to a dumbstruck Shirley and Oli.

"I couldn't get an all inclusive for the price we wanted to pay, sorry, cos that would have been well good," Gail explained.

"Aye, we'd have had all our drinks and food in an all

inclusive. Never mind, this one you've found should be ok, Gail love," Susan said gratefully.

Shirley just looked at Oli and shrugged. She had no excuse, in fact she would be at a loose end for the week, as that was when most of her loved ones were going to be away Friday to Friday on the school trip. Shirley and Oli both had the week off work anyway. She wouldn't feel too guilty about spending just a hundred and thirty quid on a holiday for herself, either.

"What kind of holiday is it gonna be for that kind of money?" Oli whispered to Shirley, the factory girls oblivious as they chatted amongst themselves and flicked through the brochures to see what Falaraki was like.

"Who's lined up to go, girls?" Shirley asked nervously.

"Well me and Trace, me sister – me mum said she'll have little Wesley so long as Trace takes precautions and doesn't come home up the duff – you and Oli, Angie, Gail, Kelly – cos her fella is working away in Ireland now so he won't even know she's gone, which is handy, eh?" she said hardly pausing for breath. "Jacqui, Ali and Lucky Jeanette, that makes ten. Perfect, eh? What d'ya think? We were hoping you two can come otherwise we'll have to pick two out of the other miseries here. Come on, it's you two we want, say yes, please. We'll have a boss time," Susan went on in an effort to convince them to say yes.

"Hey, it'd be handy having you two there to do our hair an' all. We'll still pay yer, but in drinks, eh?" Ali laughed.

5pm
We finished a bit early cos I've got the school meeting tonight. I'm gonna have to get Fi into it now, plus I 've

got to drop the bombshell that I'll be sunning it up in Falaraki while her, Shaz and Jason will be freezing their wotsits off on an environmental project in Wales. I said I'll pick Mo up an' all on the way. She said she didn't want to go really but I've bribed her with a quick drink for me, her and the kids on the way home.

I still can't get over it, I'm off on me hollies!

Oh, and what about me mum, what the hell will she have to say about it all? I dread to think. Anyway I best be off and pick up that Mo.

Shirley leaned across and popped back the little pink diary in the bedside drawer; she would fill in the next instalment after the meeting.

9pm

I didn't know what to do with meself when we walked into the school hall. It was dead busy, loads of parents and kids there. Everyone was staring at us. Mo looked as if she should have been going to Kings Cross not a school meeting. Some of the dads, well I thought their eyes were gonna pop out. On stalks they were. As for the mums, well I'm sure they gave their fellas some earache later. Mind you, only the 'anything will do' type. Mo is hardly class. I was dying to have a go at her meself after the Jason thing, but I bit me lip for the sake of the trip. Jason sat in the front next to me, bless him, and never said a word to Mo all the way.

"Aww, he's a shy one your lad, isn't he Shirl', remember me offer, Jason love," she said as she got out of the car. I could have killed her, but I need her on my side if I'm going to persuade the kids to go off on this trip.

Anyway we sat down to listen to sexy David give his spiel!

"Well, it all sounds dead boring to me," Mo said at the end.

"Hey, what d'yer mean Mo, the kids will have a great time. It'll be a wonderful experience for them. Something to put on their CV for when they leave school," I said to her all miffed.

"CV my arse. That reminds me, you promised us a V and T didn't yer on the way home?" Mo said to me.

"I'm looking forward to that Mo," I lied, really I was dreading it.

I rallied everyone up and thought I may as well get the drink over and done with.

"Aye, come on then you lot, have you got everything you need now or do we need to ask Mr Wilmore anything?" I said hoping that I could have a last close up look at him before the dreaded drink.

"Nah mum, we're sorted now. I think we'll have a boss time. I'm really looking forward to it," Fi said enthusiastically.

I couldn't get over it. Where the hell had all the enthusiasm come from?

"Flamin' 'ell, what's changed?" I asked her, shocked.

"Well, Shirley, I don't know if you noticed but there are some well fit lads going on this trip. I think Fi has set her sights on one of them," Shaz said looking round the hall and checking out the talent.

"Come on, let's ask that Wilmi summat, Shirl'. I

wouldn't kick him outta bed, would you, girl? Oh, aye, yeah, I'd lift the blanket for him no danger," Mo said walking over to my David.

She'd already tried it on with me son, now the big tart was after me fella. The cow.

"So, we're off for a little drink now if you fancy it, you know we could go and chat about the trip. Aww, this is me pride and joy, Shaz, me daughter, well of course you know that. Mind you, we're always mistaken for sisters, aren't we babe?" Mo said as I walked over at the tail end of her conversation with David. God knows what she said before that.

"I'd love to chat to you lovely ladies, and of course you Jason, but I'm afraid I've got an appointment with the physio, I need to be in tip top condition for next week. Thank you all anyway," he said, dead polite, smiling at me.

"What a shame, did you see the way he kept staring at me? I'm in there I tell ya." Mo said, all excited.

"I hope he'll be able to make it, with his back an' all that. I'm looking forward to it now. Bloody typical, now I wanna go something's bound to go wrong," Fi said all narky.

"He will be able to go. His back is fine now," I said to her.

"How do you know?" Jason asked staring at me.

"Well probably, otherwise he wouldn't have been at the meeting, an' if not they'll get someone else to go instead. You'll not miss out," I said all flustered. I thought I might have given the game away a bit.

So off we went for a drink and we had a laugh with Mo. God she is a case, I'll give her that. Jason got his drink then left us to it. Went to play pool with some of his mates. Well it was a good excuse to avoid Mo.

I'll have to go and tell the kids now about my holiday. God knows what they'll say when I tell them where I'm going. I think I may just get away with it cos they both seem well up for their trip. It's now or never.

Shirley closed her pink diary, made her way downstairs, thinking that a nice hot chocolate might make the news a little sweeter. She filled a jug with milk before putting it in the microwave, three minutes later she carried three frothy hot chocolates through to Fiona and Jason who were both lounging on the sofas.

"Aww, Mum, I feel dead tight now about leaving you next week. You've taken the week off work an' all, haven't you?" Fi said, obviously feeling guilty. The hot chocolate trick was working.

"Oh, sorry Mum, I'd forgotten all about that," Jason said reaching out for the mug Shirley offered him.

It is lovely that they love me so much and worry about me being on me own, Shirley thought.

"Well, I was meaning to have a word with you about that," Shirley said, thinking she might be able to milk the situation.

"Look, I've only just found out today, but you know the girls in the factory, well they've booked ten tickets to go away to Falaraki next week. Dead cheap the trip is and they wanna know if me and Oli want to go with them."

She didn't let on that she had already said yes though.

"Well, I think you should go. It'll be great for you and you'll have a right laugh with them girls and Oli," Fi said enthusiastically.

Great, one down, one to convince, thought Shirley.

"Jason?" she asked hopefully.

"Why not, Mum, it's better than sitting here on your own. Yeah, you go and have a great time. I'll have to have a word with you before you go, mind. Make sure you know all about what precautions you need to take."

So it was all settled, well apart from telling her mum and, of course, David. Shirley hoped that they had won the auction. They must have though, the factory girls had said if she and Oli didn't hear from them they had won. So, it all looked as if it was all going to plan.

Saturday, 15 March
10am

Had the all clear from Oli this morning. Gail won the auction so we're all set for Friday. I can't wait. I'll have to pop into town later to get a few bits for the holiday. I think I'll take me mum in as well. I can tell her then. She's bound to have a bit of shopping to do for Auntie Dilys. If I make an effort with her, maybe take her for a cup of tea and a bit of cake, she'll be made up for me. Who am I kidding?

Walking around town laden with bags of shopping for Auntie Dilys, Shirley's mother was a little put out on receiving the news.

"Well it's all a bit sudden this trip, Shirley. What's brought it all on? I can't understand it." Her mum was obviously a bit miffed that her beloved daughter was going away and hadn't invited her along.

"Well, you know we had that little win on the lottery, well it's just a little treat for me. The kids are away. I'd only be stuck on me own, cos all me mates are going," Shirley said, realising as she said it that she had put her foot right in it.

"On your own, on your own! What about me?"

"Oh, you know what I mean. Don't you want me to have fun?"

"Of course I do, Shirley, love. I know you work very hard, but I thought what with the kids being away it would have been a good opportunity for you me and Auntie Dilys to maybe have a few days away," her mother said warmly. "The over sixties have got a trip going next week. They've got three seat left – cos Albert Rowlands has gone in to have his prostrate done and Brenda Smith has fallen and broken her hip, and Brenda Smith always takes her daughter with her, every year. God, her daughter is marvellous with her."

Well done Brenda Smith's daughter, here's the George Cross, you deserve it, girl, Shirley thought to herself.

"You go, don't worry about us. You enjoy yourself," her mum went on obviously still upset at having her own plans turned upside down.

"You two can still go, you don't need me cramping your style. You'd never cop off with me there. The fellas would know how old you are then," Shirley said trying to make light of the situation.

It was no use; Shirley's mother was not impressed with her daughter's forthcoming trip. But Shirley was determined that nothing would stand in her way, now. She had initially had her reservations about the holiday but having got used to the idea, was now psyched up for the trip of a lifetime – with those girls it was bound to be memorable at the very least! Poor old Falaraki didn't know what it was letting itself in for…

9pm
Just got a text from David, he wants us to meet up tomorrow. He's been told by the physio no strenuous exercise until after the trip, just in case anything goes wrong. Apparently after the setback with the bog seats he's got to be really careful. A nice long stroll is highly recommended though, so we're meeting at twelve, having a bit of lunch and then a nice walk. It's all worked out well cos me mum has asked the kids over to do a few odd jobs for her for most of the day. Cos she said she'd pay them, they're well up for it. Well, she can't complain too much now about her useless daughter, cos she has produced two useful grandkids.

Sunday, 16 March
1pm
I've just dropped the kids off at me mum's, they're going there for dinner today. Apparently, as everyone else is gonna be away, her and Auntie Dilys have decided to go on this over sixties' trip, though she has been losing sleep worrying about how she'll cope with Auntie Dilys in her state.

"So, where is Auntie Dilys today, Mum?" I asked her.

"Oh, she's gone out for the day with Dick from over the road, just to get a few things for the holiday. She wants a new case," me mum went on.

"Oh well, there you go. She's able enough today. She'll be fine," I told her.

"Well, you never know when it will strike," me mum said, looking all serious.

"What will strike? What's up with her?" I asked.

"What's up with her? What's up with her? Shirley, she's a very ill woman, your Auntie Dilys, there's all sorts up with her," me mum said, obviously still prickly over the holiday business.

Well, ill when it suits, more like, I thought but I knew I'd best keep me gob shut.

I'm off to pick up David now; I'll break the news to him today.

Arriving outside David's cosy little terraced house, Shirley felt the butterflies in her stomach turn somersaults, she was so excited about seeing him. Out of the glossy, dark blue front door he came, obviously as eager to see her as she was to see him. Shirley didn't even have time to get out of the car.

They decided on a little drive out into the country and found a lovely little pub about half an hour out. Roaring log fire and beams: really cosy and romantic. Shirley told David about her little trip with the girls and he said he wished he was going with them. He wasn't cross or upset, so Shirley's worries had been unfounded. David really was different to anyone else she had been out with, anyone of them would have caused a flaming row at the thought of her going away without them.

They had a lovely walk along the river's edge and surprise, surprise, no disasters, really, everything went well. Walking arm in arm along the river bank, Shirley stopped and turned to David, gave him a proper good looking at.

"What?" He asked puzzled.

"I just can't believe I'm going out with you," Shirley announced.

"I'm not that bad, surely?"

"You're nothing like I usually go for, you know."

"You're nothing like I usually go for, either," David replied. "Maybe that's why we get on so well."

"So what type do you go for? The intellectual teacher type?" Shirley asked, just a little bit sarcastically.

"Usually, yes," he replied. "Or put another way, you could say the boring type. You're different, Shirley, you're so full of life, full of love. I've never met anyone like you before. I want to get to know you better."

"God... I don't know what to say."

"Well don't, then," David said gently, pulling her closer and kissing her.

Shirley looked up at him, holding his gaze.

"Shirley...anyone can learn how to be something like a teacher, but you can't learn how to be a kind, caring loving woman like you. I've seen you with your family, you're so natural, easy going, that's what attracts me to you... Plus you're not at all bad looking," he teased.

"Aww," Shirley said cupping his face in both her hands and kissing him tenderly.

"Now, come on, I'll race you to the car," he said, grabbing a head start.

As they turned into the lane where the pub was, Shirley noticed Comb-over's Beamer in the car park.

"I could just do with the loo before we head back," she said, thinking it'd be a shame to miss such an ideal opportunity to get some info on Comb-over.

David went to wait in the car. Shirley walked into the pub and saw Comb-over sitting in one of the cosy corners right by the fire. He was on his own, but obviously waiting for someone as he had a pint and a glass of white wine on the table in front of him.

Shirley hung around for as long as she could without drawing attention to herself. Things had gone so well on this date she really didn't want anything to jeopardise the wonderful day and her increasingly close relationship with the lovely David. She decided to video Comb-over with her mobile phone, but the footage only lasted thirty seconds and it could be any fat middle-aged man in a bright green jacket. Shirley phoned Oli and told him the situation. Oli decided to pop down to see if Dot or Comb-over was at home then ring Shirley later.

"Everything all right?" David asked, looking worried as she got into the driver's seat. "You've been gone a long time."

"Oh yeah, just a bit of a queue, you know how it is in the ladies," Shirley lied, checking out the car park.

<u>10pm</u>
David kept looking at me on the way home. I'm sure wondering what was going on. I never said a word; I didn't want to spoil a wonderful and beneficial afternoon.

Dropped him off. I won't get a chance to see him now until after we have both come back from our trips. I'll speak to him, I'm sure, but watch this space the week we're back, nothing is going to stop us then.

Picked the kids up. Me mum was all chuffed cos Dick, who will be taking the third place on the trip, has arranged for the three of them to pick up mobility scooters when they arrive at their hotel. I said nothing but thought what a waste. There's sod all wrong with any of them. I'm sure they'll cause chaos; the place will grind to a halt. Me mum and Auntie Dilys have never ridden a bike, never mind driven a car, they've got no road sense all. I wonder if they will have to take some sort of mobility scooter test before they are let loose. I really hope so.

Oli phoned after. Two reasons: one, he'd dumped Ricardo in preparation for Falaraki, plus secondly, and more importantly, he went over to Dot's. She was really upset having spent most of day in the hossie with her mum who is really poorly. She hadn't been anywhere near the pub and is allergic to wine so never touches the stuff. Comb-over had told her he was off playing golf. Oli showed her the video cos I'd sent it to him. Dot was more than happy with the evidence cos Comb-over was wearing the new coat Dot had bought him the other week purposely to make him stand out. That's dead clever that and a good tip that'll I'll pass on to future clients. Well, at least we're starting to make progress with this one. All we need now is to see the woman.

Monday, 17 March
6pm
Oli was giving Ricardo the cold shoulder today. I don't think he's understood that he's been dumped cos he was following Oli around all day.

"Look Shirl', I'm not a cheater cos I know what's it's like and I wanna have fun on this holiday, guilt free.

You have a word with him, will ya?" Oli pleaded.

"All sorted," I said as I came back from chatting to Ricardo.

"Oh great, girl, what d'ya say to him?" Oli asked.

"I said you were worried about the size of yer manhood but you were nearing the end of counselling so you maybe feeling better in a week or two, best leave you alone till then. I thought I'd better leave it open just in case you wanted to have a go when you're back," I said, hoping that would be ok. It was the best I could think of at the time.

"Oh my God, thanks a bunch, now he'll think I'm a fruit cake," Oli said, all dramatic.

"No, just a fruit," I said laughing, looking at his put-out face.

TEN

Well, not much work in us this week cos it's the count down to our hollies; three days to go!!

The next few days seemed to drag for Shirley; it seemed forever till they were due to fly to Falaraki. She would just have to fill her days with work and gossip. Working with Oli made it worse as all he wanted to talk about was their trip. Shirley knew exactly what clothes, shoes, hats and belts he was taking. How he would fit it all into his bucket shop flight's miserable luggage allowance Shirley didn't have a clue. He was so excited he didn't even give Shirley a chance to list all the clothes and shoes she was taking with her. It was all about him...

Two days to go! I can't flamin' wait. Only three days of work then it's freedom from blue rinses, curlers and talking bullshit – well, ok, we will probably be talking bullshit the whole week but it will be different in the sun, I hope.

I've lined up some work in one of the homes this morning, thought that would keep us going. I can't be arsed doing anything else anyway.

Better go, Oli will be waiting.

"Listen, Shirl, can we stop at the buttie shop on the way to the home today?" Oli asked her as he got in the car.

"Buttie shop?" Shirley inquired, surprised. "What you on about, we're going to the home, you'll get a lovely lunch today, soft lad. You love the grub there."

"I thought I'd get a tuna on brown today for me dinner, I'm slimming," he announced.

"Slimming," Shirley laughed. "Slimming what? There's nothing of yer."

"Well, I thought I'd lay off all the calories these last three days before we go away, like. I was gonna have a detox beforehand, but I can't be arsed so I'll just cut down me calories. I want to look the belle of the beach in me Speedos. Look, I've even bought one of these for me pudding," he announced, proudly holding up a cereal bar.

"Bloody hell, what flavour is that, then?" Shirley asked, horrified.

"Wood shavings and hamster poo," Oli replied grimly.

Once in the welcoming environment of West Haven, Shirley and Oli were overwhelmed by the comforting aroma of home cooked food.

"I bet you're looking forward to that cereal bar now, Oli," Shirley smiled.

"I can always save it for me tea. We'd best stick to having our dinner here, babe; we don't want to upset Matron, do we."

"Oh, Shirley, Oli; lovely to see you both again. Look, I've told the kitchen staff you're here today so your dinner will be ready. I'm off today on a course so it's my husband who'll be around doing some DIY if you need anything," Matron said, greeting them.

"Ooh lovely, Matron. I was telling Shirley how much I look forward to our dinners here. Wouldn't miss them for the world, would we, Shirl'."

Oli kept himself occupied informing everyone that they would soon be off on their holidays for a week. He managed to get quite a few more customers to have their hairdone. The morning rushed by in a haze of curlers, hairdryers and hot air.

"Well, I'm ready for me toad-in-the-hole now after all that lot," Oli said, licking his lips. "I don't think that buttie would see me through. I'd probably be starving later and eat a load of crap on the way home, so it's just as well…"

"Hey, you're starting to sound like Susan now, kid, making up excuses 'n' that." Shirley winked and giggled.

"Behave, you cheeky cow. Come on, let's go, I'm starving."

"I'm glad they let us eat in the staffroom, babe. I don't mean to be horrible, queen, but I think I'd be sick if I had to eat with the oldies in that big dining room. I don't think I could do it, babe. I'm too sensitive," Oli said in a discreet low voice as they both made their way to the kitchen.

Shirley looked at him guiltily, feeling much the same way.

"Hey, look at the matron's hubbie, what the hell's he up to?" Oli asked. He'd finished his dinner and was stood up looking out of the window.

Shirley rushed to look out of the window to see the matron's husband pull up in the car with a very attractive young woman.

He got out of the car and went around to open the door for his passenger, who got out holding a massive bouquet of flowers and a bottle of champagne.

Looking around to make sure no one had seen, he quickly ushered the woman inside the family's home adjacent to West Haven.

"Who the hell is that?"

"I bet it's his fancy piece come over for the day now his missus is away on a course," Oli suggested.

"Never..."

"Hey, where's today's boss?" Oli asked one of the nurses who had walked in for her break. "I know Matron's on a course but we've been told her fella is in charge while she's out."

"Oh, Mr Starer?" The nurse inquired. "DIY'ing someone, I suppose," she replied with disgust.

"What d'ya mean, kid?"

"He's well weird, always just stares at you. His eyes don't move. It's like he's mentally undressing you with them staring eyes. He gives me the creeps. I'm not sure exactly where he is but he's just around somewhere if you need him. He said he was staying put today."

"Now look, Oli, we're not on a job like that today so forget it," Shirley objected.

"But look, it'll be good practice. Ok, so we don't get paid, but like I say, it's all good experience. Come on, let's take a look at least."

Reluctantly Shirley followed Oli along the corridors.

"Any signs of the boss?" Oli inquired of various nurses as they made their way through the building. No one seemed to know where he was.

As they neared the family's home, the very flustered suspect came out wearing just a dressing gown, his mop of black hair wet.

"One of the girls phoned through saying you were looking for me. Sorry, I was just in the shower. Is everything all right?" he blushed.

"Oh, can we come in and have a chat?" Oli asked.

"I'm sorry, it's not really convenient at the moment, the place is in a bit of a mess, and I've been doing a spot of cleaning, so there's stuff everywhere. Give me a minute and I'll come over to the home," he went on, still noticeably flustered.

"Ok, look it doesn't matter right now, it wasn't that important. You get on with your...erm...your shower," Shirley said dragging Oli from the scene.

"Why did you do that? He's up to his neck in it, we could have had him, and did you see the way he was looking at you, just staring," Oli protested.

"Forget it, we haven't been asked to, have we, and you nearly had to think of a good last minute excuse as to why you wanted him so urgently," Shirley complained.

Shirley and Oli avoided each other for the rest of the

afternoon. The situation had caused an unusual tension between the two. At every opportunity Oli rushed over to the window to see if anything interesting was developing. Shirley began to think he was getting a bit obsessional about the whole detective thing – it was a good job they were having a week off in a couple of days.

"For your information, I saw that woman standing in the window in her dressing gown and then she closed the curtains, they were closed for two hours. She's only just opened them five minutes ago," Oli said smugly when they met up together at the end of the day.

Shirley shrugged her shoulders.

"Oh, you're still here, kids," Matron announced brightly popping her head through the door of the lounge.

"Oh, and you are a bit early, aren't you?" Oli asked.

Shirley looked on in horror as Oli took it upon himself to inform Matron of her husband's activities.

"What? I'll kill him!" she screamed and hurtled out. They watched her run across the courtyard to her house. Oli and Shirley followed in hot pursuit.

"Darling," Mr Starer greeted the matron warmly. Standing in his doorway he was immaculately dressed, dry hair and no dressing gown. "You're a bit earlier than we thought but here's your surprise." Arms wide open he welcomed her into the house.

Oli and Shirley nervously stood outside. Suddenly came a loud scream and the pair ran inside to see what had happened. They were shocked to see the matron with tears streaming down her face hugging the attractive young woman.

"It's Melanie, our daughter. She's been travelling for twelve months. Flew in from Auckland this morning to surprise her mum for Mother's Day. I sneaked off to the airport this morning to pick her up and hid her away inside till her mum got home. Had a chance to catch up on a couple of hours kip but she's jet-lagged, poor kid," Matron's husband explained with tears rolling down his face.

"But I thought..." Oli stumbled over his words.

Shirley looked at him horrified. She looked around the beautiful home. The living room was gleaming; obviously Matron's husband had been hard at it sprucing the place up ready for the arrival of their beautiful daughter. The bouquet of fresh flowers Oli had seen Melanie holding was waiting on the table and a bottle of champagne stood invitingly in a glistening silver ice bucket. The table was set for a lavish supper with the best silver and china laid out in anticipation.

"Sorry," Shirley mumbled. "It looks like there's been a bit of a misunderstanding."

"But your staring eyes..." Oli said mesmerised, looking at the matron's husband.

Mr Starer turned his head away muttering to himself.

"He's got a glass eye, Oli; he got shot by an air rifle when he was a kid," Matron announced. "He can't help his staring eye; he's got a bit of a complex about it, actually, so we try not to mention it," she added sympathetically, looking over at her husband.

"Well, we best be off then, eh?" Oli added sheepishly.

"Yeah, sorry everyone. You enjoy your celebrations..." Shirley added hopefully.

"I bloody told you, didn't I," Shirley moaned as they drove back home. "We'll be lucky if we ever get asked back there again."

"Sorry, I think we need a bit more practice."

"We?" Shirley objected.

"Ok, me. I just got carried away with it all. I'm eager to get a result, that's all. This Comb-over thing is on me mind an' all."

"Well, let's forget it for now, eh. We've got our holiday to look forward to the day after tomorrow. Let's just put it down to experience. We can concentrate on Comb-over when we come home," Shirley said warmly, squeezing Oli's hand, she didn't want a row, especially with a fun week in the sun on the cards.

"Ta, Shirl'. You're a star."

Thursday, 20 March

10pm

One day to go. We're off tomorrow. Just finished all me packing. Managed to get it all into two cases. Well, I've got one case of clothes and one case of shoes. Me mum and Auntie Dilys got off this morning and I've already had a phone call saying they're having a whale of a time. The scooters are great, me mum even said she's thinking of going for driving lessons when she gets back cos it would be so handy for her not having to rely on buses.

All the kids' stuff is packed, sleeping bags, the lot. I do feel a bit guilty, me in a fab hotel and them in a hostel. Spoke to David earlier, he wished me a good time and said he was looking forward to getting to know the kids a bit better this week.

I popped round to West Haven this afternoon on me own. I took Matron and her fella Mr Starey eyes a big box of chocs to say sorry, like, for the misunderstanding. We have to go there every week, it's good regular money for us so I wanted to smooth things over with them, make sure they would still have us there.

They were nice as pie. I think they were so chuffed to have their Melanie back for a bit that they were willing to let it go. They were made up with the chocs. I couldn't help looking at his staring eyes, though. I don't think I made it too obvious. They even offered me a glass of champagne, looks like they've been on it since yesterday. I said no cos I was driving, like, but it shows we've been forgiven.

I should charge Oli for the chocs, dock it out of his wages. I'd never do that, though. I love him too much and he was genuinely sorry. If we're going to make a go of this new sideline we really are going to have to get our act together.

Anyway all's well that ends well and we've got our hols to look forward to tomorrow. I'm sure I won't sleep tonight, I'm that excited.

Friday, 21 March
7am
The kids have to be in school by eight this morning, so Oli and I are gonna get to it straight away, we only had a half day down today anyway. I feel very tearful at the thought of saying goodbye to them. I 'm really gonna miss them. I've never been away without them before. It does make me feel a bit better knowing they're with David, though.

We've got Sapphire first thing then on to the factory girls for eleven latest. They are due to shut down at one for the Easter holiday and old Comb-over's due to leave just before eleven so it should all work out well.

Oli spoke to Dot yesterday and Comb-over has decided to go off on a golfing holiday from today for a week, apparently he's going to Spain, leaving poor old Dot to look after her mother. Oli told her we'll definitely get onto him next week when we're back.

Shirley and Oli made their way past the supermarket shopping trolley left in the third floor hallway of Sapphire's block of flats. Shirley and Oli were used to the mess by now. Shirley didn't really mind, she was familiar with it after years of picking Fiona up from Shaz's house. Oli, on the other hand, did not have to endure such living accommodation, but even he was able to turn a blind eye when work called.

"So, off sunning yourselves, are you?" Sapphire asked them.

"Aye, yeah, that's why we're so early, queen, sorry," Oli apologised.

"You haven't got space for a little one, have ya?" Sapphire asked laughing.

"A little one? Aye, where?" Oli asked looking around the room.

"Cheeky bastard... Hey, enjoy yourselves and don't do anything I wouldn't do, will ya?"

"So, we've got a free rein then, kid," Oli winked at Shirley.

After leaving Sapphire, her new bob gleaming, it was onto the factory .They did a sweep of all the girls ready for the holidays. They didn't want to be stuck doing hair on their first night that was for sure.

"So, what's the name of our hotel?" Oli asked Gail as he was doing her hair.

"One of them foreign names, not sure how you say it, Allocatedon arri val I think," she said, deadly serious.

"Is that like something on sea in their language?" Ali asked.

"Allocated on arrival, you daft cow, that means we find out the name when we get there," Oli said, shaking his head.

"God, I hope it's ok, I mean, you hear all about these things on the telly," Shirley said nervously.

"Well, what d'yer expect for what we paid?" Oli asked.

"It'll be lovely, mark my words, we'll be drinking cocktails in the warm sun twelve hours from now," Gail said with confidence.

There were oohs and aahs of excitement from all the girls.

"What's happening with Angie? Where we meeting her, then?" Shirley asked.

"Well, we all thought we'd all meet up in the pub over the road at four, we need to be in the airport at six so we'll have a few bevvies before we go," Susan informed them.

"Oh God, that doesn't sound too hopeful, 'specially since you lot said Angie's been in the pub since dinner time. She'll be more than in the holiday spirit by then, I'm sure."

There was just enough time after finishing with the factory girls for Shirley to go home, grab a quick shower, change and finish packing before making her way to meet up with everyone at the pub. Keeping to the planned arrangements they all met up at four. Angie was well away, sat by the bar in a bright pink bikini top and matching sarong. On her feet she had matching pink flowery flip-flops and the same flower in her hair. She had so many beads and bangles on that every time she moved it sounded like a one-man band.

"Friggin' 'ell, look at the state of you," Oli said laughing.

"I'm not pissed, I'm fine," she slurred, raising her glass.

"Not the ale state, the friggin' dress state. Look, love, no way can you go on the plane dressed like that. I'd die of shame. You've got to cover up or they won't let you on," Oli said looking through her tiny holdall.

"Look at me feet, though. Me sister gave me a pedicure ready for me hollies," She said happily pointing out her feet.

"Never mind your sister; you need a farrier to sort out them trotters," Oli muttered as Angie flashed her feet in his face.

"You haven't bought a lot with you, have you Angie love?" Shirley pointed out as she watched Oli go through the tiny holdall.

"It's too friggin' hot there. You only need a bikini, sarong and something for the night," Angie said defensively.

"Here, put these on," Oli said. He'd managed to find a tiny skirt and top for her, they looked the most promising from the selection of scanties in the bag.

"Hey, not them, that's me best clubbing 'n' pulling gear," Angie protested snatching the garments.

"Well, they'll have to do, cos I can't find anything else with more material," Oli complained. "Now put them on or they'll not let you on the friggin' plane."

"Never fear Susan's here..." Susan announced bursting in on the conversation and handing over a voluminous bit of cotton jersey.

"Susan, babe, you've always been famed for your T-shirts. God love yer, you never let us down," Shirley said relieved that Angie would be covered up a little more.

Susan had been into town to get holiday T-shirts for the whole gang. White, to show off their tan, with bright pink glittery writing on the front proclaiming 'Falashaggy Babes On Tour' and their names on the back. They each had one, even Oli, and Susan insisted they wear them for the flight.

"Now these are our official T-shirts to be worn going and coming home, so don't lose them," she said proudly.

Oli got out his camera; he said he wanted to record all the events of the holiday as they happened. He had even treated himself to a video camera. The girls had to walk around the pub strutting their stuff for the camera, showing off their new T-shirts. The regulars, a group of old men, just looked at them shaking their heads. The regular after-work drinkers started to call in not long after and cheered and whistled at the gang, much to their delight. It only encouraged them and they put on a display for the gathering crowd.

They had booked a Classy Cabs minibus to take them to the airport. They had just two hours to sober Angie up enough to fly. Oli checked through her bags again, but there was no sign of a passport.

"I'll phone her sister," Susan said. "She'll have to go round her flat and look for the passport."

Fifteen long minutes later Angie's sister phoned back to say she had eventually found the passport on the table with all Angie's holiday money! She promised to pop round with it just before the taxi was due.

They had to ban Angie from any more alcohol in the airport; they only got away with it by telling her that it would be better to save herself for all the great cocktails in Falaraki.

"Hey, Oli babe, I meant to ask you, where's your cat while we're away?" Gail asked. "Cos you usually have Shirl, look after him, don't ya?"

"Don't mention it, babe, or you'll start me off again. In tears I was this morning saying tara."

"Aww, fending for himself is he, love?" Gail asked sympathetically.

"Fending for himself!" Shirley exclaimed. "Oli's only booked him in for the week in a five star cattery in Cheshire. He even had a taxi ride there this morning. Mixie'll be having better accommodation than us lot don't you worry."

The journey turned out to be a bit of a nightmare for Shirley. Four hours wedged in-between Susan and Ali was not her idea of getting into the holiday spirit, so Shirley made Oli swap (he's the thinnest) and she bagged herself a lovely aisle seat, with plenty of space to stretch her legs. How Oli got through the flight Shirley wasn't sure. Angie flaked out as soon as she sat down and started leaning and dribbling all over him. Ali said she felt too claustrophobic to have the table down after her food so as soon as she'd finished eating the table was up and poor Oli had all her rubbish on top of his empties. As well as all that, he had Angie's dinner just in case she woke up and needed something to soak up all the alcohol.

"Hey, just as well you're skinny Oli love," Ali said

laughing.

"Mmmm, I suppose," he said pulling a face at Shirley, who smiled and waved back at him.

Shirley had managed to get a seat next to Kelly and Lucky Jeanette, who was sat in the middle. Shirley had decided that Kelly should have the window seat since she had never flown before.

"So, you haven't told your fella about this holiday then Kelly, love?" Shirley said, once they had taken off.

"Nah, I do feel a bit guilty like, what with neither of us flying before, but Gail said I'd be best not telling him, what with him working away he'll be none the wiser, will he?" she said. Not the brightest spark Kelly, more looks than brains but harmless enough, thought Shirley.

"So, you didn't have to clear this trip with anyone then, Jeanette?" Shirley quizzed her. A very dark horse by all accounts, Jeanette, she hadn't given that much away, yet anyway.

"Well, seeing as we're away from home and in the holiday spirit, I'll let you in on a secret. Don't tell the rest of them, though."

She'd had a few in the pub earlier and it must have loosened her up a bit. Shirley and Kelly huddled closer.

"Me fella won't be able to do sod all about me being here. He's away working for the queen," Jeanette giggled.

"Aww, your fella's working away an' all Jeanette. That makes two of us," Kelly sympathised.

"Well, Kelly love, I think Jeanette's fella is doing a different kind of work," Shirley went on eager to get the ins and outs of this particularly juicy bit of goss'.

"Aye, sewing mail bags," Jeanette laughed.

Kelly just looked confused.

"He's banged up. In the nick," Shirley spelled it out to her.

"Aww...what for Jeanette?" Kelly asked.

"GBH, he's been in for about three years now, he'll be out in a few months. God help me then. Fun time over."

"What happened, Jeanette? Sorry, I know, I'm dead nosey, aren't I?" Shirley giggled.

"Well...found out I'd been playing away from home, didn't he. He's got a bit of a temper, my old man. Didn't get him anywhere though, did it. I've had three fun-filled years, thanks very much." And with that she was out like a light.

"I don't think she meant to tell us all that, too much ale I reckon, but I'm glad she did. Don't let on though, babe," Shirley said quietly to Kelly who looked on open-mouthed as if she was in a dream.

Shirley wouldn't tell anyone – except Oli, of course – and with that thought she snuggled up in her seat. Time for a little snooze herself before they landed on fun beach...

The girls got off the plane in a state of high excitement to find that there was no transport to the accommodation included in their holiday price.

"Hey you lot, that bus over there is going to where we wanna go. I just heard that couple over there ask. Let's cadge a ride," Angie suggested, making her way towards the coach.

They looked at each other, Oli shrugged his shoulders, and they all followed like lambs over to the bus.

"Names please?" a tall thin male rep said, holding his clipboard in front of him. Immaculately dressed in the tour operator's official uniform with a badge revealing that his name was Neil, and his tanned face and hands he looked the perfect example of how a rep should.

Angie confidently announced all their names as if the group were really meant to be on that bus. Confidence was something that she wasn't lacking.

"I'm very sorry but I have no record of you on my list," he said looking down his paper frantically.

"Well, there must be some sort of mistake, cos we are all booked in to stay for a week in the Anemi hotel. Look we've given all our paperwork to them on the 'allocation on arrival' desk, so if you don't mind we need to get on. We're wasting valuable drinking time here," Angie went on making a start by stepping onto the coach.

"Well, we are running late, so ok, on you get," the rep said looking anxiously at his watch.

"Nice one, babe," Oli said to Neil the rep as they all piled on and found seats ready for their half hour trip to the hotel.

Shirley sat next to Oli, so she could discreetly give him the low-down on lucky Jeanette. He was suitably appalled.

Exhausted by the unaccustomed heat they arrived at the hotel to toss up who was going to sleep where. They had two apartments next door to each other. Fortunately for Shirley, it ended up with her, Oli, Angie, Susan and Trace and Kelly in one, Gail, Jacqui, Ali and Lucky Jeanette in the other.

"All the babes together in one and all the mingers together in the other, eh?" Susan said laughing.

"Well, I hope you lot behave yourselves, I don't want any trouble," Shirley said teasing them.

"The hotel isn't bad really. I can't get over the price. We've been really lucky. It's got a pool, a lovely bar area and entertainment every night... Live music and karaoke," Oli said to Shirley when they'd had a chance to have a little look around their new surroundings.

Shirley had remembered to pack her little pink diary, she was hoping to record a few fun times during the week. She could then revel in recalling the memories whenever she wanted to, especially on days when things weren't going her way or were just plain boring. She was going to write them down in order to remember every last detail, otherwise, what with the sun and the booze, it might all get a bit hazy.

11pm

Well, we've finally arrived and the place is pretty good really. I feel absolutely knackered now but apparently we've got to all be ready by midnight to meet up in the bar ready to go clubbing. According to the girls we have to: as this is our first night it'd be a waste to go to bed!

To be honest, I'm ready for me bed but what can I do? I'm gonna need a holiday to recover from this one.

The first night got off to a good start – they asked around and found all the best places to drink and the most economical to eat at. The first of the lightweights was Shirley, who made her excuses and headed for bed around four, some of the others, however, found a second wind and were lively until seven o'clock. It was obviously all set to be a very exhausting week.

<u>Saturday, 22 March</u>
<u>2pm</u>
Just come up to the room for a bit of a cool down and a nap. God, it's hot here.

Our first night was well good. We found a great bar that's open all night. I got in at four, left the others to it. They were back at seven. Angie, Kelly, Susan and Trace haven't even bothered coming up to the room. They've just plonked themselves on sunbeds by the pool.

'Well, I know from last time I came, these sneaky bastards run down early and put their towels on to save them. Well I'm making sure,' Angie said to Oli, getting herself settled for the day.

'She's asked if we will take down her factor two when we go,' Oli said to me as he got into bed.

'Bloody hell. Mind you, this will be great won't it having the rooms to ourselves if those four decide to sleep down there for the week,' I said to him.

So, a little cool off for an hour or so then back to shallow fry in the sun.

<u>7pm</u>
I don't think that Ali is gonna cope very well in this heat. She spent most of today flaked out in her room. It's too hot for the poor cow. Lucky Jeanette keeps having to take a walk in the shade an' all. She's been off most of the day, God knows where.

"Hey, d'ya think I'm starting to have a white bit?" Oli said checking his arse in the mirror.

"Well, you've got a red bit, love. What factor did you use?" I asked him.

"Factor eight. Angie tried to get me to use her

factor two but I said I'd leave it till towards the end of the week," Oli said rubbing aftersun on his red bits.

Shirley laughed and carefully hid her diary in the pocket of her case. She didn't want to risk anyone having a look, not even Oli. It was her little bit of private fun. Suddenly the apartment door was flung open and Angie walked in, after nearly ten hours of full and no break sun. She had her sunglasses on her head and an ice cream in her hand.

"Ooh, eh, do I need cooling down. Have I caught anything yet?" she said walking robot-like towards the mirror.

She stood there and screamed, "Oh my God, look at the state of me!"

Her face was bright red and she looked as if she was wearing white glasses.

"Oh, we'll be able to do something with it; we'll put a bit of make-up on it. No one will be able to tell, love," Oli said getting out her make-up.

Kelly was next back, another one who had overdone it. She'd gone topless and burnt her boobs, Susan and Trace were the same. The four of them looked like lobsters fresh out of the pot.

"You'll have to lay off the sun tomorrow, now," Oli warned them.

"What? No way. That's one reason we're here, that, the fellas and the cheap ale. Oh no, we've got to get a tan. We'll just have to suffer. There's no way we could go home without a tan. No one would ask us where we've been," Angie said horrified at the very thought.

"I'm with you, girl, a bit of aftersun and we'll be sound.

Now come on: Danny the waiter said he'd have our drinks lined up for ten tonight. Just enough time for a snooze, shower and a glam up," Susan said eager to get back to full on drinking and flirting.

While their roommates were having a short snooze, Oli and Shirley thought they would take a look in at the others. They didn't want the other girls feeling they'd been left out.

Ali was still flat out on the bed in her bra and knickers with a flannel on her head. Gail and Jacqui sat out on the balcony sharing a bottle of wine.

"Very sophisticated," Oli announced as he sat down.

"Get stuck in, love," Gail said pouring them both a glass.

"Ah, this is a bit more like it, a nice relax," Shirley said enjoying the quiet company.

"You all right, Ali, queen?" Oli shouted through to Ali.

"Aye, I'm ok if I'm lying here. Just taken a couple of painkillers. I'll be all right to go out later, you know. It'll be cooler then. It's just this heat in the day," came the disembodied voice from the other room.

"I think it's her weight, poor cow, not built for this climate…" Gail whispered.

"Not a pretty sight, is it, but she didn't know what else to do with herself," Jacqui added.

"Hey, you've one missing," Shirley realised, changing the subject.

"Aye, yeah, Lucky Jeanette, she's another one. Got ants in her pants that girl. We've seen nothing of her all day," Jacqui said.

"Aww, she doesn't feel left out, does she?" Shirley asked concerned.

"Don't know."

"I think the heat's getting to her an' all. It's not everyone can do with it, yer know," Gail said.

They finished their drinks and Oli and Shirley decided to have a little wander around the complex. They hadn't had much of a chance to see it when they were with the girls, they were too keen to spend time in the bar.

"Oh my God, I thought that fella over there was Combover, then," Shirley announced looking over at a man who was the spit of him, "I must be getting as obsessed as you!"

"Well, he's in Spain; I wonder what he's getting up to over there? We'll have to sort that one out when we get back, you know," Oli replied.

"Another late one tonight, Oli. I'm not sure if I can stand the pace for a whole week. Angie's put us down to sing tonight in the bar before we head off clubbing. She's after Danny the barman."

"Well, I think he's after you. Will you be good while you're away or are you gonna wander?" Oli teased her.

"Behave. I think I'm in love, so there'll be no wandering from me," Shirley answered firmly.

<u>8pm</u>

I wonder what David's up to now. I am missing him but not as much as I'm missing the kids. God, I hope they're ok. What about me mum and co. I wonder if they've been stopped for speeding. I must try and enjoy meself and loosen up. I'm on me hollies and let's face it nobody knows me, do they? I've got to get ready in a minute; them girls are still flat out though. They've asked to be woken up at nine; they said they need an hour to get glammed up. I don't know how they'll be, though, after all that time cooking out in the sun. Blistered to hell, I bet.

We're gonna have something to eat first, to line our stomachs before we go. That was my idea. I think everyone else was happy to have a kebab at the end of the night, but I put me foot down.

Sunday, 23 March
11am

Lucky Jeanette didn't join us last night for the meal, which was a bit odd. I'm dead worried about her but the girls say she's dead perky in the room when she does come back. She's told them that she's quite private and likes to go off sightseeing and that on her own. Strange! Oli thinks there is definitely something going on with her, has done ever since that day we saw her when she said she was cleaning. Maybe she is an escort and has got a job over here. I can't believe it though, would anyone actually pay her?!

The cocktails were flowing last night and we've found another bar now. Two sex on the beach cocktails for the price of one. Angie, Susan and Trace have copped off with some waiters from the place we ate at last night and have arranged to meet up with them later tonight.

The tans are coming along nicely. I'm sticking to me factor fifteen as recommended. Oli's gone for that an' all now after his sunburn but the other four – God help us. Angie has bought some carrot oil from the shop round the corner and the fearsome four will be plastering it on all day.

So another day of shallow frying was on the menu. The factory girls, well all except Jeanette who was doing her own thing and Ali who was still bed bound, continued their routine of poolside sleeping off the night before, sunbathing and then a snooze before a night out on the town. They'd decided the best solution for the night time lack of sleep, and to ensure they returned home with the best tan the finest carrot oil could provide, was to find the sunbeds nearest the pool and lie there semi-conscious all day.

"Look, it says on it. There's no sun protection in it at all, it'll stain your skin, I tell ya," Shirley warned reading the back of the carrot oil label. Angie, Susan, Trace and Kelly, though, were determined to keep using it for the rest of the week.

"Well, all the red bits have gone now," Kelly said inspecting her body in the mirror.

"That's because they've been stained orange!" Shirley told her.

The four planned to wear white later that evening, to show off their tans.

They were meeting at the bar at nine to have something to eat and then off round town again! Lucky Jeanette had decided against it at the last minute because she had a headache.

The evening got off to a flying start with cocktails and karaoke in the hotel bar, before heading across the road for traditional fish and chips. Then it was on to their favourite bar. Buy-one-get-one-free cocktails were in full flow. The factory girls got very friendly with the bar staff and invited them back to the hotel for some late night partying.

The once silent hallway soon turned into a makeshift nightclub as music blasted from the open doors of the girls' two apartments. So many people had been invited back the party spilt out into the hallway.

One by one, other guests started to appear from their accommodation – a few joining in the party, but most to complain. One heavily-built woman dressed in an orange bikini top and tiny sarong made light work of the cheap wine the girls had bought back with them.

"Hey, girl, save some for someone else," Angie said snatching the bottle from her.

The party got louder and louder and soon the manager was called. In broken English he tried to warn the group that they would be asked to leave. But it was only Shirley and Oli who took any notice of him. Suddenly, out of nowhere, Angie appeared arms flying everywhere.

"You've been eyeing up my fella all night, you cow," Angie shouted at the orange bikini-clad woman who looked at her horrified.

The hotel manager tired to calm the situation but was caught up in the crossfire as Angie tried to lash out at the woman, catching him on the side of the head. He fell to the ground from the impact, so Shirley and Oli rushed over to the rescue and dragged him in onto Ali's bed, where he lay recovering for the next two hours. The party carried on for a while, before gradually coming to a halt as the guests one by one collapsed anywhere there was a space.

ELEVEN

<u>Monday, 24 March</u>
<u>3pm</u>
We've all just come from a meeting with the manager after having a first and, cos it was so serious, final warning.

"They can't kick us out; we don't fly home till Friday. Where would we go?" Angie said dead cocky.

"Oh yes they can. They don't care where we go, do they? If we've broken the rules and other guests have complained about us we're out," I told them.

Last night, or should I say this morning, about five o'clock Angie, Susan and Trace decided to bring their waiters back to our apartment for a party. They brought half the restaurant with them.

The people next door complained, well to be honest the whole of the floor complained along with the guests two floors up. There was a hell of a racket.

The manager was called and accidentally got punched by Angie...who was actually trying to punch one of the women guests cos she thought she was after Angie's new found fella.

On top of all that the maids have complained and the manager has given us a bill to cover the cost of new sheets, cos four lots have turned a horrible shade of orange.

We spent two hours begging and pleading with the boss to let us stay. Lucky Jeanette is the only one in the clear cos she was nowhere to be seen, in her room with a headache, the lucky cow.

Oli reckons she's copped off so we're gonna have a little wander round the place later to see if we can spot her. I need to clear me head anyway. I think we'll take a walk down onto the beach; there's a lovely cool breeze down there, normally. Maybe Ali should come down tomorrow. She can't spend every day of the whole week in her room, surely.

Shirley dressed in her red bikini and matching sarong, and put her hair into a high bun held together with a big red floral hair bobble to maximize her back area for full on sun coverage. Oli, stylish as usual, wore the tiniest white shorts, white leather flip flops and carried a towel in his hands.

"Come on then, let's be having yer," he said, ready for his trip to the beach.

Shirley gave a twirl and they both headed off arm in arm to the beach. Once there, they settled themselves down on a sunbed under one of the umbrellas, but only after paying for the privilege.

"Stand over there, babe, and I'll get a photo of you with the sea in the background," Oli instructed getting his camera ready.

"Oh, yeah, lovely," Shirley said posing.

"Friggin' hell," Oli whispered.

"What d'yer say? I can't hear you," Shirley shouted over to him still trying her best to hold the pose.

Oli looked as if he'd seen a ghost.

Suddenly he started snapping away, taking loads of pictures but the camera wasn't pointing in Shirley's direction.

"Hey, soft lad, I'm over here. What you doing?" Shirley said waving and dancing up and down like a fool.

Suddenly he stopped and ran over, arms flapping to Shirley. "Quick, look at that!"

"What? Where?" Shirley asked looking around the beach.

"Over there, Lucky Jeanette has copped off, friggin' look," he said tugging at Shirley's arm.

Frustrated that she couldn't see what he was talking about Oli grabbed Shirley's head and pointed it in the right direction. Shirley couldn't believe her eyes: Lucky Jeanette in her black and white tankini, laughing and splashing in the water with Comb-over!

"Well, what d'ya make of that?"

"I can't believe it. Did you get the photies?" Shirley asked eagerly.

"Yeah, a load of 'em. Oh my God. I can't believe it either," Oli laughed.

"Well, we can't say a word to the girls. It would blow our cover. But what do we do, shop lucky Jeanette or let her get away with it and let poor old Dot down. Where do our loyalties lie, Oli?" Shirley asked confused.

"Let's have a drink and a think on it," he said grabbing Shirley's arm and heading to the beach bar.

Tuesday, 25 March
10am

Another near miss at breakfast this morning. Everyone decided to go to the restaurant for brekkie today. We got there just as it was closing but luckily Danny the barman was on so he said we could have something. Angie decided to pile a load of rolls, butter, ham and cheese in her bag for a bit of lunch for us all later. The deputy manager saw her and made her empty her bag there and then. She'd even shoved in the last three boiled eggs. They'd cracked, so we'll have to put up with the smell from her bag from now until Friday. We were lucky he wasn't going to take it further he said.

They'd all decided to meet up about an hour or so after breakfast in the main reception. They wanted a chance to go back to their rooms and get sorted for the day ahead. Shirley used the time to record her diary entry; Oli used the time to try on various outfits for the evening's clubbing. The factory girls, however, had a little lie down catching any chance they could get to get a snooze in, to make up for the long nights out.

"So, any plans today, Jeanette?" Oli asked while they were waiting for some of the others to arrive.

"Not sure yet, what you lot up to?" she asked.

"Thought we'd hit the water park today. Even Ali is going to venture out. She can keep cool in the pools. D'ya fancy it, Jeanette?" Angie asked hopefully.

"Well, I thought I might hang around the pool today, you know, try and top up me tan before we go home. Make the most of the last few days," Jeanette replied.

"Oh, I thought you didn't know what you were doing," Oli said sarcastically.

All the girls just looked at him wondering what was going on. The stragglers arrived, Gail and Jacqui all kitted out for a day at the water park, with blow-up beach balls and a rubber ring with an almost full sized dolphin head attached.

"I'm surprised they don't do paella here, you know," Ali piped up, changing the subject completely.

"You what?" Susan asked.

"Paella, it's a very famous Spanish dish. D'ya know, I haven't seen it on one menu. Isn't that strange," Ali said looking at the menu that was on the table.

"Well we're not in Spain, are we, queen," Angie said.

"What? Not in Spain. What? You mean Falaraki isn't in Spain?" Ali exclaimed horrified.

"No, Falaraki is on a Greek island, you daft cow. We're nowhere near Spain," Susan shouted at her.

"Bloody hell, I did wonder why it had taken us longer to get here than to Benidorm. I just thought he was taking the scenic route."

"I wondered why you were saying *gracias* to every bugger," Gail said.

"So what is Greek for ta, then?" Ali asked.

"How the flamin' hell should we know. You've no need to know anyway. They all speak English," Angie said, annoyed with poor old Ali.

"D'yer like Paella, Ali love? I can ask if they'll do you some if you want," Kelly said, feeling sorry for Ali.

"They've probably never even hear of Paeflamin'ella

before. It's all Greek salads, feta cheese and that kind of crap here. You can get pork chop and chips anywhere: Spain, here or home. That's why we've been sticking to the English food, isn't it. You know where you are then," Angie said.

"What about that then, eh? Ali not knowing where she is," Oli whispered to Shirley.

"I can't get over it, I've never thought of coming to Greece before. I'll stick to me Benidorm though, it's too flamin' hot here," Ali said, fanning herself, as they left the hotel.

"Oh, here we go, kids, the coach is here, ready for our fun-filled day at the water park," Oli said grabbing his beach bag.

"We'll have to do a bit of shopping tomorrow, Oli, get some pressies for the kids," Shirley said as they made their way to the coach.

"Aye, ok, the week will soon be over. Had any more thoughts about Lucky Jeanette?"

"Well, to be honest with yer, I think I may have a plan that'll suit nearly everybody," Shirley said as they settled into their coach seats.

<u>5pm</u>
Had a great time in the water park. I even think Ali got a bit of a tan today. She sat in a rubber dinghy in the water for most of the day, cos it was so cool. We had a hell of a job to hoist her out of it, she'd been wedged in it that long. She's gorra lovely mark on her arse where it's been. At least she got out of the hotel room in daylight, though. She was getting to be like Dracula. I'm sure she's got some special cream to rub

on her arse, she's bought that many pills and creams with her. She's like a walking chemist, that one.

Angie was like a cannonball rocketing down the slide, she had that much carrot oil on her. She nearly took off.

"Hey, I thought I could see the Liver birds, then," she laughed as she rubbed some more oil on herself ready to go again.

We got back a bit early from the water park cos we thought it would be nice to have a few cocktails by our pool, they've got a Tuesday night special on. Cocktails plus Greek food. I'm quite looking forward to trying something a bit different to eat. I'm starting to get a bit sick of fish and chips or pork chop and chips. It'll make a nice change. Well, I hope so, anyway. I don't want to be up half the night with the wild shites.

I've just enough time for a quick shower before we all get off.

Most of the factory girls hadn't bothered with a shower, they had decided on the coach that it wouldn't be worth it as they wanted to carry on topping up their tans while drinking cocktails by the pool. As the carrot oil was nearly empty and was a bit on the pricey side they felt it would be a waste to shower it all off.

"Look who's over there," Angie screamed holding a large cocktail complete with every fruit under the sun poking out of it.

The group all looked over in the direction Angie indicated and in the distance, on one of the sun loungers, enjoying a cocktail was a man bearing a great similarity to their boss, Comb-over. Lucky Jeanette was on her way from the bar holding another two cocktails walking towards him smiling, oblivious to anything else that was going on, especially the fact that she'd got an audience.

"Who is it?" Ali asked squinting to see, the strong sunlight was making it difficult to see properly.

"Looks like Comb-over to me," Susan said sounding pretty convinced.

"Never, he wouldn't come to a place like this," Gail said, trying to have a look.

"I've seen some of his holiday photies, he goes to five star places, no way would he come here."

"Well it looks like him to me, come on, let's get a closer look," Angie said determined to find out.

Shirley couldn't let that happen, it would wreck all her plans. She had come up with what she thought might be a plan to help her mate Angie get her job back. If she could keep the girls from finding out about Jeannette and Comb-over, she would have a great bargaining tool. If she kept quiet about seeing Comb-over then Jeannette would have to get Angie's job back for her under threat of Dot being told about her wandering husband and his production line lover by detectives Shirley and Oli.

"Jeanette, how are you?" Shirley shouted over, trying to stop her going over to Comb-over.

"Oh...erm...hiya, you lot. You're back early," she said all flustered.

"Hey, look, we're off over that way, we think tight arse Comb-over is here. I'm gonna ask for me job back," Angie said.

"What? Where? No, no never, it can't be. Lucky or very nearly unlucky," Jeanette said.

"Two cocktails Jeanette, flamin' 'ell, have ya copped?" Trace asked.

"Aww, dark horse, eh. Is that where you've been sneaking off to?" Jacqui asked with raised eyebrows.

"Nah...um...no, no, they're both for me."

"Get away... Come on, who is he?" Angie said eager for the gossip, momentarily forgetting about Comb-over.

Thank God, Shirley thought, hopefully she'd lose interest in finding Comb-over. The girls were making so much noise that old Comb-over had looked over and spotted the excited girls. Realising that if they saw him he would be in a lot of trouble he was busy scampering off with a paper shielding his face. Shirley spotted Lucky Jeanette looking over and seeming relieved to see him go.

"Well, yeah, girls, I have copped, but he's had to go now to work. These cocktails are both for me, honest. Buy-one-get-one-free. I think you might've just missed the offer, though. Come on, sit down and grab your own. Tell me all about the water park and I'll tell you about me fella. He's a waiter," she was suddenly eager to be one of the girls after her days on her lonesome.

All the girls gave their orders to Shirley and Oli and went off to settle down by the pool.

"Jeanette, come and give us a hand getting the drinks in, will yer?" Shirley asked.

"Aye, ok," she said, looking at Shirley as if she needed this opportunity to regain her composure and invent a story about her new man.

"Aye, come on girl, give us a hand," Oli chipped in.

"You go on, girls. I'll help Shirley and Oli with the drinks, then I'll fill you all in on the juicy gossip," Jeanette said to them.

"Aye, ok babe, but remember we want to know every last detail," Angie insisted. "Hey, what happened to that fella, oh friggin' 'ell, he's gone now. We'll never find out if it was Comb-over."

"I'm telling ya, no way was that him. He'd no way come here," Gail said, convinced it wasn't Comb-over.

Back at the bar Oli ordered in all the cocktails.

"You saw, didn't you, Shirley?" Lucky Jeanette said, while they were at the bar waiting for their order.

"Aye, I did."

"How come you never said anything? You didn't land me in it, Shirley, why not?"

"Well, if you do something for us, we'll do something for you. We'll cover for the rest of this week for you going off, we won't tell his missus, your fella or the factory girls, but only if you get Angie her job back, with no payment to Comb-over for his car, neither," Shirley said seriously.

"Bloody 'ell, you drive a hard bargain, don't ya?"

"Well?" Shirley asked.

"Ok. I'll make sure, but you have to keep quiet, you know me fella's due out soon. He'd kill him – and me." She looked seriously worried by the prospect. And with that, Jeanette made a start carrying the cocktails to the factory girls who were all eagerly waiting.

"Nice one, babe, but does that mean we can't tell poor old Dot that her fella is cheating?" Oli asked, making their way a little way behind with the remaining cocktails.

"Looks like it, Oli, but at least Angie will get her job back," Shirley said flatly.

The Greek food didn't go down that well, well not as well as the cocktails. Ali seemed to enjoy hers, though. It was like a spicy lamb cooked in tomatoes and herbs. Initially she thought it looked like the dog's dinner but she ate it all.

"It's not like the pork chops down the Horse and

Crown over the road, is it?" Susan said picking at her food.

"Well, it's a bit different, mine's not bad," Shirley said tucking into her chicken kebab, chips and Greek salad. "To be honest, it's not really all that Greek, is it, with the chips and all that."

"Aye, but they're not proper chips, are they?" Karen said.

"Well, the cocktails are great, eh, kids?" Angie said pushing most of her food to the side of the plate, apart from the chips that is.

"Come on you lot, drink up, let's go to the Horse and Crown, we can get a plate of proper home made chips there," Susan said.

Leaving a messy table behind them they all made their way to a more familiar culinary eating and drinking experience.

<u>Wednesday, 26 March</u>
<u>2pm</u>
Ali spent all morning in her room, she can't step foot outta there. It must have been the lamb from last night. She's been taking something for it out of her medicine cabinet so she reckons she'll be fine to go out later.

Lucky Jeanette's sorted it all out with Comb-over. He's gonna ring Angie on Friday and ask her to come back to work after the Easter hollies. Result. Well, except for poor old Dot. I feel dead tight, but me loyalties do lie with Angie. She really needs her job back. I only wish we could nail Comb-over as well.

I can't believe we're going home the day after

tomorrow. We've had a great time. I must do a bit of shopping this afternoon. I think everyone's going. Well all except Lucky Jeanette who is shaggin' Comb-over all afternoon. The thought!!!

The rest of the group decided that as they were so close to going home they really should try once more and go traditional for their last meal and Shirley located a Greek taverna that seemed to fit the bill.

It didn't go quite to plan; they were obviously not destined to savour the intriguing Greek delicacies. Due to their unsuitable dress code the group were asked to leave the premises leaving them with only one other option.

"Well, balls to them, I knew it was a bad idea going traditional. We should have learnt our lesson from Ali's wild shites last night," Angie grumbled, storming away from the restaurant.

"That's why I was gonna stick to a plate of chips today," Ali said miserably trudging behind.

"Right, off we go for our refreshments to the Irish bar over the road. None of this foreign muck for us," Susan announced.

All the other girls made noises of agreement.

"I really fancy fish and chips now. Come on, let's go. That's what you want, innit, the weather from here with all the comforts of good old British cooking," Susan continued, marching across the road to the bar.

There were no problems in the Irish pub, they all sat outside topping up their tan enjoying 'proper food'.

"I've been on antibiotics all day today," Ali said miserably.

"Oh, why love?" Oli asked her.

"Had a bit of jip with me tooth. Found 'em in me medicine cabinet from last time I had summat wrong with me so I thought I'd better bring 'em again just in case. Glad I did now," she said looking at the bottle.

"I don't know you should take them if they're that old, Ali love, they may do you more harm than good," Shirley said taking the bottle from her to look at the label.

"Behave, they're fine; I'll have one Ali an' all cos I've got a bit of a sore throat after all that singing," Susan said reaching for the bottle.

"No chance," Shirley said putting the bottle in her bag. I'll chuck it out later. Those girls are a liability, she thought.

"Hey, we haven't got any holiday insurance, remember. We don't want any of you lot taking ill over here. Best leave off girls. Suffer in silence. Be brave," Oli said dramatically.

Shirley knew they were all taking a risk with the holiday insurance, but if they had taken it out it would have cost more than the holiday itself, plus Gail was meant to sort it out but she'd forgotten.

6pm

Well the nerve of some people. We were asked to leave a Greek taverna this afternoon cos we refused to put our T-shirts on. Well, we didn't have any to put on anyway. How could we? The fella said he knew it was hot but we were unsuitably dressed to eat in his restaurant. We weren't even in, we were outside! I ask ya, how else are you meant to top up your tan so close to going home. We'd walked all round the shops in our bikinis and Oli in his Speedos, no one had complained, although we did get a few looks. I thought they were looking at Ali's ring mark from the dinghy still on her arse.

<u>Thursday, 27 March</u>
<u>10am</u>
Well, our last full day. God knows where the week's gone to. What a great time. Even Ali's started to come out more now in the day. I think she's getting used to the heat now it's time to go home. She said she will come with us again, only next time we have to go for two weeks so she can acclimatise the first week and go for it the second.

There was another near miss this morning at brekkie when Susan nicked some family's toast. She didn't realise you had to make your own. Just walked up to the machine and took the lot. Apparently that's what she's been doing all week. This family were well narked. She just walked past in her bikini looking down her nose at them.

I overheard the woman say that Angie walking around in that get up had put her off her food. I can see her point!

As it's the last day, today we're gonna spend the day by the pool. The single girls want a last go with the waiters, me and Oli want to top up our tans and Ali wants to try and get a bit of one. Tonight is a wild night on the town. We've all decided to put on our holiday T-shirts. It'll save us packing them then cos we're gonna wear them on the flight home.

Lucky Jeanette made an appearance on the last day.

"So, Jeanette, are we gonna get a look in at this hunk you've been shaggin' all week?" Angie asked.

"Sorry, girls, he's flying home, about now," she replied looking at her watch.

"Eh? I thought you said he was a waiter," Susan pointed out looking confused.

"Oh erm, yeah, he is, but he's off on his holiday an' all," she mumbled.

"Aww, we've missed him then, what a shame," Oli said. He was still a bit miffed with Jeanette but he didn't want her to blow the cover story.

"Are you gonna keep in touch or was it just an 'oliday romance?" Kelly inquired smiling.

Jeanette just shrugged her shoulders and looked at Shirley and Oli. "Anyway, I've got the day with you lot today," she said, shaking off any guilt she felt.

"Mmm, good enough for you now, are we?" Oli said sarcastically.

"I'm just popping to the shop to get some more carrot oil. D'yer know what, we've gone through eight bottles of that stuff this week," Angie informed them all. "I didn't want to fork out on another one, but it is for a good cause, me tan."

"I'll come with you, babe. Trace, make sure all our stuff is where we left it. If anyone's moved our towels and taken over kick 'em off," Susan instructed.

After the first couple of nights sleeping outside to save their sunbeds, the girls had taken to getting the best places all sorted: tables, umbrellas, sunbeds, the works – by putting their towels, hats and magazines out ready the night before. All to guard their space, and it was God help anyone who moved in on them.

6pm

As brown as I'm gonna be now, I think. The four lobsters now look like four carrots. They really have taken on the colour of the oil. They're all made up with it, though. They've had to buy four lilos to sleep on cos they can't wreck any more sheets. They've already paid the manager for one lot. The four of them lie on a lilo each, slipping and sliding all around the place all night long. They make a hell of a noise. Oli made them sleep out on the balcony last night. At least the beds are not wrecked, though.

I'm getting ready early tonight. The girls are already starting off downstairs before we go. I think they're going for Sambuccas before they all go onto them fishbowl things.

Shirley was just putting the finishing touches to her make-up and Oli was in the shower, when there was mad knocking on their door.

"I'm coming, keep your hair on," Shirley shouted opening the door.

"Too late for that, Shirley, love," Susan said pulling a face.

Susan, Trace and Kelly stood in the doorway. Kelly was crying her eyes out. By this time Oli was out of the shower wanting to know what on earth was going on.

"She's had a bit of an accident with a flamin' sambucca," Susan announced rubbing Kelly's shoulder.

Kelly stood in all her finery with a very singed fringe.

"She was lucky, though, it nearly had her eyebrows," Trace said, trying to make it sound better than it was.

"Let's have a look at you, babe," Oli said pulling her into the room.

"Can you do anything with it?" Susan asked eagerly.

"Course we can. We'll have to take it a bit shorter and maybe spike it up a bit. It is the latest now in France, due to hit us by the summer anyway," Shirley lied.

"What will I tell Simon? He's home next week. He'll go mad. He loves me hair. Very particular about it. He'll find out I've been away," Kelly sobbed.

"Sod the friggin' hair how are yer gonna explain that tan, you daft cow?" Oli put in.

"Oh no, I never thought, what am I gonna do?" Kelly added dopily.

"Tell him you've been on the sunbeds in Sunny Days ready for him coming home," Susan said delighted to have found the ideal excuse.

"Nah, they've closed that place down. They had cameras in the rooms. They were putting the pictures on the internet. Got their own website, the lot. Police came last week and closed it," Trace said putting the kibosh on that.

"Say it's from a bottle, then, or spray on, like the wags," Shirley said thinking of the carrot oil. Well that way she wouldn't be lying either!

Shirley and Oli managed to sort Kelly's hair out. Made the best of it, anyway, and the group were ready for the Falaraki bar crawl of their lives.

<u>Friday, 28 March</u>
<u>10am</u>
Not long got in but we have to leave the room by ten so it's a quick dash up to finish packing. Angie and Susan

are flat out on the sunbeds by the pool, so it's been left to me and Oli to finish off their stuff.

We had a fantastic night. A great way to end a fab holiday. Our flight leaves at two so we've got to be in the airport by twelve. Angie managed to sort out a cab for us, compliments, of the management. I know – you'd never believe it, would yer! God only knows how, but the manager said a taxi would be here by eleven. I think it's his way of making sure that we actually leave. Angie has told everyone in the hotel she loves it here and wouldn't mind missing the plane and staying on. Maybe he's got wind of it!

We're all meeting up at half ten downstairs. We all want to say our goodbyes to the staff and some of the guests. Angie, Susan and Trace need to get addresses and that. They've told some of the waiters to call in and see them if ever they come to Liverpool!

All the hotel staff stood on the steps waiting to wave the factory girls off.

"Aww, innit lovely. We've made such an impression on them. They all wanted to wave us off. I think I'm gonna cry," Angie sniffed.

"Making sure no one's left behind, more like," Shirley whispered to Oli.

"We've changed their lives forever," Susan added, close to tears.

"Mmm, there's no denying that, kid," Oli replied.

"I must admit I'm looking forward to seeing David and the kids and everyone, but I do feel a bit sad about leaving all the fun and laughs behind," Shirley admitted to Oli as they waited for the taxi. "I do feel a bit teary,

Oli, do you?"

"I do, kid. Now, don't get me going," Oli said, rubbing his eyes.

"Wait for me," shouted Ali struggling to squeeze down the stairs.

"Where the hell did you come from, kid?" Oli asked her.

"Well, I thought I'd nip the loo, just to sort meself out," she said looking all hot and bothered.

"What's up with ya? You're walking like John Wayne. Has the ale affected your legs, love?" Oli giggled.

"Oh no, love, if only. I'm in a hell of a state. A lady's complaint; red raw, I am. I'll be glad to get out of this heat," Ali said raising her eyebrows.

Oli looked horrified. Ali had taken so many pills and potions over the week they'd given her a very unpleasant side effect and they had to watch her wriggle and squirm all the way to the airport.

"There's no way I'm sitting next to her all the way home. Anyway, I did it on the way here. Someone else can do it," Oli said, putting his foot down, when the taxi pulled up outside the airport.

<u>1pm</u>
Well, we've finally arrived at the airport. The girls are all in the bar and Oli and I are going to have a little shop. I want to get some nice smellies for Fi, Jason, me mum and David. I can't wait to see them. I wonder how they've all got on in Wales. Bet they won't have a tan!

"We'll have to round them all up now, Oli. We have to go

through customs in a bit," Shirley said closing her diary and stashing it safely in her handbag.

"Well, I hope they've been looking after Angie. We don't want a repeat performance of the trip out," Shirley said looking around nervously.

5pm

Back in wet, cold Liverpool, finally. Although I thought we weren't going to make it. We rounded the girls all up in the airport and set off for customs. Fortunately they had been good and no one had had too much to drink.

We all put our bags on the belt thingie for them to go through the camera to be checked and then we started walking through the machine. Well, there was a hell of a noise when Angie walked through. She was called over by this really gorgeous looking Greek fella. Well, her face was a picture, grinning from ear to ear.

"Hey, girls, am I in for a treat or what?" She walked over to him ready for her body search, arms out and legs akimbo ready for action. Then, as if from nowhere, this butch woman walks over to her and does the search. The loud bleeping noise got louder over Angie's boobs. She had a face like thunder as she pulled out the bunch of keys hidden in her bra.

"Thought you'd have a last little groping from the Greek fellas, eh love?" I asked her stifling the giggles.

"Well, that back fired on yer, queen. She had more of a moussie than Father Christmas," Oli said, loving every second of it.

"Should be working in a friggin' circus not an airport," Angie said all pissed off.

"Looks like she enjoyed it, though, babe."

"Lesbian..." Angie mumbled as she flounced off.

Oli made sure we had good seats on the way home. Trace sat by the window, Oli in the middle and I sat on the aisle. It was great cos Trace is tiny, and Oli and I are just normal sized, so we had plenty of room. It was fantastic. I looked over and Susan, Angie and Ali, the three biggest in the whole plane were all sitting together in a row! I did feel sorry for them but I wouldn't swap with them. I don't mind flying so long as I'm on an aisle seat and have someone small by the side of me.

"What are those lot gonna do when the food comes? Ali's wriggling about enough now, how will she be when she has to have her tray on her an' all?" I asked Oli.

Oli just looked at me.

After we'd eaten the food, who came along the aisle holding her tray but Ali.

"You couldn't do us a favour, Oli love, could ya, hang onto me tray till they come for it. We're like sardines down there and me in my state an' all."

Give 'em an inch!!! Oli, Trace and I ended up with all of their empty trays on top of ours to give them more room! Flamin 'ell.

"Anyone up for a few bevvies later?" Susan asked once we'd landed and got through customs.

"Not for me, ta, I've been away from me kids long enough. You lot go, though," I said. I really couldn't be arsed.

"Not for me, kids, I'm gonna catch up on me beauty sleep," Oli said to them an' all.

So we all got dropped off. Now I have to wait for the kids to come home.

Shirley wandered around the empty house, it felt good to be home. First things first, put the kettle on. She hadn't enjoyed a decent cuppa for a week. She made a start on her unpacking and put a holiday wash on.

All the presents she had bought for the kids were taken out of her case and lined up awaiting their new owners. Then she heard the anxiously awaited sound of a bus pulling to a stop outside her house. Through the window she saw David get out of the minibus dressed in full waterproofs and heavy walking shoes. Even in that get up, Shirley thought he looked gorgeous. She watched as he went around to the back of the minibus to open up the door for a very tired-looking Jason and a very bedraggled-looking Fiona. Shirley was beside herself, and trying desperately to avoid the temptation to run out of the door, rush over to him, grab hold of him and give him a big kiss she had missed him that much. But the sight of her tired-out kids brought Shirley to her senses and, realising how much she had missed them, too, she rushed out of the front door arms wide open to welcome her beloved offspring home.

"Well...how d'yer get on?" Shirley asked eagerly.

"Brilliant, mum, it was amazing," Jason said looking exhausted.

David piled the bags caked with dry mud onto the pavement, said his goodbyes to Jason and Fiona, managed to give a sly wink in Shirley's direction and got back into the rowdy bus. She'd have to give him a ring on the mobie later.

"How about you, Fi?" Shirley went on, flushed.

"Amazing. It was well good. I didn't wanna come home. That Wilmore, he's great an' all. He was so different outside school. He's a right laugh, isn't he, Jason?" Fi said as they waved the bus off.

The bus replied to their generous waving with a rendition of 'She'll be Coming Round the Mountain' on the horn as it drove away from the house.

Music to my ears, thought Shirley. They had had a great time and loved David. Happy, Happy Days! Shirley smiled to herself.

Later that evening Shirley received a very welcome text message from David telling her he'd had a great time, thought the kids were fantastic and could they meet up in the week. She was chuffed to bits.

TWELVE

Saturday, 29 March
10pm
A really quiet day today. Just a chance to catch up with the kids and take me photies into town to be developed. I took them to that one hour place cos I couldn't wait to see them. I've asked Oli over tomorrow with his so we can have a gossip and a look.

Sunday, 30 March
10am
Oli's coming over this morning so we should have a good laugh looking at the photos. Apparently he's had a text from Angie who was dead excited. She'd got a letter waiting for her when she got home with an apology from Comb-over informing her that she had her job back.

"So, that bit of the plan has worked, then," Shirley said to Oli, handing him a mug of tea as they both settled down to relive the holiday highlights.

"Aye, it just leaves us with a right mess for poor Dot, doesn't it?" Oli said standing by the window flicking through the photographs.

"I know, I wish I could sort something out for her. I feel dead guilty, like, but we had to get Angie her job back cos our loyalties are with her first," Shirley sighed.

"Any more news on next door, babe?" Oli said looking out of the window as he watched Pam get out of the car.

"Nah, nothing although it was mad with cars here last night. I don't know where they all came from," Shirley replied.

"There must be something going on, Shirl'."

"Well, sod that for now, we need to think of a way to sort out poor Dot," Shirley said taking the photographs from Oli and flicking through them.

<u>3pm</u>
Just had a phone call from Lucky Jeanette saying she wants to see me and Oli urgently.

I said it would have to be quick cos I've got me mum and auntie Dilys coming over for tea at five. I thought I'd better make an effort, and they want to tell us all about their trip and show us their pictures. Well, I'll have to hide some of my pictures, well, most of them, in fact. Lucky Jeanette said it won't take long but she needs to see us both face to face.

In great trepidation Shirley and Oli made their way to

Lucky Jeanette's because she wanted to confide in them. They were sworn to secrecy.

"It's all over between me and that Comb-over," she sobbed.

"Oh my God, why?" Oli asked shocked, they'd been so lovey-dovey in Falaraki.

"Well, I wanted you to know the truth; you two have been so good not letting on and all that. I've got no one else to talk to about it. It's only you two that know anything. I wish there was some way of telling that scumbag's wife," she said.

Pausing and then taking a deep breath, she went on, "I can't. I have to keep it all hush-hush cos my fella will be out soon. If he gets wind of any of this…well…"

"What's happened, love?" Shirley asked.

"Well, you know he left a day earlier than us. He was gonna sort out Angie's work and that…" she muttered.

"Yeah, and he has," Oli butted in.

"Well, anyway, we were gonna meet up last night. Our first night back after the holiday. He came to pick me up and said he'd got a surprise for me. We were gonna go to a party. I was made up, I thought great, I can show off me tan. When we got there, though, I nearly died. It was one of them wife-swapping parties."

"Oh my God, where was it?" Shirley asked shocked.

"Down Lloyd Street."

Oli and Shirley looked at each other. So it must be true: Ted and Pam, Frankie and Fay – Lloyd Street was Shirley's street.

"So I told him, I'm not into that kind of thing. Told him it was all over. I just walked out and got a cab. He was well into it. They're planning a big one next Friday. They said it's gonna be the party of the year. He said he's going with or without me. I told him it's without. I want nothing more to do with it or him."

Shirley and Oli left Lucky Jeanette to it and promised not to tell a soul.

"Hey, kid, get the camera at the ready and make sure you're available on Friday," Shirley said to Oli as they left Jeanette's house.

8pm
Well, me mum and auntie Dilys turned up with a new spring in their step. They'd had a wonderful few days. They didn't really want to know about our holiday, just rattled on about theirs. I did try and tell them a few clean funny stories, though I only had three photos that were ok to show them, but they just kept changing the story back to theirs!

"So, how did you get on? No one was ill or anything?" I asked them.

"Ill? Ill? We were on holiday. There was no time for being ill, was there? Anyway, your mother and I are very fit for women our age. Albert said so, didn't he, love?" Auntie Dilys said, full of confidence.

Well, the holidays seem to have done everyone good, then.

Exhausted from the holiday and still stunned from Jeanette's revelations, Shirley planned to spend the next couple of days unwinding not forgetting to plan how she and Oli would be able to catch Comb-over out at the next Lloyd Street extravaganza.

<u>Monday, 31 March</u>
<u>6pm</u>
Still no work or school. We've got another week off. Everyone seems exhausted so it looks like we'll need this week to recover.

I'm still thinking about this party on Friday. So Karen was right. She'd be a good one to have on board really, she works in an ideal place, gets to see people all day long. Only trouble is, she can't keep her trap shut so we could never trust her. She'd blow our cover no danger. The whole street would know what me and Oli get up to in our spare time, and we can't be having that.

<u>Tuesday, 1 April</u>
<u>10am</u>
I still can't get over all these goings on in me own street. Half me neighbours involved an' all. You never can tell what people get up to, can ya? I mean what goes on behind closed doors and they say the quiet ones are the worse.

Me tan is starting to fade a bit. I'll have to get some fake, I think, to keep it going a bit longer. Now I need to plan how I'm gonna nail Comb-over. I think I may pay Karen a call at the paper shop; she might have a bit more info. Only trouble is she wants to know the ins and outs of the cat's arse that one.

Shirley decided to try and get a head start before Friday so she went up to the paper shop and saw Karen.

"Hey, I've heard on the grapevine there's a party going on this Friday," Karen said, probing.

"Party where?" Shirley asked, knowing full well...

"Next door to you. I overheard the pair of them chatting in here yesterday. That Fay and Pam. Whispering they were, but I've got good hearing, me. I heard them say they've had a bit of interest so it should be a good do."

"I'll take a roll of film from you an' all today, Karen," Shirley said, thinking that with luck she would need it.

Wednesday, 2 April
7pm

Well, I don't believe it. Fay has just come over asking if I'll do her hair on Friday morning. She's got a do on and wants to look her best! She said she knows that I don't normally do it, like, but fancies trying out a new look.

8pm

Just had Pam on the phone – she wants me to do her hair on Friday an' all!!

Well, I might get a bit of gossip before the event with a bit of luck. Oli's spoken to Dot about Comb-over. She told him he'd come back from his trip with a lovely white tan mark. She did ask him how come he'd got a swimming trunk tan line when he was on the golf course. He just said that he was playing golf in swimming trunks; everyone was, cos it was so hot. As bad as us lot walking round the town in ours!!!

11pm

Just had a text from David. He really has missed me and wants to meet up tomorrow. He's got something he wants to talk to me about! I wonder what it is. I'm dead excited. Maybe he wants to say how great me kids are and wants us to get serious. Oh my God, I'm getting carried away now. I don't think I'll sleep tonight I'm so excited.

Finally, I think things are looking up for me on the boyfriend front.

Fancy me getting a decent boyfriend. Me mum would love him, I know. Not that I've ever bothered what me mum thinks about me fellas, but David would definitely be the kind of fella me mum would be proud of me seeing.

Thursday, 3 April
10am

I'm meeting up with David in town in a minute; I've made some excuse to the kids that I'm meeting Oli. Hopefully, the last little lie I'll be telling them about my meetings with David. I'm ready to let them in on me little secret, I think.

The day started off so well. Shirley and David met up for lunch. She thought he looked great, and his back injury seemed to have improved, he appeared back to normal at long last. He went on about how well he got on with the kids and what a great pair they were. He even told Shirley he thought his own kids would like them too. Then the big news came. Like a bolt of lightning from the blue.

The long and short of it was David had been head-hunted. A school wanted him to be head of history back in Manchester, not far from his kids and also his ex-wife, although not in the same school.

"I can't believe it. I'm gutted," Shirley muttered under her breath. "So when you going?" she asked.

"I haven't said I'll take it, yet. I was dreading telling you. I feel we are getting closer. I know we've taken it really easy, but that's what has been so special about us, Shirley. We've taken our time, built up from a friendship to something much more.

"All I can say is I've been approached and I'm tempted. It would be great for my career and I'd be closer to the boys. I miss them so much. I feel torn." He looked upset himself.

"You have to do what is right for you; I don't want to come between you and your boys," Shirley assured him.

"Thanks, Shirl', you're so lovely," he said kissing her gently on the hand.

The rest of the afternoon was difficult for them both as David had to let the Manchester school know by Monday. There didn't seem enough time at all for Shirley to get used to the idea. She had convinced herself that he would take the job. She thought he would be a fool not to.

David tried to sweeten the pill by telling her they could still see each other even if he did go. Manchester wasn't that far away...

It wouldn't be the same though, would it, Shirley thought. He couldn't come over every weekend. And where would he stay? It would be way too complicated.

"Oh, you poor cow," said Oli sympathetically when Shirley phoned him to let him know how the day had panned out.

"He's letting them know on Monday. I thought I'd be telling the kids tonight about us. He'd got on that well with them on the trip," Shirley said flatly.

"And you behaved yourself an' all on holiday. What a waste," Oli said thoughtfully.

"Well, I'll be back on the market Monday, cos I'm not doing the long distance thing. It'll be the likes of Charlie and all the old scallies again for me. Why couldn't it last with David? He was just so perfect."

"Listen, kid, sorry to be so hard on yer but you've got to keep busy to take your mind off things. We've got a slimeball to catch tomorrow, remember, so come on, love, get a grip, for Dot's sake, eh?" Oli said trying to gear her up.

"I know, it will take me mind off it hopefully. I'm doing Pam and Fay's hair in the morning ready for the party. So if you wanna come over to give us a hand..." Shirley said trying to get into it when all she really wanted to do was sit on the sofa and sob into a box of Mansize.

<u>Friday, 4 April</u>
<u>9am</u>
The swinging pair is due at ten o'clock. I've asked Oli over in case I miss any clues they give away.

At ten o'clock precisely there was a knock on Shirley's back door and in waltzed Fay and Pam.

"Yoohoo. It's only us," Pam said walking in without waiting for an answer. They both made their way into the living room where Shirley and Oli awaited them eagerly.

"I'd like a new look, Shirley, I want to look ten years younger," Pam instructed as she sat down.

"Why don't you go dark, Pam? That would take years

off you," Shirley suggested.

"We'd have to strip you first, like," Oli said brushing her hair.

"Oh it's a bit early for stripping, Oli," Pam giggled.

Fay gave Pam a roll of the eye!

Shirley couldn't believe it of Fay, she was so quiet and she looked over at Oli who looked as if he was thinking exactly the same thing.

"You've swapped," Oli said when they all looked at the finished product. Fay was now blonde and Pam dark.

"Keeping the theme of the night," Pam whispered to Fay, who just giggled with embarrassment and they both made a flushed exit out the back door.

"Listen, babe, I'm off into town now. I'll come over about six. Thought we could have a takeaway and a bottle of wine before we get to it. I'll bring the video camera tonight an' all. Hey, imagine if we could get in, we could make more than a few bob selling the video..." Oli said putting on his coat.

"See you later, love," Shirley said, still feeling more than a bit fed up. At least the hairdos had kept her mind occupied for a couple of hours. She made herself a cuppa and with the latest hair magazine on her lap made herself comfy on the sofa. A bit of afternoon TV was in order, hopefully she would forget about David for a while. With her afternoon planned, Shirley started to relax, however, as often happened in Shirley's house, things rarely went to plan.

Ten minutes later, there was a knock on the door and in came Shaz and Digo. Shirley smiled, if anything was going to keep her mind off David and his decision it would be listening to Shaz and Digo's stories. Fiona and Jason soon made an appearance from upstairs.

"How's ya mum, Shaz, love?" Shirley asked.

"She's sound, Shirl'; she's got a new fella," Shaz replied.

Digo and Jason looked at her as if they were both glad to be off the hook.

"Anyone I know?"

"D'ya know Kenny from the video shop?" Shaz went on, blowing bubbles from her chewing gum.

"Kenny, yeah I do. I was in school same time as him. About three years younger than me, I think," Shirley answered.

"Well, his son Bobby."

"His son? Bloody hell, how old is he?"

"Seventeen, I think. He's a right minger, though."

"So your stepdad could be about two years older than you?" Fi said, sounding more than a bit horrified.

"Suppose…" Shaz replied, not looking up from the hair magazine Shirley had intended to read.

"Minging," Jason and Digo chorused.

"Oh well, at least she's got a fella. Maybe I should go out with Mo one night, see if she can sort me out. Maybe I should go for a toyboy like her. I could go with Kenny from the video shop; me, him, Mo and Bobby, on a double date," Shirley announced.

Fiona and Jason looked at her disgusted.

"Shall I ask her, Shirl?" Shaz asked looking up from the magazine.

"Nah, you're all right Shaz, love, I'm only kidding," Shirley answered quick as you like. She didn't want to land up out of the frying pan and in the fire. Fiona and Jason looked mightily relieved.

The kids all piled out just as Oli was arriving. Bobby had

acquired some DVDs from his dad and they all had a movie night planned.

"Jason and Digo will be safe tonight, then, if Mo is with Bobby!" Oli said catching up on all the gossip.

"Have you heard anything yet, babe?" Oli asked settling down to the takeaway.

"I did have a text from David this afternoon, telling me how much he thought of me. I haven't answered him," Shirley told her bessie mate. "We agreed not to contact each other over the weekend so he could make his decision with a clear head."

"Thinking about it, we didn't get any gossip really from Pam and Fay, only Pam did say she was having a few old friends over. Old being the word. Mind you, it beats listening to some old fart talk about antiques in the over fifties club, I suppose," Oli said changing the subject as he didn't want Shirley to start getting upset again.

"I didn't reply. I know he'll go," Shirley said, going back to the first conversation. "It's too good an opportunity to miss. He'll be near his kids an' all. He's going and that's all there is to it. Come on, Oli, get that chicken korma eaten, we've got work to do. I only hope Comb-over turns up."

Once the food was eaten Shirley looked outside the front window just as a familiar car pulled up right outside the house. Comb-over...

"Quick, camera, you do the videoing," she shouted to Oli. "Comb-over's here. Quick babe, get started," she went on arms waving erratically.

Comb-over got out the car and opened the door for his passenger.

"I don't friggin' believe it," Shirley shouted.

"What, why?" Oli said, now videoing Shirley's carpet.

"Look what you're doing, soft lad, look at the friggin'

woman," Shirley shouted.

"Who is it? Not Lucky Jeanette?" Oli asked trying to focus himself on the filming.

"Oli put the video to one side and take a good look out of the window," Shirley instructed, snatching the camera from him and commencing to video the action herself.

"Friggin' 'ell."

"I know, it's friggin' Dot. What's her game? She's got some explaining to do." Shirley said still videoing the action.

"Keep it rolling, Shirl'; we can use this as evidence for that Dot wasting our time."

They carried on the filming and even took some photographs; they saw the pair of them going into the shed in the back. Dot came out but not with Comb-over, with Ted. They were all over each other.

Hanging out of Jason's bedroom window, Shirley and Oli tried not to draw attention to themselves. The party animals were too engrossed in their own activities, though, to notice anyone watching them. It was all Shirley could do to stop Oli going over to Dot and confronting her there and then.

"D'yer think she feels if you can't beat 'em join 'em, then?" Shirley asked totally confused.

"I don't know, Shirley, love, she must've forgiven him for his flings in the past and, like you say, decided to get in on the action herself. I'll be telling her, though, girl. Mark my words. I'll let her know. Now come on let's have another Dixie, see if we know anyone else."

11pm

Well what a turn up, eh? We didn't recognise anyone

else. I was half expecting Karen from the paper shop to turn up for a nosy. I've made arrangements for Oli to meet me in town. I need a few things and also it will give me a chance to look at the photies. He's gonna print them off ready then we can go and tackle Dot, see what she's up to.

<u>Saturday, 5 April</u>
<u>2pm</u>
All the photies confirmed last night's antics, so we're off to Dot's armed with the evidence. I can't wait to see her face when she finds out we've caught her fair and square.

Before heading up Comb-over's drive Shirley and Oli both took a deep breath.

"What do we do if he's in?" Shirley asked.

"We still reveal all, Shirl'. It's all his fault anyway."

Comb-over's car was nowhere to be seen as they walked up the long driveway. Oli rang the doorbell, definitely ready for a confrontation. A smiling Dot answered the door.

"Hiya, you two, long time no see. Any news?" She asked eagerly.

"Don't you hiya us. What's your game? Get off, do yer, making people traipse all across the place looking for something that isn't even there," Oli said, barging into the house.

"What are you on about?" Dot asked looking confused.

"Now, Dot, we know he's cheated in the past but you should've come clean when you decided to put it about a bit yourself, love. You've made us look like fools," Shirley said trying to be a bit more diplomatic than Oli who'd just steamed in.

"Here, put this in," Oli said giving Dot the video.

They all watched it in complete silence.

"And take a look at these," Oli said throwing the photographs over.

"I don't know what to say, I'm speechless," Dot said looking shaken.

"Aye, yeah, I bet you are. Well we still want paying, call it wasting valuable time. We could've helped loads of people in the time it took to find your secret," Oli said still ranting.

Dot looked as if she'd seen a ghost.

"Dot, are you all right?" Shirley asked, by now realising something was not quite right.

"That wasn't me, that was Olive, me twin sister," Dot managed to blurb out after a bit of heavy breathing.

Shirley looked at Oli; he looked at Shirley, both of them completely speechless. Poor old Dot, thought Shirley.

"Umm, er, sorry Dot. I feel like a right arsehole now. How were we to know though like, erm, don't worry about the money love, erm, see ya," Oli mumbled getting to his feet.

They made their excuses and made a rapid exit from Dot's house.

On the way back down the drive Oli expounded his theory.

"I'm not the marrying kind, like, but to me if you were going to have an affair with someone you'd choose someone who didn't look like your wife, right? Variety being the spice of life an' all that," Oli said.

"Well, that's Comb-over, thick as shit and twice as soft. Let's put this one down to experience, love," Shirley said grimly.

"Totally ballsed that one up, babe," Oli said pulling a face. "Sorry."

<u>Sunday, 6 April</u>
<u>2pm</u>
Back to work tomorrow, plus I'll find out if I'm to live the life of a nun for the rest of my days. Time will tell. Today David finally decides where he will end up.

Fancy Comb-over having it off with his wife's twin sister. Hey, wait till we tell Lucky Jeanette.

<u>Monday, 7 April</u>
<u>1pm</u>
Still no news. I don't know how I managed to get through work this morning. We texted Lucky Jeanette to tell her who Comb-over's latest was. Even she was shocked, but like she said maybe that's all he could get hold of last minute, like.

Shirley made sure she had finished work by the time the kids were home from school. She wanted to see if they had any information about David.

"Just as we were starting to get on, old Wilmi is on the move, Mum," Fi complained.

"What d'yer mean?" Shirley gulped.

"Everyone said he's not going to be teaching us anymore, that's what's going round school anyway. Even Dobson, one of the history teachers, was complaining he'll have more work now for a bit until they find someone to take over Wilmi's work."

"I heard that an' all. Sly or what. He was sound, Wilmi," Jason added, pouring a packet of crisps in between two slices of white bread and butter.

I can't believe it. I have to be the last to find out. The bastard couldn't even tell me himself. Well, if that's all I mean to him then I'm better off without him, Shirley thought, once she'd shut herself in the loo for a bit of privacy.

She needed support, so she went to look for her mobile to text Oli. As she was about to text Oli she noticed seven missed calls from David. And before she could start texting Oli another phone call from David came through.

"I've already heard," Shirley moaned before David even had a chance to speak.

"Oh no, you haven't have you? I wanted to be the first to tell you. Isn't it fantastic news?" he slurred.

"Oh yeah, great, well done you. I'm chuffed for you." By now sadness had taken over from anger, but Shirley knew she had to be brave.

"Can you come over to the pub, have a few drinks with us, there's a few here gutted now they've found out I've been promoted. Come over so they can be even more gutted that I've got the best girl as well. Come on, let me introduce you, let's toast my new found authority."

"I don't think so, not tonight, David; I might see you before you go, though," Shirley said trying to talk, but struggling with a lump the size of a melon stuck in her throat.

"Go? Go where, Shirley?" David said, sounding confused.

"Where? To Manchester, you dickhead," Shirley said, starting to get annoyed again.

"Manchester? Oh, I get it. You've heard, but only part of the story.

"I told the Manchester lot to piss off this morning. By dinner time word had got out I wasn't going. The head had called me in once he found out what I'd decided and offered me the deputy head post here. He didn't say anything before, crafty bastard, because he wanted to make sure I took it for the right reasons. So, Shirley, I'm staying, as deputy head of the school here, but I'm staying because I love you, so get your beautiful behind down the pub and celebrate with me."

Shirley threw the phone down, didn't even explain to the kids where she was going and rushed out.

11pm
Spent the evening down the pub with all the teachers that I'd thought were stuck up bastards. Turns out they're nearly as bad as the factory girls! I am so made up. It's all coming together at long last.

Tuesday, 8 April
6pm
Oli was made up for me. I even got the courage up to tell the kids. Turns out that now he's deputy head it will not be cool to have him as their mum's new fella after all, so it looks like it won't be as smooth as I'd hoped for.

8pm
Oli's just phoned excited as hell. We've had not one

but two requests for assistance. One is an eighty-five year old: he said he's found some old medals and a blonde toupée on the floor in his bedroom, says they're not his and now he thinks his wife has had someone else in.

"What kind of medals?" Shirley asked when she met up with Oli to go over the details.

"Five metres breast stroke? I dunno, I never asked," Oli answered sarcastically.

"Oh. Not sure if I fancy that one. What's the other one like?"

"A group of teenage girls calling themselves 'Revenge'. Apparently their boyfriends are dropping like flies cos they're all at it with some old tart called Mo. They want photies so they can name and shame her."

"Now that sounds a bit more like it..."

Other titles from Honno

About Elin by Jackie Davies

A haunting novel of love and loss

Elin Pritchard, ex-firebrand, is back home for her brother's funeral. Returning brings all sorts of emotions to the fore, memories good and bad, her own and those of the community she left behind.

ISBN: 978 1870206 891   £6.99

Bells by Jo Verity

Jo Verity was the **winner of the 2003 Richard and Judy "Write Here Right Now" short story competition**.

When Jack dons his Morrismen's bells it brings a new zest of life... and for beguiling Non. But will wife, Fay, also be tempted to play away?

ISBN: 978 1870206 877   £6.99

Big Cats and Kitten Heels
by Claire Peate

Fresh and funny; ideal beach reading

Rachel – suffering from a Dull Life Crisis – embarks on an action-packed hen weekend. But there's a 'big cat' on the loose and only a handsome Welshman in wellies between Rachel and a vicious killer...

ISBN: 978 1870206 884   £6.99

Death Studies, by Lindsay Ashford
The third title in the Megan Rhys crime series. A body turns
up, miraculously preserved, in the bog behind the golf course.
9781870206860   £6.99

Facing into the West Wind, by Lara Clough
"A tender and perceptive tale of secrets" The Guardian.
Jason may be lost and friendless, but he has a gift. He has a
face people confess to. And those confessions are going to
change everything...
9781870206797   £6.99

The Floristry Commission, by Claire Peate
A heart-warming romp through village life from a talented
first time novelist.
9781870206746   £6.99

Hector's Talent for Miracles, by Kitty Harri
Mair's search for her lost grandfather takes her from a dull
veterinary surgery in Cardiff to the heat and passion of
Spain – to uncover her own family's secrets, and those of the
intriguing Hector...
9781870206815   £6.99

My Cheating Heart, edited by Kitty Sewell
24 original stories of intrigue, infidelity and betrayal. My
Cheating Heat takes a broad look at the trials and temptations
of infidelity.
9781870206730   £7.99

Strange Days Indeed, edited by Lindsay Ashford and
Rebecca Tope
Funny, shocking and tender, this is a unique collection of
autobiographical writings about motherhood penned by
women from Wales.
9781870206839   £7.99

ABOUT HONNO

Honno Welsh Women's Press was set up in 1986 by a group of women who felt strongly that women in Wales needed wider opportunities to see their writing in print and to become involved in the publishing process. Our aim is to develop the writing talents of women in Wales, give them new and exciting opportunities to see their work published and often to give them their first 'break' as a writer.

Honno is registered as a community co-operative. Any profit that Honno makes is invested in the publishing programme. Women from Wales and around the world have expressed their support for Honno by buying shares in the co-operative. Shareholders' liability is limited to the amount invested and each shareholder has a vote at the Annual General Meeting.

To buy shares or to receive further information about forthcoming publications, please write to Honno at the address below, or visit our website: **www.honno.co.uk**.

Honno
'Ailsa Craig'
Heol y Cawl
Dinas Powys
Bro Morgannwg
CF64 4AH